WARDENS OF WISTERIA

Wisteria Witches Mysteries

BOOK #8

ANGELA PEPPER

CHAPTER 1

"There's a ghost in the house, Zed."

I cracked open my eyelids to find a sight that would send most normal people into a screaming fit. Staring down at me was a mythical beast with green scales and gleaming black eyes. It was Ribbons, the telepathic wyvern who lived in my basement.

Unlike the monstrous wyverns of storybooks, it turned out the real ones weren't much bigger than a housecat. Ribbons' body, not including the tail, was only seven inches long. That morning, he sat comfortably on my second pillow, with his bat-like wings at his sides and his green-scaled legs tucked under himself. He flicked his long purple tongue over one black eyeball and then the other.

"There's a ghost in the house, Zed," he repeated. He rarely called me by my real name, Zara.

"Thanks for letting me know," I said, my voice croaky from sleep. "Who knew you were such a good watchdog?"

He snorted in my face, emitting a puff of minty steam. Ribbons didn't appreciate being compared to a watchdog. Actually, he didn't appreciate being compared to *anything* that might be helpful to humans. He considered humankind unworthy of assistance by wyverns. That was what he claimed, anyway. His actions, however, spoke louder than his telepathically delivered words.

"The ghost is downstairs," Ribbons said in his vaguely Count Chocula accent.

"Any idea why the protective wards didn't keep this one out?"

He snorted again. "I didn't let it in."

"I never said you did, Pint Size. Do I have to drop my telepathy shields and let you read my mind all the time just so you don't get offended?"

He sniffed. "No need."

I rolled out of bed, grabbed a loose T-shirt dress, and pulled it on over my sleeping camisole. The bedroom was bright with pre-dawn light. It was mid-July, and the sun wouldn't be up until 6:00 am, but the house already felt hot. We were in the midst of a hot, dry spell, and the whole town of Wisteria was cranky from not sleeping well. I could have used a few hours more myself, but ghosts didn't stick to office hours.

Ribbons followed me, doing his duck-like waddle over to the edge of the bed. His green scales gleamed like miniature daggers in the golden light.

"The spirit must be benign," he said. "A malevolent entity would have triggered the alarms when it entered the house."

I bit back a sarcastic comment about the alarms never being triggered by a certain malevolent entity with green scales who regularly raided the kitchen and drank all my maple syrup.

Before heading downstairs to face the ghost, I checked on my daughter, Zoey. She was sleeping soundly, sprawled sideways on her bed like a starfish. She looked younger than her sixteen years, with one hand clutched to her chin and her fingers curled childishly. I wished I could take in the sweetness for one moment longer, but the ghost was waiting.

2

Ribbons led the way down the stairs, gliding with his wings outstretched and the sharp talons of his feet curled around the handrail for balance. I paused to assess the damage his claws were doing. At the rate the wyvern was shredding the wood, I would need to replace the handrail annually. He was spectacularly destructive, surfing to the lower floor that way, but what other choice was there? He couldn't fly down the narrow staircase without the claws on his wingtips gouging the walls, and he refused to take the stairs on foot because it was undignified, given his stumpy legs.

I followed Ribbons to the living room. He was right about there being a ghost in the house. A semitransparent man sat rigidly on the couch. He faced the TV, which wasn't on. He didn't stir when either the wyvern or I entered the living room.

My mouth went dry and my skin prickled. I wiped my sweaty palms on the bottom of my T-shirt dress. Despite the many ghost encounters I'd had, they still gave me the chills. In the four months since I'd become a witch, I'd been possessed by, on average, a ghost a month. That figure didn't tell the whole story, since I'd also been possessed by the spirit of a coma patient, as well as an evil genie, plus one of the four ghosts I counted into my average hadn't been entirely dead, but, long story short, a ghost a month.

At the start of July, however, I'd done something drastic to prepare myself for the next spirit. With the help of—if you could call it help—my telepathic wyvern housemate, I'd engineered a powerful spell and cast it on myself. I had, in laymen's terms, "rezoned" myself as a library. Then I'd classified any ghosts who entered me as books. In theory, the rezoning would let me control the ghosts and access their memories as easily as flipping through the pages of books. That was the theory. In practice, well, I didn't know yet. In practice, I might end up with scrambled eggs for brains. This was my first haunting since the transformation spell; it was time to find out.

"Hello," I said to the semitransparent man in what I hoped was a soothing tone.

The ghost didn't react. He continued facing the dead television.

I walked around the couch and took a seat next to him.

"My name is Zara Riddle. I'm a witch, and I'm Spirit Charmed, which means I help people such as yourself." I laughed nervously. "Or at least I try to."

He blinked and tilted his head slightly.

"Hello," I said again, and then repeated the full introduction.

He turned his head slowly, ever so slowly, until he was facing me.

He was a young man, in his mid-twenties. He had fair hair, pale eyebrows and eyelashes, and close-set blue eyes that bulged like those of a flat-faced dog. His face was skinny and angular, with a jaw that began as two sharp corners under his ears. He had the hungry look of a street kid, yet his clothes—a button-down shirt and suit trousers—were tailored, pressed, and clean. I scanned him for signs of injury. Some ghosts manifested with their death wounds visible whereas others appeared as they looked on an average day. There was no blood visible, yet there was something unusual near his shirt collar. His throat glowed slightly brighter than the rest of him. Had he died of strangulation? If he'd been choked, that might have explained the bulging eyes.

The young man's eyes widened further, as though he could read my thoughts and was horrified about being strangled.

I glanced away, feeling ashamed about assessing him so dispassionately. He was a person. A young one. And his life had been cut short, presumably through foul play. The victims of everyday accidents and disease didn't come to witches as ghosts.

When I looked up again, the young man was frowning. He wrinkled his nose, sniffing the air between us, and then lifted one hand. The translucent hand traveled slowly through the air toward my face. I braced myself for what might be coming next: him turning into smoke and swirling up into my head through my nose.

But he didn't turn into smoke. His outstretched hand passed through my face and arced down. Now his arm was submerged, elbow-deep, in my upper chest. He met my gaze with narrowed, suspicious eyes. His mouth moved, and he uttered a single word. I heard nothing but the hum of my house. He was mute, like all the ghosts I'd encountered. He repeated the word, and this time it was clear by the shape of his lips what he'd said. *Ghost.*

I actually laughed out loud. The ghost thought that I was a ghost. Me!

I turned to Ribbons, who was watching from his perch on the back of the recliner. His talons dug deeper into the upholstery, making little pops as each sharp talon passed through layers of fabric and foam. The beast was trying very hard to seem disinterested, but I knew him too well. One of his tells was tightly gripping whatever perch he was on. The more damage he did, the more interested he was. I dropped the shield from my mind and asked Ribbons telepathically if he knew anything about the young man on my couch.

"Nothing," the wyvern replied. His speech was always sent directly to my mind, where I heard it in his cartoonishly Old Europe, Count Chocula voice. He continued with a sigh, "I'm bored now. This is boring. Are you sure it's a ghost? All I can see is a bit of shimmering light."

I told him it was a ghost, and I described what I saw. Then I asked how he'd detected the ghost in the first place if he couldn't see it.

"Ask the fluffball," Ribbons said. He lifted his elongated, boxy chin in a pointing gesture, indicating the upper corner of the living room.

I followed his gaze. Sure enough, there was a fluffball up there. A white one. Boa, our cat, was perched at the very top of a bookshelf, perfectly still, watching the ghost on the couch with eyes as big as saucers. I didn't bother asking Boa what she saw. The cat was, as far as I knew, just a regular cat.

The ghost man on the couch suddenly leaned forward, got to his feet, and glanced around the room.

I got to my feet as well. "Leaving so soon? I hope it wasn't something I said."

The white fluffball on top of the bookshelf let out a low, guttural moan. Her fluffy tail whipped from side to side. The moan continued much longer than you'd expect from such a small non-magical creature.

"Something's happening," Ribbons said. "What's happening, Zed?" The frame of the recliner creaked under his sharp talons.

The ghost man turned toward the front door and walked toward me as though I wasn't there. He didn't slow as he reached me. He kept going, disappearing into me. Halfway through, his ghostly body seemed to get stuck. He responded by dropping a shoulder and pushing through, angling his upper body like he was moving furniture. The sensation of the ghost passing through me was unpleasant, and also familiar. It was the same sticky, tugging feeling of pulling oneself out of a dream on purpose. Then he was finally out of me and on his way to the front door.

In a flash of white, Boa soared from the bookshelf, ricocheted off the couch, and landed on the wood floor with claws extended. She skittered after the ghost at top speed, chasing him all the way to the front door. The ghost, who seemed only mildly concerned about his cat pursuer, passed through the front door with no resistance. Boa, being a solid cat, smacked into the door head first.

I immediately scooped her up and checked that she was okay. Her body was rigid, but she gradually melted in my arms and gave me a soft, sweet meow.

"I know," I said. "There was a ghost in the house. You did a very good job protecting us." I kissed her on the top of her head. "Good kitty." She gave me a fierce purr.

Ribbons made a throat-clearing sound in my head. "It's getting away, Zed. I see a ball of light crossing the street."

I clutched the cat to my chest. What was I supposed to do? Run around my neighborhood at dawn, chasing a ghost? No way. I was going back to bed.

"You have to follow it, Zed."

"Get out of my head," I said sourly.

"I didn't have to read your mind. It's all over your face. Come on, Zed. Get the ghost. You know you want to."

He wasn't wrong. I'd always felt a strong need to help people. It was what had drawn me to my vocation as a librarian—besides all the books, of course. Once I'd become a witch, my compulsion to help others had only gotten stronger. Never mind that this compulsion had gotten me injured plenty and killed at least once. The ghost had come to me for help, and going back to bed now wasn't an option.

Boa meowed softly as I set her down. I grabbed a pair of sandals.

Seconds later, I was out the door, along with the wyvern, who flitted silently from tree to tree, following me. If any of the neighbors happened to look in Ribbons' direction, they would have seen whatever bird their minds thought appropriate. His glamour was powerful magic. I was very familiar with him, and yet, at times, even I saw him as a crow or an owl.

Ribbons urged me on excitedly. I followed the ghost as he casually walked down the middle of the street. A car suddenly pulled out of its spot and careened toward me. I had to jump out of the way. The car sped away without stopping, almost as if fleeing a crime scene. I made a mental note of the car's plate number. I didn't get every digit before it turned, but I got a few.

The ghost was now off the street, walking up a driveway. He turned toward a freestanding garage that had been converted into a two-story apartment. The ghost walked up the external stairs to the apartment, and then passed straight through the door.

"You have to follow him inside," Ribbons urged. "Do it, Zed."

I walked up the stairs, but paused at the door. I rubbed a trickle of sweat from my forehead. It was one thing to try to communicate with a ghost who came to me, but now I was the pursuer.

Ribbons, who was in a tree that overhung the garage apartment, shook a branch impatiently, raining down leaves around me. "Do it, Zed."

"Behave yourself," I hissed. "I'm not breaking and entering."

"At least knock on the door."

I crossed my arms and stared up at the gloomy shape in the treetop. "Are you truly that bored? You want me to bang on this door and confront a potential murderer?"

"Zed, I respect you too much to lie."

I snorted. Ribbons had no problem lying, especially if it was to blame someone else—usually the cat—for something he did.

"Yes," Ribbons said in his Count Chocula accent. "I am that bored. Knock on the ghost's door and see what happens. Do it."

I raised my fist to rap on the door. More leaves rained down around me. But despite the wyvern's urging, I didn't knock. Not because I was afraid I couldn't protect myself—I could, thanks to my defensive fireballs, among other spells—but because I didn't *have to* enter the apartment to see inside. There was a large picture window next to the door. The curtains hadn't been drawn, probably to promote air flow through the opening on such a warm night.

On the other side of the window was a small living room. The TV was on, flickering light around the room and illuminating the room's only occupant. And the occupant was—

Both of my hands flew up to cover my mouth.

The body of the room's occupant was dressed in a pair of slacks and a button-down shirt, not unlike the one the ghost had been wearing. Except this shirt was red. I might have assumed the shirt was made of blood-red fabric if it was not for one important detail.

The body sitting on the couch, facing the TV, didn't have a head.

No wonder the spirit's neck had been glowing.

The poor young fellow had been beheaded.

CHAPTER 2

Ribbons dropped from his tree branch and landed on my shoulder with a startling thump.

He took in the grisly sight before commenting, "I'm no expert on human biology, but I believe an injury such as that is not repairable."

I shook my head. "Cheeky wyvern. Yes. Head removal is pretty serious and generally not repairable."

"Don't let my pessimism stop you from trying to get that human's head back on and working." He reached across my face to point one of the claw-like fingers connected to his wings at the garage-apartment's door. "Go on. Use your magic to open the door so you can practice those healing powers of yours. It'll be fun. You haven't healed anyone in ages. Do it, Zed."

"Not gonna happen," I said. "I can't bring back the dead. I'm a witch, not a necromancer."

"But it's such a clean cut. You could at least stick him back together and see what happens."

"You're assuming the young man's head is even in there." I touched the tip of my nose on the window as I peered around the living room. "Where is that head? It must have rolled away, but it can't have gotten very far on its own."

"Ooh! I'll help you find it. I'm good at finding things," Ribbons said excitedly. "Let's go inside." Multiple pricks of pain shot through my shoulder as the wyvern curled his protractible claws into my flesh.

"Let's *not* go inside the blood-soaked crime scene." I took a step back from the window and turned toward the stairs. "If you really want to help, I'll mention you by name when I talk to Detective Bentley."

He made a disappointed croaking sound with his throat. "Bok bok," he said, doing his bad impression of a chicken.

I ignored him and made the sensible choice to walk down the stairs, away from the headless body. Sure, I was a witch, but I was also a librarian, not a police detective.

As I crossed the street again, I scanned the area for signs of anything unusual. Beacon Street looked, sounded, and smelled pretty much as expected for 5:45 am on a Saturday morning in July. The only thing strange was the color of the rising sun. It was crimson red. There were a few forest fires burning in the region, and the smoke had been hanging over the town all week, blotting out the distant mountains and darkening our skies. I hoped some rain would come soon and help the firefighters extinguish the blaze.

I turned my head to say something to Ribbons about the fires, but my shoulder was empty. He'd flitted back up to the treetops, presumably to keep watch over the crime scene when the local law enforcement arrived.

Back inside my house, I made a phone call and reported what I'd seen. I considered making a second call to my mentor, my aunt. She was traveling with my mother overseas, in a different time zone. I decided she wouldn't want to be bothered on her holiday. Besides, I knew Zinnia well enough that I could fill in her part on her behalf. I knew the drill. I lectured myself to be more careful, to not use magic unless absolutely necessary, and to wash the plastic dome that covered food in the microwave.

* * *

When my daughter came downstairs a few hours later, she took one look at the clean plastic dome next to the sink and asked, "What's wrong?"

I blinked innocently and sipped my third coffee of the morning. "What makes you think something's wrong?"

"You only clean the plastic thingie when Auntie Z makes you, or when something's wrong."

"I knew I shouldn't have cleaned the plastic thingie." I smacked my forehead lightly. "Why must I be such an amazing housekeeper?"

Zoey's eyebrows arched up high over her hazel eyes. "You think you're an amazing housekeeper? You must be possessed again."

"I'm not possessed."

She put her elbows on the kitchen island and leaned forward, peering into my eyes. "You still look like yourself." She sniffed. "You smell like yourself." She pulled back and took a seat on the stool across from me. "Whatever's going on, I can handle it. Hit me."

"Boundaries," I said, using my fingertip to draw a line on the counter between us. "Boundaries are part of a healthy parent-child relationship."

"But I'm not a child," she said plainly, without a hint of the whine or snark a normal kid her age might have. Zoey had always been more like a miniature adult than a child. I often joked that on the night she was born, she'd waltzed out of my womb, shook hands with the taxi driver who'd delivered her, and then corrected my pronunciation of the name of the hospital we hadn't made it to in time.

"Sixteen is not eighteen," I said. "You're not an adult. It wasn't that long ago you were putting Barbie dolls under your pillow at night, as a tribute to the Boob Fairy."

13

She rolled her eyes. "Stop trying to change the subject by embarrassing me. I know you've got something juicy you're not telling me. Ever since Castle Wyvern, you've been making those googly eyes."

"Me? Googly eyes?" I blinked innocently, as I always did when she was onto me.

"You've got a big secret and you *want to* tell me, but you know you shouldn't." She sniffed me again. "You smell more smoky than you should be."

"I was outside, where everything smells smoky. Those darn fires in the mountains are getting worse."

She jumped off her stool, poured two glasses of pink lemonade, and set them between us with solemn clunks. She took her seat and gave me a serious look.

"I'm nearly an adult," she said. "I'm licensed to drive. Plus I can turn into a fox at will. I'm not your average teenager."

"No, you are not the average teenager."

"So?"

I squirmed on my seat. She knew me well, and she was right about me keeping a secret. A big one. And it wasn't about the ghost from that morning, or even about my rezoning spell.

The reason I'd been staring at her with googly eyes was because I'd been trying to see what aspects she'd inherited from her father. Zoey's father had never been a part of our lives, not since he'd knocked me up at fifteen, and I hadn't given him much thought until recently. I had assumed he was just a regular kid, a rich brat who didn't want to take responsibility for his decisions. I hadn't known he was a supernatural being. Not until recently. I would never have guessed he was...

Zoey frowned. "What? What's going on, Mom? You're starting to freak me out."

I rubbed my clavicle to bring myself into my body, into the present moment. Zoey might be ready to hear the truth about her father, but I wasn't ready to talk about it.

What if she wanted to meet him? She was a good girl, but she wouldn't stay that way if she had one parent telling her she didn't need to be good. *Come to the dark side*, he'd say. *We have cookies.*

I took a sip of the pink lemonade. It cut through the taste of coffee in my mouth. The sweetness plus the cold made my teeth sing. Maybe I could tell Zoey about her father.*Do it, Zed.* I gave myself the command in an imitation of Ribbons' voice. *Tell Zoey, the polite teenager who mopes around the house all summer because she can't wait to get back to school in the fall, that her father is a genie. A demon. An ancient, powerful creature straight from Hell. What could possibly go wrong?*

"Okay," I said, keeping my gaze on the glass of pink juice. "There is something going on."

"I knew it. Does this have something to do with that new transformation spell you cast on yourself?"

I grasped at her question like a drowning sailor grabbing a buoy. *Pull back, Zara.*Now the cheeky wyvern's voice was gone from my head, and it was only me in there.*Look at your daughter's innocent face. Let her have the summer before telling her she's demon spawn.*

"Yes," I said eagerly. "The transformation spell. That's exactly what's been on my mind." The pink lemonade had made my mouth water spectacularly. As I spoke, saliva flew forth, spraying both my forearms and hers.

"Ew!" She squealed and rubbed her forearms on her jeans. "Say it, don't spray it, Mom!"

"Don't be so squeamish. Witch saliva is naturally antibacterial. Aunt Zinnia says it's handy for breaking down magical compounds, plus it can deodorize entire rooms." I grinned. "Rub that on your armpits and you won't need antiperspirant."

There was a flash of white as Boa came to investigate what the squealing was about. She padded across the counter like a spoiled cat despite having been told repeatedly that counters were not for kitties. She investigated our lemonade glasses, her white whiskers angling forward in an expression of do-not-want before moving on to my coffee mug, the contents of which she did like enough to take a few licks.

When she was done sampling my coffee, Boa jumped onto Zoey's lap and settled in for petting. She watched me over the counter with suspicious eyes.

"She's looking at me funny," I said. "Do you think she knows something?"

"She's just a cat, Mom. Her main concern is cat food. Speaking of which, we need more."

"Already? I just picked some up."

Zoey whispered, "I think somebody else has been eating it." By *somebody*, she meant Ribbons. It was only the two of us, plus our cat and wyvern.

"Ew. Is there nothing he won't eat?" I looked around the kitchen for the wyvern. "Speaking of whom, have you seen him this morning?"

"He sleeps in on the weekends." Zoey smirked. "And on the weekdays."

I nodded. She didn't know Ribbons had been awake before dawn, alerting me to the presence of a ghost in our living room.

Zoey looked down at the fluffy white cat on her lap. "Boa feels tense," she said. "It must be the smoke outside." She ducked her head down to give the fluffy white cat a kiss on the nose, then peered at me expectantly. "You were saying? Something about that spell you shouldn't have cast on yourself? Are you going to phone Auntie Z and tell her what you did?"

"I swear I'll tell her as soon as she gets back from her vacation."

"You'd better. Keeping secrets from your family is unhealthy." She rubbed Boa's chin. The cat gave me a smug look, as if to say she was the most beloved creature in the house. And who was to say she wasn't right? Nobody else in the house got their chin rubbed so lovingly.

Zoey prompted me again. "What's going on with your rezoning spell?" My clever offspring was nothing if not persistent.

"Nothing much. By which I mean I guess it's working the way it's supposed to. I'm a perfectly organized library for ghosts now, not a free-for-all ghost disco or whatever."

My daughter continued petting the cat with one hand and used the other to indicate I should keep talking. Normally I didn't need such encouragement.

"There's a new ghost in town," I said grimly.

She listened as I told her about the morning's events. Being woken by the wyvern. Finding the ghost on the couch. His bulging eyes and glowing throat. And then the headless body inside the apartment across the street.

CHAPTER 3

After I was done telling my daughter about the new ghost, she held her finger to her lips and asked, "Can we backtrack for a moment?"

"Of course," I said. "Backtrack away."

"When you ignored Auntie Z's many, many, many warnings about casting spells to alter yourself, did you happen to set up official business hours?"

I rubbed my forehead. Had I? My memory of that night was hazy. I'd been manic, scribbling notes and calculations in the wee hours of the morning, arguing with Ribbons while I sipped on the cocoa he'd warmed with his personal steam.

"Hang on," I said. "Let me get my notes."

I ran down to the basement, retrieved my notes from a hidden drawer in the desk, and ran up the wooden stairs quickly. I didn't like being down there during daylight hours, never mind how cozy and welcoming I found my witch's lair at night. Zoey didn't like going down at all, so she'd stayed at the doorway waiting for me.

When I got upstairs, Zoey asked, "How did this ghost get through the wards on the house?"

We returned to the island in the kitchen, and I set the notes between us. "My guess is I might have overrode something when I cast my transformation spell."

Boa jumped from my daughter's arms to the counter. She repeated the inspection of the glasses and coffee mug with the curiosity only a cat could conjure up.

Zoey read over my notes and grew very still and quiet. She hadn't yet manifested the ability to cast spells, but thanks to her keen intellect, she was able to understand the theory beneath the Witch Tongue language and the syntax of spellwork.

"You didn't specify hours, but you did use the local library as a reference point," she said. "Due to the inheritance factor, any specifics not set within the spell could have come from the WPL by default."

I checked the current time. "Speaking of which, the WPL will be open shortly, which means I will be open, too." I waggled my eyebrows. "I'll be open for business."

She groaned and shook her head. "You really know how to take the terror out of something by making it sound gross."

"Excuse me?" I put my hands on my hips. "It's not just me. Having a ghost enter your head through your nostrils *is* gross."

She didn't react. She continued to pore over my notes. "This subjunctive clause seems unnecessary," she said, pointing at a scratchy section. "And I can't make out the words. Did you write it messy on purpose so I wouldn't be able to read it?" She leaned in and took a closer look. "Does this say what I think it says?"

I yanked the pages off the counter and held them behind my back. "Thanks for your help with the business hours."

"Mom." She gave me a pointed look.

"You weren't supposed to see that part." In all the excitement of the morning, I'd forgotten about that particular clause.

"Too late. I saw it." She frowned. "It had something to do with love. Is this about your crush on Mr. Moore?"

"That depends." I turned my head and gave her a coy, sidelong look. "What do you think that clause is supposed to do?"

She spoke slowly. "Well, I know that you and Auntie Z were studying potions after what happened at Castle Wyvern. You were trying to reverse engineer that anti-love potion that made people fall out of love. And I know that some potions can be re-created as spoken spells and vice versa." She crossed her arms. "I think when you transformed yourself, you included an anti-love potion on yourself."

I slowly brought the notes out from behind my back. I gave the special clause a quick look. It had taken me hours, even in my manic state, to write the anti-love clause. She shouldn't have been able to decipher it so quickly. Something clicked in my head. She'd been keeping a secret from me, but now I was onto her!

"Zoey, you're a brilliant kid," I started off. "In fact, you've been smarter than me for a few years now. But even the smartest and most experienced witch couldn't have figured out the nature of this clause by only glancing at it for a few seconds."

Her cheeks grew pink. Oh, yes. I was onto something.

"It was a lucky guess," she said, her voice raspy as she tried to fake a casual air.

"You're familiar with this spell... because you've been planning to cast it on yourself."

The pink on her cheeks deepened in color. "There's no point," she sputtered. "It doesn't work."

"What do you mean it doesn't work?" I looked over the anti-love clause in the rezoning spell. "It must be working. The morning after I cast the spell on myself, I saw Chet, and I felt nothing." I patted my heart. "Nothing."

"It must have been the placebo effect. You felt what you wanted to feel."

"If only!"

"The placebo effect is real, even with magic."

I struck my finger in the air. "But it might have worked."

She shook her head. "Anti-love is one of those spells you need the potion for. Words alone aren't powerful enough to cause that kind of change."

"If that's true, then why don't I feel anything toward Chet?"

"Maybe because you never actually loved him in the first place. All those feelings you had came from Chessa's spirit. You were only feeling her feelings, not yours."

She had a good point. My neighbor and I had flirted a bit when we met, but any positive feelings he'd whipped up in me naturally had almost certainly been offset by his betrayal. The man had used me as a pawn in his own game, getting me to move to Wisteria so he could use the Riddle family's powers to get his fiancée back. I couldn't be too angry with him, not after learning the atrocities that had been done to the woman he loved. If I'd been given the choice to help her, I absolutely would have. No woman should have to suffer the way Chessa had.

I still had my hand over my heart. I dropped it away. "You're probably right, kiddo." I squinted at the clause one more time. "Are you sure this anti-love wording didn't do anything? I still love my friends and family, but I don't feel very much when I read fictional romance."

"You've probably outgrown fictional romance. Aren't you the one who told me that after forty, lots of women switch over to thrillers and memoirs?"

I made a choking sound. "Excuse me. I'm a long way from forty."

"But you have to admit you're not that interested in romance."

I snorted. "I don't know if you've noticed, but I don't have time for romance. I've been rather busy raising a too-smart-for-her-britches teenage daughter on my own."

"What about Leo?"

"Who?" I knew exactly whom she meant. Leo was the hunky scuba diving instructor who'd dropped more than a few hints that he was interested in seeing me again, with or without my scuba diving suit.

Zoey rolled her eyes. She knew that I knew whom she meant. "I know Leo has some sort of history with the gorgon triplets, but that was a long time ago. He was cute." She wrinkled her nose. "For an older guy."

"Even if I had time for romance, I won't be dating anyone who has a history with people I know."

"Mom." She shook her head. "It's a small town. Unless you start dating teenagers, you'll have to deal with someone's baggage. At your age, that means dating guys who have ex-wives and maybe kids."

I stuck out my tongue. "Ech. Kids." I shuddered. "Ex-wives! Double ech."

Boa, who was still sprawled languidly on the counter, reached up a soft paw and patted my arm. "That's right," I said to the fluffy white cat. "Human beings have yucky baggage, which is why I'm not going to date anyone, let alone fall in love. Love makes you stupid." I leaned down and kissed her pink nose. "And I only have stupid love for Boa." I went on, making the baby talk sounds Boa pretended not to like.

"Love does make you stupid," Zoey said with a sigh.

I pulled my face from the white fluff and shook my finger at my daughter. "You're young. You have to experience stupid love. It's the curse of being a teenager."

"Not if I can get the ingredients for that anti-love potion."

I narrowed my eyes at her. "Over. My. Dead. Broomstick."

"So, I'm just supposed to learn about magic but not do anything useful with it?"

"Exactly. It's like eighty percent of your curriculum at high school. The whole point is to exercise your mind *to be able* to learn."

Her voice got low and gritty. "I bet if I made that anti-love potion, you'd want some."

"I forbid you to make anti-love potion. Or any kind of potion without supervision by an elder witch."

She shrugged. "What's the harm in getting better at potions? I can't cast spells with Witch Tongue. I'm not like you and Auntie Z. I'm not a witch like you two. I can't do anything magic."

I raised an eyebrow. My teenager was less dramatic than most, but she did throw the occasional pity party.

"You can't do *anything* magic? Nothing at all?"

She scowled. "No."

"Except...?"

"Fine," she spat out. "I can turn into a fox."

"That's pretty magical."

"Not really. It's just what I am. Any shifter can do it. I'm just a boring, standard shifter."

The sadness in her voice finally got to me. I felt the stirrings of sympathy. Gently, I said, "Zoey, you're so much more than a shifter."

She rolled her eyes. "No, I'm not."

"Yes. You are." She was half genie. Half demon. From what little I'd been able to find about genies in my reference books, their magic wasn't compatible with the Witch Tongue we'd been learning. However, I suspected my daughter was far more powerful than she could even imagine.

The sympathy in my heart veered toward panic. What would I do if she managed to cast a spell using the demonic powers she'd inherited from her father? What if the spell went terribly, terribly wrong?

"Zoey," I said through clenched teeth. "Don't mess around with potions out of some misguided teenage angst."

She let out an exasperated sigh. "Stop calling it angst. My feelings are real."

"Yes. I didn't mean to invalidate your feelings. I know being a teenager can be hard, and I know how painful it can be to get your first crushes, but it's a part of life. Falling in love, stupid or otherwise, is part of growing up."

She crossed her arms and huffed.

I went on. "You can't protect yourself from growing up. Not with an anti-love spell."

She snorted. "But it's okay for you to cast one on yourself?"

"I'm an adult. I've already been in love."

Her hazel eyes blazed with an uncharacteristic fire. "Were you in love with my father?"

Her father. *Archer Caine.* The genie. I'd certainly felt something for him when I was fifteen. Was it love? It had felt as powerful as any magic. He'd been a boy then, with a different face and a different name. But he was still the same charming devil. He was nothing but trouble.

My face burned as though my cheeks had both been slapped. Zoey's paternity was a topic we didn't discuss, and she knew bringing it up would only hurt me.

I kept my tone neutral. "I've already been in love," I repeated. "The details are none of your business."

She was watching me intently. "Did you love my father?"

"Maybe," I said, surprising myself. Memories of that night came flooding back. I usually made a joke of it, focusing on the too-sweet wine coolers with the ridiculous name, but there'd been more to the night than that. *He* had been there. Archer Caine. His new name was blotting out my memory of his old name. Had he called himself Andrew? Or Alex? It was all blurring. Even his face was changing. The golden hair and soft, boyish features he'd worn all those years ago were being replaced with those of Archer Caine's.

There was a soft pat on my hand. It was the cat, letting me know she was ready to receive more adoration. I moved my hand to pet her, but it wasn't easy. My memories had ensnared me in another time, and I wasn't present. My hand looked foreign, like a puppet hand barely under my control. My whole body felt hot and heavy. Something inside me wanted to remember that moonlit night with absolute clarity. But I couldn't go there. I couldn't indulge in that fantasy, that false reality. It had all been a lie. He'd promised to love me. He'd sworn that I would be his and he would be mine. Forever. For... what had he said? Eternity.

There was a warning growl from the white fluffy beast, and then a scratch. The pain of talons on my forearm brought me back to the present.

I was in the kitchen with my daughter—my daughter who was the product of the night I couldn't think about. Boa was letting me know I'd gone too far. My hand had strayed into the no-touch zone on her belly.

"Boa," Zoey said. "No scratching! Bad kitty."

I rubbed my arm. The cat had drawn blood, but the scratch would be healed in a moment, thanks to my powers. "It's okay," I said softly. "That was my fault for touching her belly. We have an agreement, and I broke it."

"She's a brat," Zoey said.

"Bratty Boa."

Zoey grabbed the cat and held her in her arms. The cat went limp and purred loudly.

A minute passed, and the purring only got louder.

Zoey said, "You're not going to tell me if you loved my father, are you?"

"Do I need to? You're a smart kid."

She pursed her lips. "But I want to hear you say it."

"Why?"

Her hazel eyes burned. "Do I need to tell you why? You're smart, too."

"I..." I shook my head dazedly. "Zoey, I don't know everything. I don't know why you're so upset right now. You're going to have to give me a hint."

She narrowed her still-burning eyes. The air around us crackled. The cat stopped purring with a single hiccup.

Through gritted teeth, she said, "You do know."

"No. I don't."

"You're lying."

The pain and anger in her voice did its magic. Something within me shifted, softening. I reached across the counter to give her a reassuring pat on the arm. When my fingers touched her skin, the crackling air between us ignited. Bright blue light blazed. My defensive magic blasted from my palms, through my fingers, and straight into my daughter's arm.

The cat in Zoey's arms erupted, an explosion of white fur. She jumped straight up in the air, landed on the counter, and skittered across it before flying to the floor. Her cartoonish movements would have been funny if not for the frightened look on my daughter's face as she tipped backward on her barstool, hurtling toward the ground.

I jumped to my feet and used a web of telekinetic energy to catch my daughter before she hit the floor.

But there was no need for me to catch her. She'd changed into her fox form mid-air. She would have landed on her four paws. Now, thanks to my magic, there was a fox hovering three inches off the floor, pawing at the air and yipping in protest.

"Oh, sweetie," I said. "I didn't mean to shock you just now. Sometimes the energy builds up, like static electricity."

She yipped to be set down. I released her from the web of energy.

Zoey-Fox stalked around the fallen stool and broken glassware. When Boa had been scared off, she'd managed to knock down not one, not two, but all three drinking vessels.

Zoey-Fox gave me a hurt look. Deep down, she knew the shock had been an accident, but her fox face had a limited range of expressions. She might only have been surprised, but I read her expression as hurt, probably because of my own guilt. I should have told her about her father. I should have told her so much more.

CHAPTER 4

After the incident in the kitchen, Zoey-Fox skulked off to her bedroom in animal form. She closed her door with a soft thud that sounded, to her mother's ears, passive aggressive. My lungs ached and my eyelids felt hot. We hadn't fought, exactly, but it was as tense as things had gotten since our move to Wisteria.

As much as I wanted to go upstairs, I stayed in the kitchen. I swept up the broken dishes and mentally rehearsed breaking the big news to her.

Zoey, here's the thing. Remember how I told you that your genetic father was a bratty rich kid who didn't want anything to do with us? And that his family whisked him away at the first sign of the trouble brewing inside my belly, never to be seen from again? And how, when I hired a private investigator years later, the guy reported that the boy had never existed in the first place, so I assumed the punk had given me a fake name along with too many Barberrian Wine Coolers? Well, it turns out there never was a rich kid. There was only a demon, wearing a borrowed face and body. These days, he calls himself Archer Caine. Earlier this summer, he got a girl killed at Castle Wyvern, and I'm afraid that if you meet him, something terrible is going to happen to you. Or me. Or both of us. So, can we just forget this whole thing about your father and go back to pretending he doesn't exist? That'd be great.

What's that? I'm all the parent you need? You made it sixteen years without a dad, and your life is perfect, so why spoil it? Oh, great! I was hoping you'd say that.

* * *

I gave my daughter an hour to cool off before I called up the stairs, "Are we still going to the museum today?"

The door creaked open. "Sure," she said brightly, as though nothing had happened. Since she could speak, that meant she was in human form again. Her fox form could communicate, but only in foxy yips and barks.

She came down the stairs walking lightly, wearing a different outfit and a full face of makeup.

"Foxy lady," I said.

She stuck out her tongue.

"I'm really sorry I shocked you by accident," I said. "How's your arm?"

She looked down at her bare forearms, which were both unmarked. "Fine. I don't even remember which one you zapped."

"That must be your dormant witch powers at work. You heal quickly."

She gave me a skeptical look. "Or maybe your zaps are weak."

I laughed with relief. If she was teasing me about my powers, it meant she'd gotten over our fight already. Phew!

I pretended to be offended. "You're lucky I didn't hit you at full power. It was just a little... accidental leakage."

"All leakage is accidental. That's what the word implies. Accidental leakage is redundant."

I clapped my hands. "Correcting my grammar! I'm so relieved my zap didn't knock that particular trait out of you." I tilted my head down and muttered to myself, "I'll have to shock her a lot harder next time."

She stared at me blankly, then asked, "Did your ghost show up again?"

"No. Unlike some library patrons, he was not pacing the front lawn, waiting for the metaphorical doors to open."

"Maybe he got confused about all the various municipal buildings and went to the museum instead."

"We'd better get going and find out." I stretched out my arm and called for my purse. For a while, I had been casting a spell just to find it, then another one to float it onto my shoulder, but lately I'd merged the commands into a sort of macro spell. There was a rustling upstairs, and my pink leather purse appeared at the top of the stairs. Apparently, I'd left it in my bedroom the night before. It careened down the stairs on the handrail, only slightly more graceful than Ribbons, thumped Zoey on the buttocks, then bounced over her head and onto my outstretched arm.

Zoey shot me a dirty look. "You did that on purpose."

I held out both of my hands. "Magic has a mind of its own."

* * *

It was my first time visiting the Wisteria Museum. Zoey had been there already on a school field trip, but she hadn't seen the new exhibit featuring artifacts from ancient Egypt. The showpiece was a 13-carat emerald worth over a million dollars. Due to the value of the emerald, the Egyptian exhibit had extra security, and the museum staff allowed only a dozen people at a time in to view.

We arrived shortly after the museum opened for the day, and there was already a long line to get into the Egyptian exhibit. Zoey and I joined the line.

A little girl of about eight stood in front of us in the line. She stared up at my red-haired daughter in wonder. The girl touched her own dark-blonde hair self-consciously, as though wondering if she might be able to change her hair color and grow up to be as lovely as Zolanda Daizy Cazzaundra Riddle.

I saw my daughter in a new light, through the little girl's admiring eyes. Zoey had a heart-shaped face with a broad forehead and a pointed chin. Her quick-moving, bright hazel eyes were fringed with thick eyelashes the color of caramel. Her skin was fair and baby-soft, her lips full and naturally deep pink. Her light-brown freckles were, in my opinion, perfectly sprinkled across the bridge of her nose and the tops of her cheeks. Her hair was red and thick, falling past her shoulders but not by much. She was average height for her age, and her narrow waist always attracted the envious gaze of older women if she wore her shirts tucked in. That day she wore a loose-fitting, peasant-style blouse with threadbare denim shorts. I didn't think much of that particular outfit—it was a bit monotone and dreary for my taste—but the little girl in line ahead of us stared up at Zoey in naked admiration. Worship, almost.

The little girl's mother noticed her daughter staring and pulled the girl closer to her side. The mother confided to me, "Your daughter is such a lovely young woman. My little Rebecca thinks all redheads are mermaids." She patted Rebecca on the head.

"I was a mermaid once," I said, more to the little girl than to her mother. "I found a secret journal at the bottom of the sea."

The mother laughed merrily. "Isn't that wonderful," she said, and then turned to greet someone else in the line.

Zoey said to me, "Sweet kid." She sighed and shifted from one foot to the other. "I'm not sure coming on opening weekend was such a good idea. This line's not even moving."

"We could always come back here after hours when it's not so crowded."

"After hours?"

I grinned. "They might have high security in place, but there's no such thing as a truly locked door to some of us." I wiggled my fingers suggestively. "If you know what I mean."

She elbowed me. "Mom! You're supposed to be teaching me values, not corrupting my young mind."

I shrugged. "I blame Ribbons. He's a bad influence on the whole household. Remember, he wanted me to go into that apartment this morning. He was practically begging me to."

"I believe it. He loves stirring up trouble. And he always looks guilty."

"He does look guilty! It must be the black eyes, combined with the lack of eyebrows." I rubbed my own eyebrows. "He's got those ridges over his eyes that are eyebrow-like, but when they smooth out, he looks shocked, like you just caught him in the middle of a crime."

"I think he's up to something we know nothing about."

"Charlize said the same thing." Charlize was my gorgon friend who worked for the DWM—the Department of Water and Magic. That was the local secret underground organization. They supposedly kept an eye on supernatural disturbances so the townspeople of Wisteria didn't find out magic was real, or that monsters lurked everywhere.

Zoey leaned out, surveying the lineup in front of us. "I think we'll be here a while," she said. "Want me to get you a snack from the cafe?"

"Bless your heart. I thought you'd never ask. It's been at least an hour since I last ate."

She grinned and held out her hand for money.

"Just a coffee," I said. "Unless there are some pastries that look edible."

"You set a really high bar, Mom."

"Nothing but the best for the Riddle family." I winked at her. "And get a little somethin' for yourself."

She made grabby fingers, indicating she'd need more money. I handed over my whole wallet with a shrug. I trusted her. We often joked that my wallet was probably safer with her, anyway.

After Zoey left, a woman with four children in tow joined the line behind me. Her kids were chatting away happily about seeing the Egyptian emerald, telling each other about the magical powers it had. At the mention of magic, they had my full attention. I turned to look them over. *Uh-oh*. I quickly rotated back, angling my body away before the mother could see my face.

I knew the woman, and not in a good way. Bentley had mentioned her name: Margaret Mills. She was the rhinoceros woman with gray frizzy hair who'd chewed me out last month for allegedly wearing fur. It had actually been my father, in fox form, not a fur wrap. The bossy woman and I had also bumped into each other again at the mini golf course. That interaction had not gone well, either.

Margaret Mills had taken a dislike to me from the minute she'd set eyes on me. It felt personal, almost as though she was jealous. Jealous of what, I couldn't guess. My gorgeous red hair? I peered over out of the corner of my eye. It was just Margaret and her four children. I didn't see her frizzy-haired, boxy-headed husband with the group. The lucky guy had gotten to sit this one out, apparently.

While I was pondering what might have made Margaret Mills so cranky toward me, the second-youngest Mills child declared a bathroom emergency. A moment later, all five were gone in search of the restrooms. To my relief, some new people I didn't know joined the line behind me.

The new people were a group of four women, about my age—thirty-two—or younger. One of them wore a new baby in a sling, and her three doting girlfriends seemed to be having a competition for Best Godmother.

Seeing them together gave me a pang of loneliness. I'd been sixteen when Zoey was born, and I'd been so busy keeping us from being homeless that I hadn't enjoyed carefree Saturdays at the museum with friends my age. Of course, there was no way of going back and changing things, not unless someone had invented a way to time travel, ha ha, so I was determined to make up for lost time now. And my social life was improving. I had many new friends at the library, plus I got along with a couple of agents at the DWM. Unfortunately, none of them were witches. The only witch in my life was my aunt, Zinnia. She would eventually have to introduce me to the members of her coven—her coven she denied having— but she kept delaying it, saying I needed more control over my powers.

For a witch, I was a late bloomer. I should have gotten my powers at sixteen, but due to circumstances—being pregnant with my daughter—the magic had stayed dormant. It hadn't emerged until I was thirty-two and living in Wisteria. I'd been working hard to catch up. Over the last four months, I'd been diligently mastering the Witch Tongue and spellwork, but I still had so much to learn. My daughter had a better grasp on the language theory than I did, which was ironic, since her powers appeared to be limited to changing into a fox. She'd inherited the shifter gene from her grandfather, which made her a shifter, not a witch, but my intuition told me she was more than just a shifter. After all, her father was —

The baby I'd been staring at gave me a startled look and pointed a chubby finger at me accusingly.

I quickly turned away from the women and the know-it-all baby. He or she was probably a mind reader. We were in Wisteria, after all, a magnet for supernaturals.

The din of noise around me picked up volume. The museum was getting crowded and noisy. I scanned the center atrium for my daughter. She was talking to a prehistoric caveman. Or, rather, a teenaged boy dressed in a prehistoric caveman costume.

After zero internal debate about whether or not to violate my daughter's privacy, I did so. I cast a spell that was relatively new to me.

The spell was a sound tunnel. It was an inversion plus modification of the sound-bubble spell my aunt and I used regularly to protect ourselves from eavesdroppers in public spaces. While the sound *bubble* spell kept energy waves trapped inside, the sound *tunnel* directed it outward and straight to the eager ear of the casting witch.

"That costume looks pretty authentic," Zoey was saying.

The boy's name was Griffin Yates. He and I hadn't met, but Zoey had mentioned him a few times in what she'd thought was a casual manner. Being her mother, I'd immediately picked up that he was her crush. I did the usual social media research. He appeared to be a regular teenager, but looks could be deceiving.

Griffin talked about his caveman costume. "It's sort of authentic," he said nonchalantly. "Some of the leather is real, but the fur is totally fake." He put his hand to the side of his mouth and stage whispered, "We have to use a lot of cornstarch to prevent chafing."

"Cornstarch is not very authentic," Zoey agreed. "What's that in your hair? Mud?"

"Chocolate pudding. At least I hope it's chocolate pudding. I was posing for some photos this morning with families, and a little girl decided to share her snack with me."

Zoey leaned in and sniffed Griffin's hair. "It's chocolate pudding," she said.

"Phew." He pretended to wipe his brow. "You must have a good sense of smell."

"Why, thank you." She struck a flirty pose with her shoulders bunched up. She moved her hands, holding the takeout coffee and pastries, down toward her knees. My daughter was flirting! My cheeks burned. I felt embarrassed for spying on her. Not enough to stop, though.

Griffin cracked a grin and glanced around. "I gotta get back to my cave. You should come see me after the Egypt display."

"Of course. I wouldn't dream of missing the chance to see you in your native habitat."

"Hey, if you're not busy tonight, you should come with us to the beach."

"Us?"

"The museum staff. We're going to build a big bonfire and take some promo photos for the website. You could be in the pictures. I'll get you a spare cavewoman dress."

She took a step backward. "Thanks for the offer, but I need to help my mom with something tonight." She nodded in my direction.

He turned his head and looked right at me. "That's your mom? I thought she was your big sister."

Zoey groaned. "Whatever you do, never tell her that. Promise."

Griffin chuckled. "Your mom looks okay." He frowned. "That's weird. It looks like she can hear what we're saying."

Zoey whipped her head, locked eyes with mine, and shot me with daggers. "That is weird," she said through gritted teeth. "It might look like she can hear every word we're saying, but I'm sure it's just an illusion. Like how the eyes in a painting seem to follow you. I'm sure she's just zoned out thinking about something else."

"If you say so." Griffin backed away casually. "So, uh, let me know if you change your mind about tonight."

She said goodbye and made a beeline straight for me.

When she reached me, I pretended to be surprised. "Back so soon? I was totally zoned out. You know how I am."

"I thought we didn't spy on each other."

"In my defence, you were in a public space. I could have just as easily walked over there and heard everything. The only reason I didn't was because I didn't want to lose our spot in the line."

"Were you using your new sound tunnel spell?"

I nodded. "My first time casting it without Aunt Zinnia's help."

She swished her lips from side to side, trying to decide how angry she ought to be.

"It worked perfectly," I said.

She frowned. "It's good to know it works. Promise you won't listen in on me again, unless it's an emergency."

I held up one hand. "I promise."

She handed me the coffee and a Danish in a waxy wrapper. "I don't know why you had to listen in. You know I was going to tell you everything he said anyway."

"I know. But look at all the time I saved you."

She took a mouthful of her own Danish and chewed it thoughtfully.

I asked, "Why did you say no to the bonfire party? It sounds fun."

"I don't know. Does your mouth ever say no when your brain says yes?"

I gave her question just enough consideration to make my cheeks burn again. Last month at Castle Wyvern, I'd said no to the monster who called himself Archer Caine. It had been difficult for me to say no, because every cell in my body had wanted to say yes. I didn't always win the yes-no struggle. I had made the mistake of saying yes on that fateful night seventeen years ago, and look where it had gotten me.

"Uh, Mom?" Zoey was giving me a concerned look. "Is everything okay in there?"

I licked my lips. There was no good time to talk to Zoey about her father, but the longer I waited, the worse it got. I would tell her soon.

"Let's go somewhere special after we're done here," I said. "Anywhere you want. How about the fancy place where they serve high tea?"

She frowned. "What's wrong?"

"Nothing's wrong. I'd like to treat you to a nice afternoon. Why's that so suspicious?"

"High tea," she said matter-of-factly. "That sounds like something you'd make fun of Auntie Z for being interested in."

"True. But I would like to be somewhere extra-civilized while I talk to you about something important."

"Like beheaded bodies and serial killers in our neighborhood?"

"Don't worry. It's got nothing to do with what I saw this morning. Nothing at all." As I said the words, I realized I couldn't be certain of that fact. Headless bodies could be connected to any number of monsters, including genies.

"Can I get a hint?" Her hazel eyes twinkled.

Just then, we were approached by a man in a gray suit. He was walking briskly and breathing heavily. It was Detective Theodore Bentley.

"Uh-oh," I said under my breath.

Zoey saw the detective and whispered, "Is he here to get a statement?"

"My phone call was anonymous," I said.

Bentley reached us. "There you are," he said breathlessly. "I knew you had to be in here as soon as I saw your rusty bucket in the parking lot."

"Rusty bucket?" I clutched my hand to my chest in mock indignation. "Her name is Foxy Pumpkin, and she's rust-free, thank you very much."

He gave Zoey a pained, apologetic look. "Miss Riddle, would you mind if I borrow your mother for a moment?"

She gave him a sweet smile and a shrug. "As long as you bring her back in one piece."

One piece? "Ouch," I said, thinking of the morning's headless body. "Too soon."

She wiped the smile off her face and nodded solemnly. "Too soon," she agreed.

I walked off to talk privately with Bentley.

CHAPTER 5

Detective Theodore Bentley was dressed in his usual gray suit, minus the tie. He'd given in to the summer heat wave and unbuttoned the top three buttons of his shirt. Peeking out of his jacket pocket was the dark gray tie he must have removed earlier.

As we walked over to a quiet area of the museum atrium, Bentley scanned the crowd with his hooded, steely gray eyes. The police detective was classically handsome, like an Old Hollywood actor. He had a square face, prominent brow ridge, and hollow cheeks. His neck was muscular with a visible Adam's apple. His lips were thin, as though all the bulk had been squashed out on purpose. His nose was thick, with a mild crookedness that suggested a history of being broken by a fist at least once. His hair was dark and lush, shot with streaks of silver, blossoming outward from the sharp point of a widow's peak on his smooth forehead. His dark, bushy eyebrows were straight when he was relaxed and curved downward when he frowned. He was frowning as he stopped walking and turned to face me.

"Tell me who did it," he said.

"Who did what? Are you talking about the..." I used my finger to draw a straight line across my neck.

"No more games," he said, his voice gruff and gravelly. "I know about all your ways, and I won't be played for a fool. Not anymore."

He seemed more cranky than usual. I still had my pastry in its bag, so I withdrew it now and waved the flaky roll under Bentley's nose.

"I bet you're hungry," I said. "You probably got the call from dispatch at dawn, which means you've been on the case these last few hours. You could use more than a nibble, but you can start with this."

He ignored the pastry and continued to stare at me with those steely gray eyes. He growled, "Zara."

The sound of my name on his lips sent a shiver through my spine. There was a strength to the detective I hadn't seen before. There was cold fire in those hooded eyes, combustion in that voice.

I lifted my chin and met his gaze. "Theodore," I said coolly. "Or should I say... Teddy B?" That was what my mother had called him last month at the castle, when they'd been dating—or whatever it was they'd been doing with each other. I suspected she'd been feeding on his blood, not the artificial serum she claimed sustained her undead state. Not that it was any of my business either way. Ew.

Bentley's mouth crushed into a flat line. I stared into the detective's cool, mercury-like eyes. The din of the crowd roared around us, sounding like a crashing waterfall.

"Call me Bentley," he said. "Things haven't changed *that* much."

But things had changed. While the detective remained a mere human with no supernatural powers, he had recently found out about magic. He knew I was a witch who channelled ghosts, and yet he hadn't yet figured out what my mother was.

"Eat the pastry," I urged. "You know you want to."

"No, thank you," he said. "I'm here on business."

"Of course you are. I'm sorry I tried to offer you a delicious pastry. I didn't mean to waste your time and be difficult."

His steely gray eyes flicked up to mine. He nearly smiled. "You don't mean to waste my time and be difficult? I thought that was your M.O."

"Ha ha." I took a sip from my paper cup of coffee. "How are things going? Did you manage to track down the head?"

He looked past me, his gaze unfocused. "We shouldn't be talking about this in public. The victim's next of kin hasn't been notified yet."

I switched the pastry to my coffee hand and wiggled my fingers in front of his face to get his attention. Once I had it, I arched an eyebrow and asked, "Mind if I put up a sound-bubble spell? It'll give us all the privacy we need."

An expression of disgust flashed across his face. Then he blinked once, slowly, and nodded. "Go ahead."

I twirled my tongue inside my mouth to summon forth the Witch Tongue, the language of witch magic. I exhaled to reset, inhaled fresh air, and cast the spell that would give us privacy. I used my free hand to guide the boundary lines. The air around us grew damp and heavy due to the spell's compression, then lightened again on a breeze that didn't exist. Now that I was more practiced at casting the sound-bubble spell, I noticed the subtle side effects.

In a deliberately loud voice, I said, "I'm ready to discuss the recent homicide! Let's talk about all the gushing blood and the headless body!"

Bentley's dark, straight eyebrows lifted so high that his hooded eyelids smoothed out. He looked past me, and then his eyebrows returned to their normal position.

"It must be working," he said. None of the people walking by were giving us a second look.

"So?" I peered up at him expectantly as I took another sip of museum coffee. "Where was the head? What happened in that apartment? Are we dealing with an Ichabod Crane situation? Or, should I say, a headless horseman situation? Should I be listening for hoofbeats?"

He stared at me.

I rolled it back to just one question. "Did you find the head?"

"We found it inside a trophy cabinet, inside the residence."

My hand went to my mouth. A head in a trophy cabinet. That was some next-level serial killer stuff. Suddenly, I wanted to run away and be somewhere else. I wanted to shower.

Since becoming a witch, I'd witnessed a lot of gruesome things without reacting the way a normal person would. But the idea of a head in a trophy cabinet was downright profane. It was even worse than the headless body sitting on a couch. At least a body belonged on a couch. A head belonged on a pillow, or with its body.

"That poor young man," I said.

"Did you know him? His name was Ishmael Greyson."

"Ishmael Greyson?" At the mention of the name, a few puzzle pieces clicked into place in my head. The last name was familiar. "He must be related to Arden Greyson."

"You know Arden?"

"Not well. I know his dog, Doodles, better than I know Arden. I've bumped into them—the old man and the dog —around the neighborhood a few times."

"Did he say anything about his nephew?"

"He did mention that he's always helping out his family. He's got a niece he loaned money to for some business venture. Now that I think about it, he did mention a nephew who was staying with him." I swallowed hard. My throat was burning. I looked down at the floor. "I guess that was Arden's apartment-garage?"

"It was." Bentley sounded more friendly when I wasn't looking at his face. He continued, "Ishmael is Arden's great-nephew. He was only twenty-six."

I murmured, "Such a shame." I nudged a pebble across the museum's floor with the toe of my shoe.

"Now, if you'll just tell me who killed the young man, I'll be on my way."

I looked up into Bentley's eyes. He had a hard expression. The muscles on his cheeks bulged as he clenched his jaw.

"I don't know who killed him," I said, my voice rising in pitch and volume. "Honestly, I don't know anything about his death."

"Come on, Zara. I thought we were past the games. I know about your powers, and the way you talk to ghosts."

"Bentley, I'm not holding out on you. Not anymore."

"But you knew about the body. You disguised your voice and blocked your phone number when you called it in, but we both know it was you who made the report. There's got to be more to the story."

"Just a tiny bit more. It all started when my, uh, *pets* woke me up before dawn. I checked on Zoey, then went downstairs, where I found a ghost sitting on my couch. I tried to communicate with him, but he seemed to think that I was a ghost, not him."

Bentley cocked his head. "That's odd."

"Yes and no. Ghosts are usually confused. They don't experience time the way we do. They're slipping between worlds, caught up everywhere and nowhere at the same time. Plus, they don't necessarily know they're dead."

"Did the ghost have his...?" Bentley gestured to his head.

"Yes, he had his head on when he was in ghost form. Thankfully. He had ears and a mouth, but he couldn't hear me or speak to me. We weren't able to communicate. I only sat with him for a couple of minutes, five minutes tops, before he got up and left. He walked right through me, then out the front door."

"Is that normal?"

I chuckled. "Normal is just a setting on the dishwasher."

He didn't miss a beat. "Is that typical?"

"It's not *atypical*, but keep in mind I have limited experience with ghosts. I'm a late bloomer, remember."

"Did you summon him back? With a spell?"

"Of course not. I wouldn't even know how. I pulled on some sandals and followed him across the street. He led me over to his place."

"At which point you entered the residence?"

I smiled, feeling I'd won a point for showing some restraint. "I didn't go inside the residence. I only looked in the window. Then I went home and called in the report." My smile broadened. "Like a good witch." *Zara tries to be a good witch!*

"And where is the ghost now?" Bentley winced. "He's standing behind me, isn't he?"

I hadn't seen the ghost since making the phone call to the police, but I looked around, just to be certain. "He's not here," I reported. "He's been gone since the sun came up."

"Is that normal? I mean typical? They disappear in the daytime?"

I scratched my head. "I don't know."

"What aren't you telling me, Zara?"

"The thing is, what happened this morning is both typical and atypical. It's normal for ghosts to show up and mess with my life. But usually it's because they turn into smoke, go up my nose, get into my head, and sort of..."

Bentley cocked his head. "Possess you?"

"For lack of a better word, yes. They tend to possess me. But they aren't in full control the whole time." I patted my collarbone. "I'm still me most of the time. But they do talk sometimes using my mouth, repeating things they said when they were alive."

"And?"

He'd sensed there was more, and he was right. "They influence me in subtle ways. For example, Winona Vander Zalm got me to throw dinner parties. Remember her?"

"I do recall the Vander Zalm homicide. And I recall that you knew who killed her." He blinked. "So, tell me who killed Ishmael Greyson."

"The thing about the Vander Zalm homicide is I didn't find out from the ghost of Winona herself. I had to figure it out by doing research, talking to people, and putting together clues."

"That sounds a lot like my job."

"It sure does." I grinned. "I've been doing your job for a while now, and not getting paid."

He rubbed his square jaw and took a thoughtful moment before saying, "This Greyson case will get closed faster if we work together for a change." There was a note of accusation in his voice that rubbed me the wrong way.

"That's not fair," I said indignantly. "I've been cooperating. I've been good." *Zara tries to be a good witch!* "Did my mother say something about me being uncooperative?"

He gave me a blank look. "Your mother?" All the color dropped out of his face.

"Yes. My mother. The woman you were hooking up with last month. Zirconia Riddle. She looks like me, except older and meaner. Also, her hair is black. You don't remember? Her name is Zirconia. Repeat it after me. Zirconia."

"Zirconia," he said slowly, numbly. "Cubic zirconia is a type of synthetic gemstone."

"And she's a person."

He mumbled incomprehensibly. We weren't getting anywhere.

I waved a hand to dismiss the topic of my mother. As much as I wanted to fill in the gaps in Bentley's memories, he might have been better off not knowing he'd served as a blood bag snack for a certain creature of the night.

Bentley came out of his daze. He picked up where he'd left off, saying, "You will be on the Greyson case, as my partner."

"Your partner?"

Now I understood what he'd meant about us working together for a change. He'd been trying to get me on board. Funny how it had come across as an insult. Was I oversensitive, or was he just bad at asking for help?

I clarified. "Are you asking me to play detective with you, Bentley?"

He winced again.

"I mean *be a detective*," I said quickly. "Not *play detective*. I'll take it seriously. I promise." I touched my collarbone. "Zara tries to be a good detective!"

His expression remained doubtful. "I'll believe that when I see it." He gestured toward the exit. "We'll head over to the crime scene now, where you can do some of your ghost business."

"Let me say goodbye to my daughter first. I can't just ditch her here. What kind of mother do you take me for?"

Gruffly, he said, "I'll be waiting in my car." He ducked his head as he glanced up at the atrium's high ceiling. "This place gives me the creeps."

I patted him lightly on the shoulder. "Yes, dear. Let's leave the scary museum with the bright lights and the priceless emeralds, and go visit the bloody crime scene of a recent decapitation. That'll be much less creepy."

He shrugged off my hand and headed for the exit.

CHAPTER 6

On Beacon Street, crime scene vehicles were taking up all of the street parking in front of the Greyson residence.

Bentley rolled past slowly and parked the car at the end of the block.

He turned off the engine but didn't move to step out right away. I could hear him breathing. With the air conditioning off, the car immediately started heating up under the bright sun.

"We have a mixed crew working the investigation," he said in a neutral tone. "A few of them are in the know, like us, but the majority of the technicians haven't been made aware of any supernatural elements. Zara, what I'm trying to say is I'd prefer that you keep a low profile in there."

"A low profile? Darn. There goes my plan to make a grand entrance."

He didn't ask me to elaborate, but I did anyway.

"I was planning to fly in on a broomstick, shooting blue fireballs from my hands."

He kept staring straight ahead out of the window.

I followed his gaze. There was nothing of note on the street, other than rubberneckers trying to get a glimpse of what was happening behind the crime scene tape.

After a moment, he spoke in a soft voice. "I remember driving in that old car with you."

"The old car?" My car was old, but he hadn't been inside it, so he must have been talking about our car chase at Castle Wyvern.

Bentley rubbed his forehead with one tanned hand. "Zara, I don't know which of my memories are real." He sounded exhausted, beaten.

"But you do remember driving in the convertible Cadillac?"

"Was it a Cadillac?" He massaged one eyebrow and then the other. "Who's Lucille?"

"The car!" I exclaimed. "The Cadillac was named Lucille. We borrowed it from my buddy, Nash."

"Yes." His voice didn't sound so beaten now. "We were chasing someone."

"A genie," I said, my mouth tasting sour. "There was a nasty ol' genie who took someone hostage. He kidnapped a woman with black hair."

"A woman with black hair? I remember her now." Bentley dropped his hand to his lap. "She was someone we both knew."

"That's right." The woman with the black hair was my mother. He'd been involved with her, but her mind-wipe glamour was still in effect.

He turned to me slowly and then startled, as though he hadn't expected to find me in the passenger seat.

"Your clothes," he said, blinking rapidly.

I reached down and smoothed the slim pencil skirt of my suit. Bentley had noticed I wasn't in my usual colorful attire. Earlier that morning, I'd consulted my closet with an outfit-picking spell, as I usually did. My closet had suggested the conservative gray suit that I only wore for job interviews. The wool was lightweight, but I'd still found it an odd choice for such a warm summer day. I'd taken my closet's advice anyway, since my closet knew best. Now I understood why. Bentley and I were both in conservative gray suits. We were a team.

"You look nice," he said. "Not like a clown."

"You sure know how to give a compliment."

"It's a good suit. You should dress like this more."

"You're only saying that because I look like your twin."

"Like my twin, but prettier."

"Well, obviously." I waved away his compliment.

He cleared his throat and looked down at my legs. "You look so pretty."

I snapped my fingers in front of his face. "Hey, mister. My eyes are up here."

He stared at me, his eyes glazed. Was his dazed look caused by trying to access his glamoured memories? The stress of the morning's homicide? Or the sight of my pale calves below my pencil skirt? Probably all three.

I didn't know what to do about him complimenting me. Bentley had looked at my legs before, and even said the odd flirtatious thing, but I hadn't thought much of it. We had a playful routine of teasing each other. Whenever he bumped into me around town, he would suggest I was up to criminal activities. Then I would get back at him by ordering all the rainbow sprinkle donuts at his favorite bakery so he couldn't get one. That was our thing. This new thing, with him giving me genuine compliments, was new. New and weird. But not bad.

I snapped my fingers again. "Are you okay?"

"Excuse me," he said gruffly, turning toward the driver's side window. "My mind must have drifted on me."

"No kidding. It was caused by your eyes drifting down to my legs."

He cleared his throat. "I did see your legs."

"Bentley, if we're going to be a crime-solving duo, you shouldn't ogle my legs like that."

He snorted. "Looking and ogling are very different."

"How so?"

The corner of his mouth twitched up. "Ogling is strictly against Wisteria Police Department policy."

"Good to know. I'll try not to be so ogle-able."

He didn't move to get out of the car yet, even though it was heating up in more ways than one.

"You were saying it's a mixed crew in there," I said, turning and looking down the street toward the garage apartment. "How are you going to explain to the non-magical folks about me being there?"

"I have a plan. I'll tell them you're a behavioral consultant with a specialty in deviant behavior."

"That's not far from the truth," I said seriously. "I can always tell when a patron in the library is trying to hide food or use the computers to find weird porn. Fun fact: A lot of people who do one of those things, do both of those things. What's that all about?"

He nodded. "It's true. People who violate one boundary violate more than one."

I reached for the door handle but didn't open it yet. Once I opened the door, I'd be on the case. Partnering with Bentley in an official capacity was going to change everything. Was I ready? Judging by his hesitation, even Bentley wasn't ready.

"You might know the victim's sister," Bentley said. "Her name is Carrot Greyson."

I didn't know the woman. "Did you say *Carrot*?"

"Yes. There are a lot of odd names in the Greyson family, not just Ishmael. You must have heard about his sister, Carrot. She worked with your aunt at City Hall until quite recently."

My jaw dropped. Aunt Zinnia worked at City Hall? She'd been so secretive about her work that I'd assumed she didn't have a job at all. Zoey and I had a theory she used her short-range psychic powers to make money as a day trader on her computer.

I closed my jaw and said, "Aunt Zinnia never mentioned anyone by that name." I looked down and traced a circle on my wool skirt. "Remind me, what's my aunt's job at City Hall?"

"She's the head of the Wisteria Permits Department Division of Special Buildings. She took over in February, shortly after the second death in the department."

"Right," I said with fake casualness. "The second death." I had a million new questions to ask my aunt.

I looked over to see Bentley staring at me, a bemused expression on his face. "You didn't know," he said. "All that business at the Permits Department happened before you moved here, and you didn't know."

I snorted. "You're new here, too. You don't know everything."

"But I have access to the redacted reports now. I know what happened to my predecessor, Fung." He crossed his arms and leaned back. "And you don't know." He looked as pleased as I'd ever seen the man.

I tilted my nose up in the air. "I'm sure if my aunt had wanted me to know, she'd have told me. It's probably for my own protection she didn't mention it."

"Sure," he said flatly. "You can ask me about the case later, if you really want to know."

"Thanks." I did want to know about Zinnia's past, but I wanted to hear it from her, not Bentley's version. Not the watered-down, doctored version. Even if he did have access to more detailed reports now, there was a slim chance even they told the whole story.

Bentley unfastened his seatbelt. "We should probably get into that crime scene before we melt in this car."

"Ready when you are."

He nodded, and we opened our car doors in unison.

Partners.

CHAPTER 7

The apartment over the garage contained about what you'd expect for a bachelor of twenty-six. That is, other than the headless body, which was being zipped up in a coroner's bag by three people in white suits when we walked in.

The furniture was all black leather, dark wood, chrome, and glass. The tiny kitchen's counter held up a stack of empty pizza boxes. The inexpensive bookshelves held very little reading material besides magazines about tattoos, hunting wild game, and weapons. The plain white walls were decorated with three tribal-patterned woven blankets and a framed illustration of a jaguar. The walls were also marked by two bright-red streaks of blood spatter.

Bentley gestured to the red streaks. "As you can see by the spray pattern on the wall, the victim was decapitated here."

"Here," I repeated, my dry mouth making smacking sounds. "Right across the street from my house."

He continued in a business-like tone, as though I truly was the criminal behavior expert he'd introduced me as. "The spray pattern isn't arterial. That means it didn't spurt from the body, but was caused by the movement of the weapon slicing through the air."

"Hmm," I said knowingly.

The detective shuffled past a worker in a white suit and got behind the sofa, which sat squarely in the middle of the room. "The killer must have stood here, behind the sofa, and sliced off the victim's head like this." Bentley swept his hand over where the body's neck had been, then flung his hand into the air triumphantly. "And that's when the blood ran off the weapon and onto the walls."

I'd seen enough blood spatter analysis on crime shows to understand what he was demonstrating.

"Did the killer fling their arm out twice?" I asked. "There are two distinctive blood streaks on the walls."

"Good eye. And what does that tell you? The double streaks?"

I gave it some thought before answering. "Two weapons, maybe? Or even two killers?"

"Perhaps. Or we might be looking for a killer with an artistic side. Someone who appreciates symmetry."

"Like an artist?"

He mimed scooping blood with his non-dominant hand and then flinging it onto the wall. "A painter."

I made a disgusted noise.

The three other white-clad people inside the small space barely glanced our way. Like myself and Bentley, they wore the so-called "bunny suits" that reduced contamination of the crime scene. The suits were white overalls with hoods, made of a non-woven material that would not be my top choice for clothing on such a sweltering day.

I tucked my chin down to catch a trickle of face sweat on the inside of my suit.

Bentley watched this with an amused expression. "You can always step outside for a moment if you don't feel well."

"If you can take it, I can, too. Riddle women are tougher than we look."

He raised one straight eyebrow. His facial expressions were more exaggerated, more comical when viewed through the oval opening of the white suit.

"Riddle women *are* tough." He frowned thoughtfully. "Yes. My predecessor, Detective Fung, mentioned that fact in a number of his secret reports."

"Where is this Fung person now?"

"I don't know."

"You probably need a higher level of clearance to get *that* report." I felt a slight chill despite the sweltering tropical environment inside my Tyvek bunny suit. "Maybe it's for the best you don't find out what happened to the man who had your job before you."

"There's a rumor he's enjoying a much-needed vacation somewhere beautiful."

"Right." I crossed my white-suited arms and tapped my green-gloved fingers on my bicep. "And every kid's old dog goes away to live on a farm."

"We all believe the lies we need to get through the long, dark nights," he said vaguely.

I murmured noncommittally and looked around the crime scene. The shock of the blood—both the sight and the smell—was wearing off. I was able to pick up more visual details now that I was past the initial horror. An unplugged black electrical cord caught my eye.

I pointed at the cord. "That big television is unplugged now," I said. "Did someone connected with the investigation unplug it?"

Bentley looked over the cord and the television. "I wouldn't think so. Why do you ask?"

I was mindful of the people working a few feet away from us and edited my speech. "The person who called in the initial report said the television was on. They saw it flickering when they looked in the window."

"Ah." He nodded. "Someone might have bumped the cord with their foot."

Given the location of the outlet, that didn't seem likely. I walked over to the media stand and leaned down to look at the second thing that had caught my eye. It was a metallic box, no bigger than a coffee mug. I waved for Bentley to come join me.

He trotted over. In a whisper, he asked, "Do you see him? The ghost? Is he here now?"

"No sign of the ghost, but I think I found a clue." I gingerly picked up the cube with my gloved hand. "They use these high-tech projection boxes at the DWM," I said at a quiet volume. "The units are not supposed to leave the premises."

"Are you sure that's a high-tech item? It looks like one of those useless decorator things real estate agents put in show homes, right next to the bowl of acorns."

"Look closer." I tilted it so he could see the tiny lens. "It projects images, like a regular projector, except it's super-tiny, and with no detectable power source."

He leaned back, nodding appreciatively. "If it does what you say, it's quite the gadget."

I turned from the black TV screen to the blood-soaked couch. Thankfully, the black leather showed the blood only as a sheen. "Since the TV appeared to be on to our witness, Ishmael Greyson must have been using the box to watch something, maybe even projected onto the screen of his unplugged television."

The muscles on Bentley's face twitched with excitement. "We need to find out what he was watching," Bentley said.

"Are you sure about that, Detective? Whatever he was watching might be irrelevant." I set the cube back exactly where I'd found it, the spot marked perfectly by a dust-free square patch. "Judging by the lack of dust under the box, it's been here in the apartment for a while. And the killer did leave the projection unit behind."

"True." His face drooped. "So, it would appear this little gadget is not a clue, after all." He let out an impatient huff, as though I'd intentionally gotten him excited over nothing. "Are you getting anything at all from the ghost? That is what I brought you here for."

I put one hand on my hip. "Is that all I am to you? A ghost magnet? You said you wanted a partner."

"I said we should work together instead of separately."

"Well, I'm trying to be cooperative."

"Then do your job," he said curtly. "You talk to the ghosts. I'll do the detective work."

I shook my head. "I can't figure out what my mother sees in you."

"Who?" His pupils dilated wildly.

"Never mind." I turned away and scanned the crime scene. "Be quiet and don't aggravate me while I look for the ghost."

He huffed again, but didn't speak.

After a moment, I reported my lack of results. "I don't see any sign of Ishmael's scrawny ghost, but I'm sure he'll be back eventually. With my other ghosts, they always stuck around until I figured out what happened, or got them justice."

"That's reassuring news."

"Easy for you to say. You don't have to get possessed by a ghost."

He sniffed. "That's not true. Detectives have their ghosts, too, Zara. A case like this has a way of taking over your life until it's closed."

Now it was my turn to huff indignantly. "That's not the same thing. It's your *job* to solve crimes. It's not your personal curse that comes as a bonus with your powers."

He guffawed. "Don't dismiss me like that just because I don't have any of your type of powers."

"Oh?" I stepped closer and looked him in the eyes. "What makes you think you don't have any powers, Detective?"

He was temporarily speechless. Got him!

"The town could have brought in any ol' detective," I said. "There's got to be a reason that the powerful entities that secretly run this town picked you, Mr. Theodore Dean Bentley."

He continued to say nothing. His pupils dilated and contracted wildly.

Oops, I thought. *I broke Bentley.*

By now, the other three bunny-suited people had gotten the body loaded into the zippered bag. They carted it outside, then closed the door behind them. Bentley and I were alone in the crime scene.

I pointed my gloved finger at the cube and changed the topic back to the clue I'd found. "You wanted me to help, and I am helping. This little box is a clue. It means Ishmael was connected to the DWM."

His pupils returned to normal, and he nodded slowly. "It would appear that way."

"You're not surprised he's connected to the DWM?"

"I'd be more surprised if someone in this town got murdered and *wasn't* connected to the DWM."

He made an excellent point. We probably should have started with that assumption. Point taken for our next case, if there was one.

My whole face tickled. I ducked my chin into my hood to catch another drip of sweat. "You know, they claim to be the good guys."

"So I've heard."

The heat rose inside my suit. I was breathing heavily. The blood-stained wall seemed to be closer now than it had been a minute ago. My pulse whooshed in my ears. The temperature inside my bunny suit reached inferno levels. I felt bile coming up my throat.

"Thank you for pointing out the cube," he said evenly. "That was helpful."

"You're welcome," I said, swallowing hard to keep my stomach contents down. There was no ghost in the tiny apartment, yet there was a lingering energy. A malignant hatred that I could practically taste.

"You can take a break now," he said.

"I don't need one," I lied.

"Of course not." He smirked. "But take one as a favor to me. I'd like to be alone in here for a moment."

"If that's something you'd like to do, I suppose I could step outside for some fresh air."

"Thanks for doing that for me," he said, still smirking.

I walked to the door as slowly as I could manage.

The air outside was just as hot as the interior of the apartment, but it smelled infinitely better.

I pushed back my stifling white hood and took shelter under the welcoming shade of a tree.

I hadn't been enjoying the shady spot for long when I was joined by someone I'd never met before—the town's coroner, Dr. Jerry Lund.

CHAPTER 8

I unzipped my suit to the waist to get some air circulation. I stood in the shade of a tree outside the garage apartment, enjoying the fresh air and debating whether I should cross the street and return to my house or go back into the crime scene. I kept glancing up at the tree branches, expecting to find a nosy wyvern demanding the inside scoop, but Ribbons either wasn't around or wasn't in the mood for boring human business.

Something white emerged from the side of the garage and moved toward me. It was a short person in one of the crime scene bunny suits.

"There you are," the man said in a friendly tone, as though he knew who I was.

"Hello," I said to the man in an even tone. I didn't know who he was, but he certainly wasn't Bentley. Not unless the detective had shrunk a foot and become bow-legged.

"You must be Riddle," the man said.

"If you insist," I said with a smile. "Zara Riddle."

"That makes you the witch."

"I've been called worse." I gave him a tight smile. Apparently, he was one of those *in the know*.

"Lund," he said, waving one green-gloved hand. "I'd shake your hand, but I'm not done collecting specimens."

"Lund," I repeated. "And what are you?"

He narrowed his eyes playfully. "Do you mean what, or who?"

I shrugged, equally playfully. "Surprise me."

"I'm the M.E. The medical examiner. Jeremiah Lund. Some folks call me Jerry, but most folks call me Lund."

"Lund," I said again. "Would that make you Dr. Lund?"

"You can call me that. I am a doctor, yes, among other things." He waved a gloved hand vaguely. "You can call me Doctor, but don't call me Doc. It makes me feel like one of the seven dwarves. I may be vertically challenged, but I don't have a white beard or glasses."

I fought a devilish grin. Now that he'd asked me not to call him Doc, the temptation to do so was almost overwhelming. Thanks to his height and his bow-leggedness, he really would have fit into a collection with six others.

The man pushed back the hood on his white suit, giving me a better look at him.

Dr. Jerry Lund, the medical examiner, was a short man, though not quite as short as one of Disney's seven dwarves. He was round in the middle of his body, but with skinny arms and legs. He had a wide, heavy-looking head with soft features. His hair was fair and thin, damp and disheveled from the suit's hood. His face was clean-shaven, and he had a very wide mouth with thick lips that gave him a bullfrog appearance. His eyes were wide-set, light-blue, and bulging. I was reminded of the victim's bulging blue eyes; I swallowed hard, hoping the young man who'd met with such a grisly end hadn't been a relative of Lund's.

I was about to ask him if he knew Ishmael, but he spoke first.

"Bentley says you live across the street," he said, amiably enough.

"In the red house on the corner. I've lived here since March of this year. Almost four months. I've met a few neighbors, but I didn't know the victim. Did you know him?"

Lund's large, soft features didn't move much. "Greyson worked for the same organization that employs yours truly." He was careful not to mention the DWM by name. "I worked with the kid."

"I'm sorry for your loss."

"No need to be sorry," he said neutrally. "I knew him, but he wasn't a friend. It's a large organization."

"And how big is the organization?"

"That depends." He winked at me. "How long is a piece of string?"

"Nice evasion. Do they teach all of you how to do that on your first day underground?"

"Never mind my training." He waved a hand. "You are the witch, right?"

"Guilty as charged."

"Great. Now, tell me what you need to channel the ghost. I'll see that you get what you require. What'll it be? A pound of flesh or a bucket of blood?" His bullfrog mouth twitched into a smile. "You want the heart? Don't be shy. We're all on the same team these days, it seems. I'll set aside the heart for you."

"That's a very generous offer, but I don't need anyone's heart." At the mention of hearts, the rapid beating of my own caught my attention. Ever since it had been turned to stone and then back to flesh again by a gorgon, I had been sensitive to the topic of hearts.

He looked me over. "If you don't need any flesh to channel the dead, you must be as powerful as they say."

"Who's been telling you I'm powerful? Not Bentley."

"The people we both work for."

I laughed lightly. "I don't work for those people. I'm just a librarian."

"You're just a librarian, you say." He gave me a wide, bullfrog smile. "Does a librarian typically spend her Saturdays at blood-soaked crime scenes?"

He had me there. "Today's a special day," I said slowly. "I came along to give Bentley a hand."

"Librarian or otherwise, it's good that you're around." His expression grew serious. He blew a lank of damp hair out of his eyes. "Ms. Riddle, I want you to know that we all appreciate everything you've done for the organization. You—" His voice cracked, and his bulging blue eyes glistened. "You got rid of Bhamidipati, that flying sack of crap."

He meant Dr. Bhamidipati, whom most people called Dr. Bob. The DWM doctor had been violently dispatched of earlier that year. Sack of crap or not, the man wouldn't be flying anymore. Or even breathing.

Lund went on, seething through gritted teeth. "If I'd known what that monster was up to, and using our facilities, no less, I'd have ripped him apart myself."

"He was a bad man."

"Very bad. And thanks to that serum he created, he was also huge and powerful in his shifter form."

"What kind of bird was he, anyway? I swear he was bigger than a condor."

"He was a sparrow."

"Shut the front door!" I couldn't hide my surprise. "A sparrow," I muttered in disbelief. "That must have been one strong serum. Do all the shifters at the Department take it to make themselves bigger?"

"It's... not recommended. Dr. Bob was conducting some tests outside of the facility, overseas, and what few notes we've been able to locate have served as warnings."

"I guess the shifters can't pass for regular animals if they're three times the size they're supposed to be."

"Exactly."

I shook my head. "Dr. Bob was a super-sized sparrow."

"Magic and science make strange bedfellows," Dr. Lund said, his eyes shining in a very mad-scientist manner.

"Some things probably shouldn't get in bed with each other at all," I said, sounding not unlike my overly cautious aunt.

Lund blinked the sheen from his eyes. "It's a shame there wasn't much left of the giant sparrow's body for me to examine. I would have liked to have seen the effects the growth serum had on his internal organs. Also, I would like to have seen... what made him tick."

What made him tick? I didn't know what the medical examiner meant, but I definitely got a sense of it from the way his gloved fingers twitched excitedly. I'd seen that same finger-twitch before. It happened at the library, when shipments of new releases arrived, and the librarians crowded around for the unboxing, fingers twitching in anticipation. To a coroner, cutting into a body must have been its own form of unboxing.

Lund continued talking, squinting as he stared past the shade of the tree, into the sunny distance. "The dead share their secrets, if you know where to look." Another finger-twitch. "But look who I'm talking to." He focused on me again, looking upward. "Being a witch, you must know all about the secrets of the dead."

I shrugged. My instincts told me to divert the topic away from myself. "Dr. Bob sure didn't help your organization's reputation as," I made air quotes, "*the good guys*, did he?"

Lund scowled. "What's that supposed to mean?" He stepped closer to me so the big tree's leaves shaded the blazing afternoon sun from his eyes.

"Never mind," I said. "I'm sure there are a lot of great people working at the department."

"A lot of great people, yes."

I decided right then to cast another fishing line. Information was hard to come by, and my new friend could be a helpful resource.

"Great people such as Dr. Ankh?" I asked.

His expression froze again. His wide mouth barely moved as he asked, "You know Dr. Ankh?"

Did I know the necromancer who'd brought my mother back from death? Not very well, but I had shared a hot tub with her briefly.

He pressed on. "How do you know about Dr. Ankh?"

"She's the one who showed me the DWM's fancy little projection box," I said lightly. "The same kind that Ishmael has in his apartment, by his television."

Lund's posture relaxed as he exhaled. "Yes. Bentley pointed that out to me. As you might have guessed by now, Greyson shouldn't have had the box in his residence."

"They're not supposed to leave DWM premises."

Lund looked left and right. "Yes, well, *some people* believe the rules don't apply to them."

"Such as Dr. Ankh?"

He pressed his thick lips together in silence. I wasn't going to get any more dirt on my mother's savior.

I asked, "Why do you suppose Ishmael Greyson had the device in his apartment?"

He shrugged. "It might have been something as simple as watching unreleased movies. We have a subdivision that monitors mainstream media for potential security leaks. In fact..." He trailed off into a croaking sound. "No. I shouldn't say."

"Ishmael Greyson worked for that department," I guessed.

Lund blinked up at me and then admitted, "He did. He was only a junior agent, so he filled in across a few departments. He reviewed media when he wasn't needed in legal." Lund narrowed his eyes as he gazed up at me. "You're easy to talk to, Ms. Riddle. Is this a spell?" He withdrew a pen from an inner pocket and prepared to give it a click. It was a MPCG, a multi-pulse click generator. The agents used it as a defense against witch magic.

I held my hands out innocently. "Just my natural charm, I swear. You can click your pen if you'd like."

He slowly put the pen away, unclicked. They had a limited number of charges. "I trust you," he said. "For now."

"What about Greyson? Do you think he was up to something at the department that got him killed?"

"He was clearly up to something. My final report is pending, but I believe we can rule out suicide." He chuckled darkly.

"And what do you have for motive so far? Any suspects?"

"I'll leave that part to you and Bentley. My specialty is the body." More finger-twitching. "Finding out its secrets."

Curiosity got the better of me, and I had to ask the question burning on my mind. "Dr. Lund, if I may be so bold, are you talking about finding magic? Can it be found inside the body?"

His eyes twinkled, catching the dappled sunlight beneath the tree. "There are signs, if you know where to look."

"I'm going to go out on a limb and guess that testing a body for supernatural powers is a bit... invasive?"

Another bullfrog smile. "You could say that."

"Does this testing of yours involve chopping off the head?"

He let out a staccato bark of laughter. "No, no, no," he said. "Whoever did that to Ishmael Greyson wasn't looking for anything." He swiveled his head and looked around nervously. "However, I suppose it's possible they were about to look for something within the body, but then you scared them off."

"Me? Are you suggesting the killer was still inside the apartment when I came by?" I didn't ask the question that followed in my mind. Had the killer seen me? My skin prickled all over.

"The killer might have still been around," Lund said casually. "I'd put the time of death at 5:00 am. The body's temperature had barely dropped when we arrived." He stared at me, unblinking. "How was it you came to be on the victim's stairwell shortly before dawn?"

"His ghost paid me a visit at my house," I said. "I thought you knew all about me."

"If it's all the same, I'd like to hear your version."

"Okay," I said, and then I repeated the whole story. Judging by Lund's lack of reaction, he didn't hear anything that surprised him. As I stepped back through the sequence of events, I remembered something I hadn't mentioned to Bentley. How could I have forgotten?

"There was a car that pulled out in a hurry," I said.

He showed interest in that fact. "That could be something."

Just then, Bentley emerged from the apartment, came down the stairs, and joined us under the tree.

"Tell him about the car," Lund said to me, nodding to Bentley, so I did. As for the license plate, I hadn't caught the letters, but I was certain of the last four digits. "It was 2319."

Bentley asked, "Are you sure?"

"Absolutely. It's my favorite four-digit number."

The two sweaty-haired men in bunny suits exchanged a look.

Lund said, "I'll bite. You have a favorite four-digit number? Is it your bank card password?"

"No," I lied, making a mental note to change my password. "Here. It makes more sense if I show you. Paper? My purse is in Bentley's car." Lund produced a notebook and pen, and gave it to me. I wrote 2319 in block letters. I flipped the paper over and held it up to the dappled light. "See how 2319 in reverse looks like it says PIES?"

Bentley's mouth opened with surprise.

"Neat-o!" Lund exclaimed, peering closer at the paper. "Once you see it, you can't un-see it. PIES."

"But more importantly, that's enough to narrow it down and get a suspect from the plate, right?"

Lund shrugged. "Like I said before, I'm happy to brainstorm, but I'm no detective. I'll be busy digging through the victim's entrails." He gave me what started as a wink but turned into a blink, his eyelids out of sync with each other in a way that seemed amphibian. "For my coroner's report," he added dryly. "Not for my personal enjoyment."

Maybe just a little personal enjoyment, I thought. The man was passionate about his career.

Bentley took the paper from me. "We'll call this in to the station from the car," he said, shifting his body to indicate we should be leaving now.

"You don't need my help for that," I said. "I'll get my purse, then I should probably walk across the street and return to my house."

Bentley raised an eyebrow. "Is that what you want to do?"

"It's what I *should do*. Ishmael might already be there in ghost form, sitting on my couch. If he's not there, I could always find something to do in the house while I wait around for him." I stuck out my tongue. "Like housekeeping, or laundry."

The detective narrowed his steely gray eyes. "You don't strike me as someone who waits around for anything."

He was right. I hated the idea of doing laundry while waiting for a ghost. Particularly the part about doing laundry. Laundry was no picnic. I'd recently learned several spells for stain-removal and button-strengthening. But instead of making laundry a breeze, it had only increased the level of attention involved in doing that particular chore.

"Waiting around sucks, but isn't patience a big part of investigation?" I asked.

"Patience, but not waiting around," Bentley said.

I sighed. "If you want my company so bad, you could ask. *Zara, would you please drive around with me on your day off? I'll treat you to lunch!*"

His eyebrows rose. "Lunch is the furthest thing from my mind."

"Then I guess I'd better come with you, to make sure you eat something and keep up your strength." I grabbed the paper from his hands. "Let's get this number called in and find out who was in that car. If I hadn't jumped out of the way in time, they might have made it a double homicide. That means we're dealing with a potential serial killer."

"We might be," Bentley said, unzipping the white bunny suit. I'd been joking, but he sounded serious, which made me nervous.

"We might be?" I shot a panicked look at Lund. "Are there other headless bodies popping up around town? Don't hold out on me, Lund. I don't appreciate being kept in the dark."

Lund said evenly, "This is the first headless body I've seen in a great number of years."

"But not the first one ever," I said.

Lund dismissed my line of questioning with a head shake. "This case is unrelated to anything local or recent. Most decapitations occur during vehicle or industrial accidents. When the victims meet with foul play, there's typically a sawing pattern on the bones." He mimed using a hacksaw to saw through material. "Ishmael's head wasn't sawed off. It was sliced." He made a smooth, swift slicing motion with one hand.

"The attacker must have been powerful," Bentley said.

"And the blade must have been extremely sharp," Lund said. "It went through the tissue and bone in one smooth motion."

"Like a guillotine," Bentley said.

"That narrows it down," I said. "There can't be many people in town who own a guillotine. We'll check the guillotine registry, find all the local guillotine owners, and question them about their whereabouts last night."

They both nodded as though taking my suggestion seriously. For a long moment, nobody gathered under the shade of the tree spoke. Before long, I wondered if perhaps there was a local guillotine registry after all.

At last, Dr. Jerry Lund broke the silence. "Guillotines work with gravity, slicing vertically. We're looking for a weapon that cuts horizontally. Greyson was alive when he sat down on his sofa for the last time."

"You mean a sword?" Bentley asked.

"Or a scythe," I said.

They both looked at me.

"A scythe," Bentley muttered. "A scythe?"

"Now, there's a thought," Lund said. "A scythe can be swung with speed, though I'm not sure about the angle. Even with the victim sitting, his neck was still four feet above the floor." His nostrils flared and spit flew from the corners of his wide mouth as he grew more animated. "I'll have to do some tests on a meat dummy." He rubbed his hands together. "This is so much better than a standard mauling or gunshot wound."

"Great," I said. "If the scythe theory pans out, you've ID'd the killer."

They both gave me a puzzled look.

"I'll give you a hint," I said. "He carries a scythe and wears a black, hooded cloak."

They continued staring at me.

"The Grim Reaper," I said, holding out one hand to let them know I was joking. Whatever happened to gallows humor at the crime scene? These guys were not on the same page as me.

Lund tipped his head to the side. "The who?"

I grinned. "Don't pretend you don't know him. The Grim Reaper. Death personified. History's most notorious serial killer. Sooner or later, he comes for every single one of us."

Lund chuckled darkly at my joke, as I'd suspected he would, once he finally understood it.

"Because the Grim Reaper carries a scythe," Lund said, nodding.

Bentley groaned and clapped his hand to his forehead, which was sweaty and thus made a satisfying slap.

CHAPTER 9

My comment about the Grim Reaper had been a joke, but as we drove away from Beacon Street, I wondered if there was something to the idea.

Were we looking for a robed skeleton carrying a scythe? Scythes weren't used much in modern times, but they were as ordinary as toasters back in the Middle Ages, when Europe was largely an agrarian society. I imagined the idea of a man carrying a scythe had probably come first, and then the name. The Grim Reaper. But he wasn't the only personification of death.

Around the world, humans had been creative in their depictions of an entity who reaped souls. The Greeks used an image of twins, shown side by side, one being Sleep and the other Death. The twins were young men, named Hypnos and Thanatos respectively. Was our chief suspect in the Greyson case a twin named Thanatos? Possibly. But he wouldn't be carrying a scythe. In ancient Hellenic societies, Thanatos was painted with either a sword or an upside-down, extinguished torch. The torch wouldn't do much to detach a person from their head, but the sword might.

I pictured a hooded man standing behind Ishmael Greyson as the young DWM junior agent watched unreleased movies obliviously. The assailant swung a two-handed sword, slicing Greyson at the juncture of his scrawny neck. Blood flew from the sword as it arced, painting a dark-red streak on the apartment's white wall. One bony hand released the hilt of the heavy sword and swept back the dark hood, revealing a glowing skull with hollow eye sockets.

A voice came from the car's speakers, jarring me out of the disturbing vision.

"That narrows it down," came the voice, which sounded young and female. "All the way down to, yup, a single vehicle registration."

Bentley replied warmly, "Thanks, Persephone. I knew you'd be able to track this one down."

My ears buzzed. Did I have Greek mythology on the brain, or was Bentley talking to someone named Persephone? As in, the daughter of Zeus, queen of the underworld?

There was the sound of typing over the speakers, then she reported back, "I've sent the name and address of the car's owner to your phone."

"Don't keep me in suspense. I'm driving right now, on my way to notify the next of kin. What's the name of our speeding driver?"

"Maisy Nix," said the voice on speakerphone. "That's Maisy, like Daisy, and Nix is spelled N-I-X."

Bentley took in a sharp inhale. The woman on the other end of the phone call wouldn't have heard him gasp, but I did.

"Repeat that," Bentley ordered gruffly, sounding less warm and more like the stone-cold commander of a fleet of starships.

"Yes, sir. The vehicle matching your description and partial license plate number, 2319, belongs to a local business owner, Maisy Nix. She runs Dreamland Coffee. There are two locations. She might be at one of the locations right now."

"Yes," he said dryly. "I know who that is and where she works. Thank you, Persephone."

The call ended, and the car's speakers reverted back to playing music from the radio.

"Maisy Nix," I said. "I believe I know her."

"That doesn't surprise me." His tone was dripping with accusation.

"What do you mean by that?"

He stared straight ahead through the windshield. "Maisy's name has turned up in a few reports. She was on my radar for suspicious activities before the incident at Castle Wyvern. She was one of the leads I was chasing down before I found out... well, everything." He frowned and chewed his lower lip. "I haven't given her much thought since then."

"I don't know her that well," I said. "I've only spoken to her a couple of times at Dreamland. They do make the best coffee in town, possibly the whole world."

He glanced over at me. "She doesn't live in your neighborhood."

"You know where she lives?"

"Like I said, I was looking into her, due to her connection to suspicious cases."

"You think she's a shifter, or a gorgon, or a witch?"

"I think she's... something."

"Do you think she's a Grim Reaper?"

He chewed his lip a bit. "How about Lady Death? Isn't that a thing? Something to do with dice?"

"You're thinking of Lady Luck."

"Either way, she does make an impression."

"She is tall," I said, which was an understatement. Maisy Nix was statuesque, beautiful, and commanding, like an actress who might play Wonder Woman.

"Tall women are strong."

"I guess she might be strong enough to do some damage with a scythe or a sword." I quickly shook my head. I'd liked Maisy. I didn't want her to be a Grim

Reaper or a Lady Death. "But there must be some other reason she was on my street this morning."

"Why? Why must there be another reason?"

"Because she's a nice woman. She was always friendly to me. Not like someone who goes around chopping off heads."

"When I met you the first time, you seemed like a nice woman, too."

I made an offended sound. "You're so rude sometimes, Teddy B."

"Don't dish it out if you can't take it back." He clicked on the turn signal. "Let's see if she's at the coffee shop now."

"Now?" My pulse quickened, but not from fear. I was excited. Things were really moving along with this case. At this rate, I could have the bug-eyed ghost of Ishmael Greyson on his merry way before dinner time.

Bentley took a few turns, and soon we were driving through the alley behind the downtown location of Dreamland Coffee. Jackpot. The same car I'd seen that morning, with the 2319 license plate, was sitting in one of the staff parking spots.

Bentley kept driving. And when we reached the street, he didn't turn back to park in front of the coffee shop.

"Change your mind?" I asked.

"Just wanted to get a positive ID on the vehicle. If we like Maisy Nix as the Grim Reaper, we should get some more information before we talk to her. Right now she has all of the information and we have none."

"Assuming she has any information at all. She might have been visiting someone in the area. Maybe a boyfriend."

"Maisy Nix is forty-five," Bentley said. "Ishmael was only twenty-six. He was too young for her, if that's what you mean."

"Some mature women like dating younger men. My mother, for example."

He frowned at the street ahead. "It's odd that you're always mentioning either your mother or your aunt to me. It's like you're trying to set me up. Exactly how old do you think I am?"

I replied without hesitation. "Fifty."

He took his eyes off the road long enough to shoot me a dirty look.

"I didn't mean it," I said. "You don't look fifty. Except maybe when you're scowling."

"I turned forty-two last week."

"Happy birthday. What did you do to celebrate?"

"After twenty-one, there aren't any birthdays worth celebrating. What's so great about getting older?"

"It beats the alternative," I said. "Ishmael Greyson won't be getting any more birthdays."

Bentley made a grumpy noise. "This is why I'd rather not discuss personal matters with my partner. I was simply sharing my opinion with you, and now you've brought up the murder victim and painted me as the bad guy just because I didn't order a bouncy castle and throw a block party for my birthday. You made me sound ungrateful to be alive."

"Are you?"

He turned up the volume on the car stereo.

As we drove, I wondered if Bentley had always been so gloomy about birthdays or if dating the undead, humorless woman who was my mother had changed him in some way.

There was another incoming call. He answered it. The young woman—whose name definitely was Persephone—confirmed that Greyson's great-uncle, Arden Greyson, was indeed the owner of the garage apartment and main house. The police hadn't been in touch with Arden yet, but he had been spotted out on the ocean on his little yellow boat. *Probably with his dog and his pointy trident,* I thought. According to Persephone, Arden must have left to go fishing at dawn, before the police had showed up at the house.

"I'll stop by the marina next," Bentley said.

"No need. We've got someone there waiting to talk to him when he comes ashore."

"Great. Keep me posted. I'm nearly at the victim's sister's place now."

"Oh, dear," Persephone said.

"What is it?"

"Nothing. Uh, nothing case-related. I just feel bad for you that you're the one who has to give people bad news. It must be so hard."

Coolly, Bentley said, "It's all part of the job."

"I know, I know," she said. "But if you need someone to talk to, I'm around."

The detective cleared his throat. "Persephone, I have someone in the car with me."

She blurted a curse word, followed by an apology.

"It's fine," he said. "I'll speak with you later."

After the call ended, I could only hold back for so long.

"You're having a torrid affair with Persephone!" I squealed.

"I am not."

"She thinks you are."

"She's just a girl. Girls get crushes. It doesn't mean anything."

"You'd better watch out for all those pretty young things who work under you. One of them's going to get you, and put a permanent smile on that grouchy mug of yours."

He shot me a deadly look.

"You won't know what to do with yourself if you turn happy," I said.

"I'm not going to turn..." He sighed. "Thanks for the warning, partner."

"Any time."

A moment later, we were parking in front of Greyson's sister's workplace, a tattoo studio located on the main floor of an old house.

"Carrot Greyson is a tattoo artist?" I asked.

"Yes. Why? Do you know anything about that?"

"You said the person who made the two blood streaks might have an artistic flair. Is she a suspect?"

"It's a homicide investigation, Zara. Everyone's a suspect."

"Even me?"

"That would be quite the twist, wouldn't it?"

I held up one hand. "I didn't do it. I swear."

"How can you be so sure? You've admitted that you allow spirits to possess your body."

He actually had a point. I said nothing as I mulled it over. A spirit had made me sleepwalk at least once before. I'd even sleeptoasted. Had I sleepmurdered?

"It wasn't you," Bentley said. "I don't know what happened in that apartment, but I know in my heart that it wasn't you."

"How do you know?"

"You're a good person. Good people aren't perfect, but they don't murder, not even when they're being influenced by someone else."

"Thanks," I said. "Partner."

We got out of the car and prepared to interview the victim's sister.

CHAPTER 10

The studio was named Time Traveler Tattoos. I'd expected it to have a pun name, like many of the small businesses in Wisteria, which included such gems as Open Toad Shoes, Salt and Battery Seafood, Doggy Style Pet Groomers, Stalk Market Flowers, Hairforce One, and the Shady Lanes Bowling Alley. I was surprised by Time Traveler Tattoos' intriguing name as well as its eye-catching logo, which featured a woman in a flapper dress and steampunk goggles riding a strange flying contraption.

Bentley and I walked inside, and were cheerfully greeted by the owner and tattoo artist, Carrot Greyson. The young woman, who had dyed orange hair the color of freshly pressed carrot juice, stared at me with big, bugged-out blue eyes.

Bentley introduced us by name.

"Zara Riddle?" Carrot asked. "You must be Zinnia's niece."

"I am." I was glad Bentley had warned me that Zinnia had worked with Carrot at City Hall.

The orange haired woman cooed, "You look exactly like her!"

And she looked exactly like her brother, except female and still alive.

Before I could say anything awkward, Bentley took her by the elbow and said in a low and serious tone, "We need to sit and speak privately, Ms. Greyson. I'm afraid there's some bad news."

"B-b-bad news?" Her large eyes glistened.

Bentley signaled for me to stay where I was, in the lobby, and whisked Carrot through the doorway into some back area. The old house was deadly quiet. If other people worked at Carrot's tattoo studio, they weren't in yet that afternoon.

I stayed in the front waiting area, in what must have originally been the home's mudroom. Ishmael's ghost hadn't made an appearance, but I kept an eye out for him as I surveyed the place.

The interior of Time Traveler Tattoos had a bold, red-and-black scheme, starting with the checkerboard floors, then extending up the walls in alternating stripes of red and black. There was a shiny red sofa next to the front door. I took a seat on the end of the sofa. The red fake leather squeaked under me.

I checked out the reading material on offer. It was all tattoo magazines. I picked one up, but couldn't focus on the page long enough to read, so I held it loosely on my lap while I gawked around. The reception area's front counter was sleek and black. The counter was lined with a tidy row of glass apothecary jars. The jars held candies, but only red ones. There were red jelly beans, red licorice whips, red jawbreakers, red saltwater taffy, and red gumballs. My mouth watered for the candy, but I stayed where I sat. I wasn't a customer. I was an unwanted guest bearing very bad news.

I crossed my legs, smoothed down my gray wool skirt, and tried to look professional in case the victim's sister happened to glance my way.

Carrot Greyson had certainly created a welcoming tattoo studio. It was just edgy enough to increase the thrill of being tattooed, yet it was also homey and relaxed. She had a trio of ferns growing in a macramé plant hanger, and a small box of children's toys tucked under a side table. The boldly striped walls were decorated with black-framed prints from various eras. There were illustrations of airplanes from the early days of aviation, portraits of white-wig-wearing aristocrats, and a number of patent applications for perpetual motion machines and time traveling contraptions. My gaze swept from one delightful illustration to the next until I landed on a drawing of a jaguar. The print was the twin of the one I'd seen that morning at Ishmael's place, next to the spatter of his blood.

Ishmael Greyson.

I'd never heard his name before that Saturday. It had sounded so strange at first, but now it was too familiar. His name wouldn't stop echoing in my mind. I looked around Time Traveler Tattoos for the ghost with the bulging eyes and the skinny, glowing neck. I still couldn't see or sense him.

"Ishmael," I whispered. "Ishmael Greyson, are you here?"

There was no response.

I decided to cast a threat detection spell I'd recently learned from my mentor, Aunt Zinnia. The spell revealed the invisible or hidden, within certain parameters that Zinnia hadn't defined clearly. I suspected she'd been keeping me in the dark on some spells to prevent me from becoming overconfident. But I'd seen her cast the spell, and I'd kept pestering her about it until she taught it to me recently.

To cast the spell, I waved my hand as though I was sprinkling powder in a circle around myself. The spell also came in powdered form, with the magic already built in, but we'd used up my aunt's supply during lessons and she hadn't yet made another batch. Zinnia told me the spell would work at least one time on a newly made ghost —one time only, then the spirit became inoculated against the spell. Until now, I hadn't needed any spells to see ghosts, but there was something different about Ishmael. Or something different about me.

The old house was quiet, yet an even deeper hush fell around me as the threat detection spell settled. I held very still and waited. No ghost.

Darn. The spell hadn't reveal anything new, and yet... the gleaming checkerboard floor did appear more dusty than it had seemed a moment before.

I cast the spell once more for good measure, this time twitching my non-dominant fingers at the upper corners of the small waiting room.

Still no ghost.

I looked over at the jars of red candies. *Those sugary candies are the only threat in this waiting area*, I thought with a chuckle. My mouth watered. I forced my eyes down to the magazine. *Zara is a good witch. Zara doesn't help herself to delicious red candies that are for customers only.*

Cut to: twenty minutes later.

Wouldn't you know it, yours truly literally had her *hand in the candy jar* when Bentley returned to the waiting room. Busted.

"I need your help," he said, then shook his head. "I can't leave you alone for a minute, can I?"

I held out a handful of red jelly beans. "I was planning to share. Here. Take some."

"They look moist from your hand."

"So? Don't tell me you're a germaphobe."

"Just because I'm selective about what I put in my mouth, that doesn't make me a germaphobe." He hand went to something at his neck, a lump under his shirt collar.

I stuffed the jelly beans in my mouth. He was right about my hand being moist. The candy coating left a red sheen on my palm that I had to lick clean, much to Bentley's horror.

CHAPTER 11

The sticky candy clung to my teeth as I asked Bentley, "How'd it go?"

"She took the news as well as could be expected." He rubbed his chin. "I'd like to try the rest of the interview with you present. Since you're here already, I might as well put you to use."

"You make me feel so special."

He nodded for me to follow him. "She formed a bond with your aunt when they worked together. Due to your similar appearances, I believe Miss Greyson may be more comfortable with you present. I've explained to her that you're acting as a special behavioral consultant on the case."

"And she bought it? Wow. You're good."

With no trace of humor whatsoever, he said, "I am good."

I followed him through the tattoo studio, past reclining black leather chairs that would look right at home in an edgy dentist practice, and then into a small office.

Carrot Greyson was wiping her eyes with a crumpled tissue. Bentley and I sat on two guest chairs that were a bit too close together. We bumped arms until we each leaned to the outside.

"Ms. Greyson, I'm so sorry to be meeting you under these circumstances," I said, offering her my hand for the second time because I didn't know her well enough to offer a hug. She shook it limply.

"You look so much like Zinnia," she said. "I feel like I know you already."

"If you know my aunt well, you may know more about me than most people do." For example, she might know that the Riddles were witches.

She frowned. "I don't know her that well. We worked together for over a year, but she's very private about her personal life."

"Ah," I replied. Zinnia was private about her personal life. Carrot Greyson didn't know my aunt was a witch.

She went on. "I didn't even know Zinnia was dating someone in our office until..." She trailed off, her weepy eyes unfocused. She seemed to stop breathing for a full moment before taking in a gasp of air and then gushing, "It's all been so terrible lately. Everything. I thought I could get away from all of that death and start fresh by opening this place, but we can't ever escape our fates, can we?"

I glanced over at Bentley for permission to dive in with my questions. He gave me an almost imperceptible nod.

"What do you mean by *our fates*?" I asked gently. "Do you think that whatever happened to your brother has something to do with you?"

"I don't know." She scrunched her face. "Do you ever feel like you're cursed?"

"Yes," I answered without hesitation. I'd been told I was Spirit Charmed, but it often felt more like Spirit *Cursed*.

Bentley interjected. "It's normal to feel that way after a string of bad luck. I'm sure you're not cursed, Ms. Greyson." He looked directly at me and explained, "Earlier this year, two of the people Carrot worked with at the Permits Department died by violent means. The cases have both been closed, and there's no reason to believe those incidents are connected to what we're talking about today."

I nodded. The cases had almost certainly been connected to my aunt, and I was dying to know how, but now wasn't the time.

"Let's say you are cursed," I said to the young woman with the skinny face and bright orange hair. Bentley groaned, but I went on. "Do you have any thoughts about who might have cursed you? Or why?"

"I'm not crazy," she said. "I know things like curses aren't real." She smacked herself lightly on the forehead. "Stupid Carrot." She gave herself another smack before she dropped her pale hand away. "I shouldn't even say stuff like that as a joke. People always tease me about my beliefs. My boyfriend hates it when I tell him about my dreams."

I leaned forward. "Your dreams?"

"In my dreams, sometimes I'm myself, but other times I'm like a camera, or a silent passenger inside an animal." She rubbed her collarbone, running her fingertips over the tattoo that marked her pale flesh there. It was the paw of an animal with sharp claws. "The Greyson family comes from a long line of psychics and monster hunters," she said. Then she smacked her forehead again. "Stupid Carrot. I shouldn't have said that. Now you both think I'm crazy."

In unison, Bentley and I both said, "Not at all."

Bentley took over. "There are many things in this world people don't speak of, let alone understand. Did you have any of these dreams last night?"

"No. It was so hot upstairs." She dabbed her eyes dry and explained, "I live on the top floor of this place, and there's no air conditioning, as you might have noticed."

"It's not so bad on this level," Bentley said.

"No, but heat rises," she said. "The heat must have knocked me out, because my dreams were only blackness, except for when I was watching a movie." She smiled briefly through her tears. "I dreamed I was watching a movie that hasn't been released yet. Isn't that funny? My mind must have made it up from the trailer."

Bentley and I exchanged a look. Did Carrot have a psychic connection with her brother? Rather than wonder to myself without any answers, I went ahead and asked, "Did you and Ishmael share a bond? I've heard that some siblings can sense things about each other in ways that can't be explained by science."

"We aren't twins," she said. "He's a year older than me." A tear sprung from one eye. She caught it with the crumpled tissue. "He *was* a year older, anyway. Now I'll catch up to him, since he won't be getting any older."

"Oh, sweetie." I got up from my chair, leaned down next to her and gave her a firm hug. "I'm so sorry for your loss," I said into her orange hair. She hugged me back, and I held tight on until she let go.

When I returned to my seat, she was looking at me with her head cocked. "You're different from Zinnia," she said. "You look like her, but you're not her."

"Thanks, I guess."

Bentley cleared his throat and tapped a short pencil on a notepad he'd produced from a jacket pocket. "Ms. Greyson, I'm afraid we must press on. In cases such as these, time is of the essence."

"Of course," she said. "What else do you need to know? I already told you that my brother didn't have any enemies or people who'd want to hurt him. He's never even had a girlfriend, as far as I know. He doesn't have any close friends in town. He likes to work and save his money for traveling." She wrinkled her nose. "He lives for safaris. The kind where they shoot big game."

I picked up on her distaste easily. "You don't approve of that," I said.

"I'm a vegetarian," she said.

"But your brother liked hunting," I said. "Big game."

Under his breath, Bentley said, "The most dangerous game."

Carrot looked at Bentley and I looked at her. Judging by the confusion on the tattoo artist's face, she didn't understand what he'd meant by his comment. But I knew.

"The Most Dangerous Game" was a famous short story by Richard Connell. It was first published in 1924, and became the basis for a number of film and television adaptations. In the tale, a big-game hunter in search of a jaguar in the Amazon finds himself on an isolated island in the Caribbean, where there's a role reversal. He becomes the one being hunted for sport. Not by a big cat, but by another man who's grown bored of hunting animals and moved on to man, the most dangerous game. Hence the title.

Somewhere in the quiet studio, a phone began ringing noisily. Carrot jumped to her feet, excused herself, and ran to answer it.

Once Bentley and I were alone, I said to him, "If Ishmael Greyson was hunted for sport, it wasn't very sporting of the hunter to nab him on the sofa of his apartment."

"No," Bentley said slowly. "The real sport would be an intellectual one."

"You think?"

"Getting away with the perfect crime." He flicked his gaze around the small office. The walls were a muted brown, unlike the bold red and black of the main showroom. The walls were decorated with more of the same vintage prints, including a few illustrations of jungle cats. "The victim had a print of a jaguar on his wall," he said.

"He did," I said. "And Carrot has a tattoo of a big cat on her breastbone. A cougar, I believe."

Bentley gave me a perplexed look. "This must be why they don't tell new detectives about all the magic in this town. Once you open your mind to the peculiar, it's hard to think inside the box again. Look at me. I'm planning to look up a novel from the 1920s as part of my research for this case. I might be losing my mind."

"It was a short story," I said. "Not a novel. 'The Most Dangerous Game' was a short story."

He shook his head. "You can take the librarian out of the library..."

Carrot returned to the office looking even more pale. She waved her cell phone apologetically. "I'm going to turn this off for the rest of the day. The rumor mill is churning. People have seen all the police cars at Uncle Arden's house." She gasped and held her fingers to her lips. "Does my great-uncle know?"

"He's been informed," Bentley said. He tapped the notepad again. "For my records, where did you say you were last night?"

She pointed at the ceiling. "I was here, up in the apartment."

"When did you leave? Have you left the building this morning?"

"Yes. At about ten o'clock this morning, when I drove to the discount warehouse to buy paper towels." She pursed her lips. "You go through a lot of paper towels in the tattoo business."

"Were you alone last night?"

Her cheeks flushed pink. "My boyfriend was here. He stays over sometimes." She patted her cheeks with her hands. "He says I've been a source of comfort for him, ever since his father passed away recently. He won't talk about it, but I get the feeling something bad happened."

"Violence?" Bentley asked. "Did his father live in town?"

"No. Overseas. I never met him, unfortunately." She patted her cheeks again. "It's such a shame. I hear he was a great man. My boyfriend idolized his father."

Bentley tapped the paper again. Every time he tapped, Carrot's posture relaxed and her focus returned. The tapping was not unlike a hypnotic suggestion.

"And your boyfriend's name is?"

"Sefu Adebayo," she said, and then spelled it.

Bentley kept his gaze down on his pad and asked casually but carefully, "How did your brother feel about you dating Sefu?"

She shrugged. "He was happy for me. They got along well enough when both of them were helping me paint and decorate this place."

"Did the two of them ever socialize without you being present?"

"I don't think so. Why? Sefu didn't have anything to do with what happened to Ishmael. He's the most gentle person you'd ever meet."

"And Sefu was here at the house with you the entire night?" Another tap on his notepad.

Her cheeks flushed a deeper pink. "Of course he was. Is this what you call profiling? Are you suspicious of him because he's black?"

"I didn't know he was black."

She crossed her tattooed arms. "It shouldn't matter that he's black. He told me he's had problems with cops all his life, since coming to this country. I didn't want to believe it, but now I see it."

"He's new to this country?" Bentley looked at Carrot steadily. She didn't answer. He flicked his gaze down to the notepad. "Adebayo. Is that an African name?"

"Yes. He's an American citizen. African American." Carrot reached for a paper takeout coffee cup on her desk, took a gulp, grimaced, and then spat into a garbage can next to the desk. "Sorry," she sputtered. "That was yesterday's coffee."

I jumped up, went to her side, and patted her back as she spat the sour remnants into the wastebasket. The container was full of takeout cups with names written on the side in black felt pen. Half of the cups had the name CARROT written on them in bold block letters, and the other half had a variety of names. I reached in and fished out a few of the cups she hadn't spat on.

"Are these cups from customers?" I asked. The name FISHTAIL caught my eye. "There's one here for Fishtail. That's an odd name. Fishtail." I shrugged. "But I suppose this is a tattoo studio. You probably get some unique people in here."

"That was Ishmael's coffee cup," Carrot said sadly. "The woman at the coffee shop never got his name right. Look." She fished out more paper cups and showed us the names. There were cups for GMAIL, ISHTAR, SCHLOMO, and a dozen other variations or misinterpretations of Ishmael.

"Cute," I said. "I guess it was a running gag?"

Carrot shook her head. "Ishmael hated it. He only kept going there because they make the best coffee in town."

I looked over at Bentley. He had his poker face on, but it hadn't escaped his notice that the coffee cups were all from Dreamland Coffee.

I swallowed down a lump of excitement and asked, "Was it the owner who always misspelled your brother's name? A woman named Maisy Nix?"

Carrot said, "I don't know. He would stop by there after work and bring me a coffee. I mostly work evenings these days." Her eyes glistened with a fresh batch of tears. "Since I opened the studio, my brother and I were closer than ever, closer than we were as kids."

I picked at the cup from her desk, the one she'd referred to as yesterday's cup. I took a sniff and gave it a swirl. I didn't have my daughter's keen shifter-sense of smell, but I could tell the difference between day-old and multi-day-old coffee. Half a lifetime of surviving on leftover takeout food had honed certain skills.

"This is yesterday's coffee," I said, as much to Bentley as to Carrot. "Does that mean Ishmael went to Dreamland Coffee yesterday?"

Carrot nodded. "Around six o'clock," she said. Her forehead wrinkled. "Now that I think about it, he was really steamed up last night. Whatever they wrote on his cup made him so mad that he threw it out and had them make him a fresh latte."

I heard Bentley's chair squeak as he leaned forward. "And what was it they wrote on your brother's cup yesterday?"

"He didn't say. When he got here, the cup he had was blank." She dug through the wastebasket and pulled out a cup with no name.

Bentley whipped a plastic evidence bag from his pocket with a flourish. "I'll take that," he said, popping the cup into the bag with practiced ease.

Carrot stared at him in horror. "You think he was poisoned? Before they killed him?"

"It would explain why there was no sign of a struggle," he said.

She continued to stare at him with her mouth open. She snapped it shut and swallowed audibly. "When can I see him?"

"Soon," he said. "Someone from my office will be in touch." He glanced at me and gave me a look that seemed to say, *as soon as they fasten the guy's head back on.*

I raised my eyebrow to say, *assuming he doesn't come back to life when the head reattaches.*

He frowned back, as if to say, *I don't know what you're suggesting, Zara, but I don't like it.*

Bentley asked Carrot to review a few more details, and then we prepared to leave.

Bentley handed her an assortment of cards from his pocket. There were cards for a grief counselor, a crime scene cleaner, and a funeral home. Then he handed her some small brochures. The transaction reminded me of the basket of local business advertisements and coupons I'd received in my mailbox shortly after I'd moved to Wisteria. It was like a welcome wagon package, except instead *of welcome to your new home*, it meant *welcome to Bereavement, population one.*

CHAPTER 12

We hadn't been in the car for very long before Bentley said, "I really wasn't profiling the boyfriend in the way she thought I was."

"I believe you."

"We were talking about big game hunting, and safaris, and Adebayo is an African surname, I believe. Let's see." He used voice commands on his in-car computer to do a search on the name.

A robotic voice served up the answer. "*Adebayo is a Yoruba name. Yoruba names are used by the Yoruba people and Yoruba language-speaking individuals in Benin, Togo, and Nigeria.*"

Bentley turned to me and whispered, "These voice-activated internet searches are eerily good these days."

I whispered back, "Why are you whispering?"

"Because I don't want her to know I'm giving her a compliment."

"Why not? You should try buttering her up. Women love compliments."

He gave me a serious look. "Zara, it's a computer."

"Then why are you whispering?"

He waved a hand at me, pressed the button on the display again, and asked the computer, "What does the first name Sefu mean? S-E-F-U."

The robotic female voice replied, "*Sefu is a Swahili name for boys. It means sword.*"

"Sword!" I exclaimed, bouncing up and down in my seat. "You heard that, right? Your robot voice has just solved the case for us." I patted the dashboard. "Thank you, robot voice. I shall dub thee Lady Sherlock."

Bentley narrowed his eyes and shot me a look. "How much of the tattoo parlor's candy did you consume, anyway?"

"Not that much."

"Zara, stick out your tongue."

I did, blowing a little air so it made a funny sound.

"Your tongue is completely red," he said.

"That's the color of tongues, silly."

"You know what I meant."

I flipped down the sun visor and checked my tongue in the tiny mirror. It was stained by the dye in red candy. "My tongue has been worse colors," I said nonchalantly. I flipped the visor up again with a chunky snap. "More importantly, we have a very solid lead on a suspect. This Sefu guy."

"Ms. Greyson claims her boyfriend was with her all night. He has an alibi."

"They might have done it together."

"What's the motivation?"

"I don't know yet, but come on. The guy's first name means *sword*."

"Ah, yes. I forgot that important new section of the criminal code where we prosecute people for crimes based on their names."

I settled back in the passenger seat and crossed my arms. "Maybe I did eat too much candy." I shook my head. "Wow. Talk about a phrase nobody ever expected to hear coming from my lips. What a strange day this has been."

We drove for a while in silence.

"I take pride in not being prejudiced," Bentley said. Apparently, he hadn't let go of his hurt feelings over being accused of racial profiling.

"I already said I believe you."

"Most of us in law enforcement are just trying to do our jobs. It's a few bad apples who ruin it for everyone. Well, more than a few, but even so, I'm not one of them."

I held both hands up. "You're preaching to the choir." I thumbed my chest. "If you're talking about getting lumped in with bad apples, look over here at the genuine witch sitting in your car. The genuine practitioner of witcher-i-doo."

"Witcher-i-doo? Don't you mean voodoo?"

"It's something I picked up from Vincent Wick." I gasped. "Speaking of that particular devil, did they tell you all about Wick when you got your new level of clearance?"

He gave me a cagey look. "In what sense?"

"In the sense that he's got hidden cameras all over town, and he spies on people from his underground lair by the dump. He's a wizard of sorts. A tech wizard. No magic abilities, as far as I know. What did you hear?"

"I've heard that Wick is an independent contractor who occasionally assists in investigations, which is why his," he steadied the steering wheel with his elbow so he could make air quotes, "*underground lair* continues to operate. His role is similar to that of a criminal informant."

"Is Wick a criminal? He's creepy as all get-out, but that doesn't make him a criminal, does it?"

"Several of his intelligence gathering methods are in contradiction with modern privacy laws."

"But he's friends with my aunt, so he can't be that bad. And he helped me out when a family member of mine was hurt."

Bentley whipped his head to look at me. "Zoey was hurt? What happened?"

"Not Zoey. It was my dad. He was..." I waved a hand. "Long story." I looked out the window. "Where are we going again?"

"The coffee shop."

"Already? I thought you wanted to get more information before you interrogated Maisy Nix about her driving habits."

"I do, and I will, but we have something already to talk to her about." He patted his pocket, where he'd tucked away the evidence bag containing the blank coffee cup. "We can ask her what she wrote on the first cup that got him so irate."

"Under what pretext? Maybe you should tell me more of your plan so I don't mess it up."

"Just follow my lead." He shot me a serious look. "And don't let on that Ishmael's dead."

"I won't say a peep. Not even if I see his ghost standing there with his own head tucked under his armpit."

* * *

We parked in front of Dreamland Coffee and both looked up at the sign.

The coffee shop had a logo featuring a cuddly woodland creature—probably a chipmunk but possibly a marmot—wearing a striped sleeping cap and resting comfortably on a cloud. When I'd first moved to Wisteria, I'd mistaken Dreamland for a mattress shop based on the logo. Over the past few months, and no small number of mint mochas, the name and logo no longer seemed odd. And was it really that strange? The logo for Starbucks is a terrifying sea monster. Er, make that a sultry mermaid.

The interior of Dreamland could have had an austere, bare-bones feel, thanks to its tall gray walls of bare cinder blocks, gritty concrete floor, and exposed metal rafters. The light fixtures were the style used in warehouses a hundred years ago. But it didn't feel bare-bones at all. The tables were generously wide and made of honey-hued solid oak. The chairs and couches were all plush, upholstered in sunset shades of red, orange, and gold. Tall, arched windows flooded the space with sunshine, and were softened by curtain panels of gold crushed velvet, held back with the sort of chunky tasseled tiebacks my aunt might have used for a belt.

Maisy Nix was standing at the front counter.

"That's her," I whispered to Bentley. I could see by the set of his jaw that he already knew that. I wondered what sort of criminal cases she'd been associated with that had roused the suspicion of the detective.

Maisy Nix was equal parts tall and gorgeous, like an Amazonian warrior in a comic book. She stood over six feet tall, and though I couldn't see her feet behind the counter, I could tell by the length of her slender neck and her long arms that none of the height was coming from high heels. She had medium-brown skin, eyes the color of black coffee, and shoulder-length ebony hair, glossy and straight. Her face was angular, with a strong jaw that didn't detract from her beauty. The sharp planes of her face were balanced by a small nose and pretty lips that were ever so slightly too large on the top.

Under her orange Dreamland Coffee apron, she wore a white blouse tucked into gray trousers. The blouse wasn't the polyester-cotton blend of a uniform, but a silk blend with round mother-of-pearl buttons. The apron itself looked freshly ironed and spotless.

She covered her mouth, yawning as we approached. "Sorry about that," she said sleepily. She had a light Hispanic accent. "I had a late night," she explained.

A late night? A late night of... murder?

She smiled at me. "The usual for you? Mint mocha?"

"Perfect," I said, even though my cravings for that particular beverage had been fading since my possession by a mint-mocha-loving ghost. I would have preferred an iced tea given the weather, but we were there to get information. I couldn't stray from my usual behavior and tip her off.

She looked pointedly at Bentley and stifled a second yawn. "And for you,*Detective*?" She said the word *Detective* with a teasing tone I recognized. It was the same playful tone I'd used myself on Bentley, all those times I'd bumped into him around town. He'd had it coming, the way he was always insinuating that I was up to something nefarious. Such as witchcraft. Was that also Maisy's secret? My aunt always sidestepped questions about a local coven, but she'd never gone so far as to tell me we were the only witches in town.

I studied Maisy's face closely, and then I let my eyes unfocus and studied her... *the opposite of closely*. Seeing things on the magical plane was like trying to catch movement in your peripheral vision. You had to try not to try. It was one of the many intriguing contradictions of magic. As my gaze shifted past normal reality, the colors in my vision lost saturation and gained vibration. Maisy was still there, majestic and striking despite her tiredness. I didn't see anything unusual. If Maisy had been a gorgon, I would be able to see her hair snakes, but there were none. No devil horns or halo, either.

At my side, where my vision was blurry and my hearing was dampened, Bentley leaned forward and ordered a plain black coffee. Then he paid for both of our drinks. He asked no questions about the woman's car, or her whereabouts last night. I kept relaxing my vision and being open to seeing something. Maisy's sleek, ebony hair only revealed that she used an excellent conditioner. Since Bentley wasn't making any moves, I guessed it was time for me to roll out the slightly bigger guns.

When Maisy took her eyes off us and turned her tall, strong body toward the espresso machine to make our beverages, I quickly made a circle and cast the threat detection spell.

The instant I finished the phrase, Maisy jerked her head up and stared right at me. Her black-coffee eyes were like two bottomless wells.

"What was that?" The depth of her eyes pulled at me. "I didn't catch what you said just now, *Zaaaaara*." She dragged out my name as though we had a long and complicated personal history together, and not at all like a coffee shop owner who'd memorized the names of her regular customers.

She'd heard my silent Witch Tongue! I was thrown off by her reaction, but I was even more thrown off by the result of the spell. It splashed back at me in a cold wave of failure, like the time I'd brushed my teeth while driving and then attempted to spit out the car window only to have it come back on my face. Grimacing, I took a step back. My backfiring spell had been both startling and unpleasant.

Had Maisy countered my spell herself? Or was there a magical ward over the coffee shop? Or was there something wrong with me? Ishmael Greyson's ghost had walked through my body that morning. Had he shorted out something inside me?

Maisy, meanwhile, was patiently waiting for an explanation about what I'd "said." Two angular eyebrows arched above those coffee-black eyes.

I coughed delicately into my fist. "Nothing," I said. "It must have been my stomach making a noise."

Maisy nodded, pressed a button on the espresso contraption, and began grinding the beans. I was relieved by the cover of noisy bean grinding. Plus, it did smell awfully good.

I glanced over at Bentley. *Well?*

He avoided eye contact with me, looking down as he lifted one foot to rest casually on the iron pipe that ran horizontally along the base of the counter. The pipe was like the brass footrails found in English pubs, except black and pockmarked.

Maisy finished making our drinks and set the paper takeout cups on the counter. "Lids are by the cream and sugar," she said.

Bentley didn't touch his.

Maisy asked, "Would you like a carrying tray, Detective?"

"No need," I answered for him. "We've got four hands between the two of us."

I didn't grab the cups just yet. Stalling for time, I rubbed my palms on my hips thoroughly, as though preparing to grab the high bar at a gymnastics competition. Bentley wasn't making his move yet, so I kept rubbing my hands. The gray wool of my suit started to heat up from the friction. I slowed down before I accidentally shot off a spell.

Finally, the detective spoke. "You didn't write our names on the paper cups," he remarked dispassionately.

Maisy gave him a forced, fake smile. Her front teeth were very long, but mostly hidden by her large upper lip until she bared them this way. "Would you like me to write your name on the cup, Detective?"

"I suppose not." He peered down into the cup of plain black coffee but didn't pick it up. "I'm just curious about something."

"Oh?" She looked back and forth between me and Bentley excitedly, as though our presence was the most interesting thing that had happened that day. Now her eyes were bright and lively, and there was no longer any sign of a yawn on her lips.

"Do tell," she said. "Or I could guess, if you give me a hint. I love games." Her gaze came to rest on me. "Games of all kinds," she said enigmatically.

My cheeks felt hot. She was so beautiful. Was she flirting with me? Or trying to tell me something? She'd heard my Witch Tongue. What else did she know about me?

Bentley picked up his cup slowly, turned his body away from the counter, paused as though having second thoughts, and turned back again. In a casual, off-handed tone, he said, "I'm just wondering what it was you wrote on Ishmael Greyson's cup last night that had him so rattled."

The tall woman stopped breathing, and for some reason, I felt it in my own chest. My airway seemed to pinch, though I was still breathing. I watched her as the tendons in her long, slender neck stood out. Then she stretched upward, becoming half an inch taller, and the tendons became less pronounced. The hollow at the center of her collarbone grew deeper, and darkness pooled within the depression like an abandoned well.

She licked her lips and asked, "*Fishtail* didn't report me to the police for that bit of fun, now, did he?"

Bentley almost smiled. He had her right where he wanted her. "Ms. Nix, I assure you I'm asking out of curiosity. It's not the concern of the Wisteria Police Department what you did or did not write on a customer's takeout cup. Unless, of course, it was a hate crime, or a threat of some sort."

She turned and walked away hurriedly. Was she running? She moved quickly on those long legs.

Get her, my brain yelled. *She's getting away!* I was yelling at myself more than Bentley. I wanted to get her. My fingertips crackled as my magic readied itself.

Bentley, however, didn't even twitch. I felt like kicking him, or zapping him with one of my newest spells. I had recently mastered a biting spell that mimicked being bit on the buttocks by a toothy animal. Before Aunt Zinnia would teach it to me, she made me swear up and down to never, ever, ever use it on her. But I could use it on Bentley.

Maisy had been running, but she didn't run far. She stopped at a recycling bin full of paper cups and dug in. I remembered Carrot Greyson, digging through her wastebasket. *None of this would be happening if people were more environmentally conscious and brought their own reusable mugs to coffee shops*, I thought. Not that I ever remembered my takeout mug.

"Got it," Maisy said. She skipped back to us with an empty cup held forward like a trophy. "This is the cup that Fishtail, I mean Ishmael, wouldn't take. You'll see it's not a hate crime or a threat."

Written neatly in black felt pen was the phrase CARROT'S BROTHER. Maisy set it on the counter between us.

I nearly laughed. "That's it?" I asked. "He was all torn up about being identified as his sister's brother?"

Maisy shot me a conspiratorial grin. "I know, right? Some men! They're so terrified of us having any type of recognition or power they don't." Her right eye twitched in what seemed like a canceled wink.

"You enjoyed teasing him," Bentley said. "You knew that description would bother him, which is why you wrote it on his cup."

Maisy laughed and held out both hands, wrists together, over the top of the counter. "Guilty as charged. You'd better cuff me and take me away."

"That won't be necessary," he said crisply.

Maisy pulled back her hands, placed them on her hips, and cocked her head. "What's this all about?" She directed the question at me, specifically. "Are you two working together on something?"

I lifted my takeout cup. "Just driving in a car, going for coffee, like normal people do."

She arched one black, angular eyebrow. "Sounds like my kind of fun." She picked up a bar cloth and wiped some coffee grinds from the counter into a metal-ringed hole.

"One more thing," Bentley said, taking the previous day's used paper cup gingerly. "Where were you and your vehicle last night?"

106

Maisy stiffened. Staring straight ahead without moving, she said, "I was at the other Dreamland location, roasting coffee beans. I was there until my niece came by at dawn to pick me up." She yawned again, though it looked to me like a fake one. "I only got a few hours' sleep before coming in here. Excuse my yawns."

"Your niece had your car last night?" He repeated the make of the car and its license plate number.

Maisy Nix confirmed it was the same one, and gave her niece's name. Fatima Nix.

"Fatima? I've met her," I interjected. "Does she work for the veterinarian? Dr. Katz?"

"That's the one," Maisy said, curling her thick upper lip to reveal her long front teeth. "You'd never guess we were related, since I'm so tall and poor little squat Fatima is so *not-tall*."

I liked how Maisy described Fatima's shortness as not-tallness.

Maisy shifted forward and deftly wrung the bar cloth in her strong-looking hands. "Is there a problem? Has my niece gotten in any trouble? She's a good girl, Detective. Not the sharpest knife in the drawer, but Fatima has a good heart. She loves animals and people."

"I'm sure it's nothing," Bentley said. "We're looking for some witnesses who may have seen something unusual last night. Your vehicle was captured on home security footage not far from where the incident took place."

Home security footage? Nice move, Detective Bentley. People can't argue with hard evidence.

Instead of becoming more worried about her niece, Maisy relaxed, leaning forward and propping one pointy elbow on the counter. "Don't tell me you're chasing shadows again, Detective." She pursed her lips and gave him a flirty eye flash. In a sultry tone, she said, "You know what they say about people who look hard enough for something."

"Sooner or later, they find it," he said. "I fail to see what's wrong with that."

"There are other ways to chase shadows. Have you ever tried asking nicely?" She ran her free hand through her glossy hair in a practiced move straight out of the handbook for Flirting 101.

I reached over and patted Bentley on the shoulder. "Nicely isn't his style," I said.

She pursed her lips more tightly, narrowed her coffee-black eyes, and shot me a look that could freeze rain. "And you would know, Zara? You're familiar with the detective's style?"

"Somewhat," I said, my voice quivering and betraying my uncertainty. What was the deal with Maisy Nix? She had power in that tall body of hers, of that I was certain. But what kind?

Maisy's tight lips relaxed into a crooked smile. "Oh, Zara. You have so much to learn."

Bentley took a half step back and raised his cup of black coffee as though offering a toast. "Informative, as always, Ms. Nix."

"A pleasure, as always," she replied, her smile broadening.

His voice gritty, he said, "Try to stay out of trouble."

"Oh, Detective. I never make promises I have no intention of keeping."

My mouth dropped open. That was my line! Who did this woman think she was, stealing the lines I said to Bentley? I nearly dropped my coffee. My arms felt heavy and my body filled with jerky energy. I thought of hockey players throwing off their gloves to begin a bare-knuckles fight on the ice. I wanted to throw down my metaphorical gloves and challenge this powerful woman to a duel. If she had magic, I wanted to see it.

Distantly, I heard the tut-tut of my aunt inside my head. *Zara, be careful. Do not allow your emotions to be used against you.*

Luckily for Maisy Nix, Bentley grabbed me by my arm and steered me out of the coffee shop before I could cast the biting spell to chomp her on the butt.

CHAPTER 13

As soon as we got into Bentley's car, I started ranting about Maisy Nix. "That woman really thinks she's something! Can you believe the nerve of her? All that hinting around about stuff, but without the decency of giving us anything concrete."

"She's quite the woman," Bentley said neutrally.

I snorted. "You were right to be suspicious of her. What sort of cases was she involved with?"

"That's not particularly relevant to the current investigation."

"Humor me. What do you think she's up to?"

He started the engine and the air conditioning, then turned toward me, looking hopeful. "Never mind Maisy."

"Never mind her? What's that supposed to mean?"

"I don't even find her attractive. She's much too tall."

I pulled my head back and blinked at him. "What? Are you implying I'm jealous of that woman? That ebony-haired, black-eyed... giraffe?"

"She's not my type, but I understand she's a very striking woman. Some men might call her *perfect*."

"She's not perfect. Her upper lip is a bit puffy, which I suppose is good, because it covers those long front teeth of hers." I glanced over at the door to the coffee shop and ran my tongue over my own front teeth. "Do you think she's got rodent powers? Maybe she's a rat shifter. That would explain the teeth."

"Never mind Maisy," Bentley said again. "Let's stay on track. Did you happen to see the ghost in there?"

I pulled my gaze away from Dreamland Coffee and took a breath to reset. My aunt was right about many things, including my weakness for letting my emotions get the better of me. I hated living up to the stereotypes about fiery redheads, but I did have my fiery moments.

"The ghost," Bentley prompted patiently.

"Ishmael? No. I didn't see anyone dead in there. Why? Did you feel something? Sometimes even regular people pick up on the presence of spirits. You might have felt a cold spot, or a sudden sense of dread."

"No dread, and I didn't feel any cold spots, though it would be a welcome relief on a day like this." He leaned forward and let the cool air from the vents stream over his face.

"Ishmael isn't there now, but it's mid-day. His usual routine was to stop by after work." I paused, picturing the skinny, pale-haired ghost walking through the wall of the coffee shop to order his usual beverages. "Bentley, do you think, if we stuck around, we'd see him show up around six o'clock?"

Bentley rubbed his chin. "Doing a stakeout for a ghost would be a new one for me."

I checked the time. "It's not even two o'clock yet. We could come back in a few hours."

He made a noncommittal sound and put on the car's turn signal as he prepared to pull out onto the street.

"Are we going to visit Fatima Nix?" I asked.

"You're a quick study," he said warmly. "Are you sure you haven't done any police work before?"

I grinned at the rare compliment. "Maybe a detective ghost passed through me briefly and I didn't notice. They tend to leave some stuff behind. Residual memories and..."

"And what?"

It was hard to say the word, but I did. "Emotions." I cleared my throat. "The ghosts leave behind some of their feelings. It really isn't very considerate of them. I already have a tough time trying to deal with my own feelings, let alone theirs."

"That must complicate your life."

I let out a sarcastic whoop. "And the Understatement of the Year Award goes to Detective Theodore Dean Bentley!"

He shot me a wry smile. "You and I have a lot in common. When I'm on a homicide case, I feel possessed by it until it's resolved."

The man didn't know what possession truly felt like, but I kept my mouth shut this time and let him think he did.

He shoulder-checked before pulling the car out onto the street. "And the difficult cases always leave behind an emotional residue."

I still had my mint mocha in my hand. It was too full to put in the cup holder because the smallest bump in the road would cause it to splash. Dreamland Coffee's takeout cups didn't have the handy cap that some coffee places did. I took a sip to bring down the volume. Before I became a witch, I wouldn't have taken that sip lest I burn my tongue, but one benefit of being a witch was never having to worry about the temperature of coffee. Any burn I received healed almost immediately.

The mint mocha was perfect, as usual. I nestled it in the cup holder between us, next to Bentley's coffee. Seeing our coffees next to each other gave me a feeling. A pleasant feeling.

Bentley broke the silence. "I don't know anything about Fatima Nix, but her aunt, Maisy, certainly is an alpha type. Do you know what I mean by that?"

"Alpha? You mean like the leader of a pack of werewolves?"

"Less supernatural."

"Ah. Alpha, but not supernatural. Sure, I know the type." I listed them on my fingers. "Head cheerleaders, rich ladies with reality TV shows, and some—but not all —head librarians."

"Really? Librarians? I suppose you would know."

"Not *all* librarians."

"Right." He tapped the screen for the car's navigation, asked me for the name of my veterinary clinic, and pulled up the address so we could pay a visit to young Fatima Nix at her workplace.

He took a sip of his plain coffee and asked, "Did you detect anything magic back there at Dreamland? Or am I just out nine dollars and fifty cents for the overpriced coffee?"

"You did get the lead about Fatima driving the car last night."

"Sure, but I didn't need to buy coffee to get that."

"Now that you mention it, there was something odd that happened." I explained how I'd attempted to cast a threat-detection spell, only to have it splash back at me.

Bentley said, "Maybe your spell did work, and you're the threat. It detected you."

"Ha ha."

"Thank you."

"But you should have seen the look Maisy gave me after I cast it. That was when she asked me what I'd said, and I told her it must have been my stomach."

"I didn't hear anything."

"You're not a witch."

"And you think Maisy Nix is?"

"Well, you're the one who was onto her in the first place because her name kept popping up in your police reports."

"True."

"And... my aunt's name is also one that popped up in reports."

"Many times. More than Maisy's name, in fact."

"Right. But let me ask you this, Detective. Do any of the known DWM agents' names appear in those non-restricted reports?"

"Never," he said. "They're always scrubbed right out of the regular files."

"So, it's only the witches in town who get officially associated with local weirdness."

He made a thoughtful noise. "Being a witness doesn't necessarily mean someone's a witch."

"No, but *someone* either countered my spell or cast dampening wards inside that coffee shop."

"If you say so."

Something else occurred to me, filling in the picture. Excitedly, I said, "Also, Maisy Nix was friendly with Tansy Wick, and Tansy was a notorious hermit who didn't have many friends, besides my aunt."

"Tansy Wick," he said. "Our local supplier of magical toadstools."

"Don't stereotype. There's a lot more to potions than toadstools." I took another sip of the mint mocha coffee that had been Tansy Wick's favorite. "Maisy did know Tansy. Did you read up about that case?"

"I know only that Tansy Wick died of natural causes, and the death was ruled an accident."

I chucked. "Natural causes. More like supernatural causes."

"They don't write that in the case files," he said, sounding eager. "I have so much to learn. My world has really opened up. The wool has fallen from my eyes. I see everything in a new light now."

"You're excited about all of this stuff," I said.

"Aren't you?"

"Yes, but I'm a witch."

"And I'm a detective. Like I said, we've got a lot in common." He shot me a glance, his steely gray eyes twinkling. "We make a good team. I've been trying to figure out Maisy Nix for months, and for a mere fifteen-dollar investment, you've all but confirmed she's a witch."

"I thought the coffee was nine-fifty."

"Plus tip."

"You tip fifty percent on coffee?"

"Doesn't everyone?"

"I can't tell if you're pulling my leg or not."

"Good."

CHAPTER 14

We arrived at the Katz and Dogz Veterinary Clinic and parked on the street in front.

"Katz and Dogz," Bentley mused. "What is it about small towns and puns?"

"It gets better," I said breathlessly. "The veterinarian's name is Dr. Katz. It's his actual *name*."

"I can't tell if you're pulling my leg or not."

"Good," I said, and I jumped out of the car.

I hadn't been to the vet clinic since June, when I had to get my father, in fox form, stitched up. It was also the place where I'd first laid my eyes on Boa, who'd been staying at the vet while waiting for her "furever" home.

When we walked in, Fatima Nix recognized me right away. "Ms. Riddle! How are you?"

Other than her glossy black hair, Fatima looked nothing like her aunt. Fatima was as short as Maisy was tall. She had to step up onto a platform to use the computer at the vet clinic's front desk. Unlike the angular features her aunt bore, Fatima had a perfectly round face, olive skin, and wide-set, sparkling brown eyes. She wore glasses, a too-large pair with thick white plastic frames. The glasses were not the pair I would have picked out for her, but they gave her an adorable, cartoonish look. They did not, however, make her look any smarter than she was.

"I'm fine," I answered, though my voice pitched up as though I was asking a question. I would have been *more* fine if I wasn't there to check on her alibi for a homicide case. "How are you?"

"Tired but good." Her large glasses slid down her small nose, and she didn't push them up. "How is Miss Boa? Is she settling into her furever home with her new furever family?"

Bentley had entered alongside me and was now quietly browsing the clinic's display of materials about vaccinations and flea medication. This was now our second stop where he'd pretended to be a regular customer before breaking out the interview questions. He'd been all business at our first stop, but then again that one had been different. We'd been there to deliver the bad news to the victim's sister. It wasn't the sort of thing someone could casually segue into.

Fatima continued to smile up at me, oblivious to the reason for our business call.

"Miss Boa is definitely part of the family," I said. "She's bonded intensely with my daughter."

Fatima nodded. "Cats tend to pick favorites."

"She's not that loyal. If I have deli meat ham, I'm the favorite."

"I bet! Is she getting enough exercise?"

"Absolutely. She and my daughter can play for hours." I didn't mention that their play involved the cat darting up and down the stairs, chasing my daughter in red fox form while an overexcited wyvern screeched encouragement. If I'd told the veterinary assistant that, she'd probably think we were abusing the poor thing. Boa, however, loved every minute of it. When she finally got tuckered out from chasing or being chased, she'd flop on the floor and expose her belly trap for Round Two, The Playful Eviscerating.

"You should get a second cat," Fatima said. "Someone like you should have more than one."

Detective Bentley chose that moment to drag himself away from the flea brochures and join the conversation. "Someone like her?" He nodded his head in my direction. "What do you mean by that?"

Fatima's eyelashes fluttered behind her thick lenses. "I mean someone who's so good with pets." Her glasses slipped over the tip of her small, flat nose, and she finally nudged them back up to the bridge.

I gave Bentley a bored look. "She means someone who's good with pets," I repeated.

Fatima asked, "How is your red fox?"

"Fine, I suppose. He hasn't been in touch lately."

Fatima's forehead wrinkled. "What?"

"Just a joke," I said with a hand wave. "That little trickster I brought in for stitches was never mine. He recovered for a while at my house, got into all sorts of trouble, and now he's gone again. Back to where he came from." Silently, I added *good riddance.*

"That's such a shame. He was a cutie. You know what, Ms. Riddle? You should still pose for our Furever Family calendar. All the proceeds go to some very good pet charities. You could bring Boa. We'd love to see her again." Fatima clapped her small hands excitedly. "You know what? Her silky white fur would be a such a good contrast with your red hair."

"You think?" I twirled a lock of hair. Flattery felt good, even if it came from a murder suspect. "What would I wear?"

"That's easy. You could pull your hair forward, over your chest, and then you could hold Boa right across your bathing suit area." She looked pointedly down at a bathing suit area where a woman might hold a cat strategically if, say, that woman were nude.

I made a choking sound. "I'm sorry," I said. "For a minute, it sounded like you wanted me to pose nude."

"You wouldn't be nude." Her glasses slid down her nose. "Nobody would see, except the photographer."

There was another choking sound beside me. I turned slowly to find Bentley struggling to maintain his steely composure.

"You know what? Sign me up," I said brightly. "Pet charities are very dear to me, ever since Boa came into my life."

Bentley gave me a look of shock mingled with admiration.

Fatima typed on her computer keyboard, and we set up a time for my photographic debut.

Then I grabbed a case of canned cat food for Boa, since I was there anyway.

After I'd finished paying, and nearly forgotten the reason for our visit, Bentley finally spoke up.

"Miss Nix, I'm Detective Bentley with the WPD." He flashed his badge her way. "We're looking for witnesses to an incident, and I understand you were driving your aunt's vehicle along Beacon Street at dawn this morning. Is this correct?"

She gasped and held both hands to her mouth. "Is this about that homeless lady I almost hit with the car? I didn't hit her. I swear."

Bentley's calm, professional expression didn't change. "Describe the homeless lady for me."

"She had crazy hair, and she was wearing rags as a dress. Plus she was ranting, probably talking to the voices in her head." Fatima pushed her glasses up her nose. "Did she say I hit her? I swear I didn't. I was only there on that street because Mr. Greyson called me to come check on Doodles. The poor little guy was having a meltdown. He was barking at shadows and chasing his tail. I gave him a mild sedative, and he settled down. Then, when I was leaving, I hit the wrong button to adjust the seat, and it went down instead of up. I could barely see over the steering wheel, and then that crazy woman jumped out of nowhere, like she was trying to throw herself at my car."

I pressed my lips together and bit my tongue. I hadn't come out of nowhere, and I hadn't thrown myself at the car. Also, homeless lady? Dressed in rags? Really? My hair had a certain wildness to it before brushing, but come on!

Bentley nodded. "I see. Is it possible the dog, the one that belonged to Mr. Greyson, was barking at this woman? The homeless lady?"

I gave Bentley's foot a subtle kick. Did he not realize the homeless lady was me?

"Maybe Doodles was upset about the lady," Fatima said. "Arden thought it might have been a neighbor's cat sneaking in through the doggie door to steal Doodles' kibble. Both of them thought it was a cat."

"Both of them?" Bentley asked. "What do you mean by 'both of them?' Was Mr. Greyson's nephew, Ishmael, present?"

Fatima's cheeks reddened. "No." She answered in a near-whisper. "I meant both Mr. Greyson and Doodles."

Bentley raised an eyebrow. "Do you speak dog?"

Fatima let out a high-pitched peal of laughter. "No, of course not, but sometimes it seems that way." She looked down and adjusted her blue scrubs. "It might not have been a cat that was bothering Doodles. It could have been anything. A raccoon, or squirrels, or even a bird. I've heard there's a big raven that lives on that street."

Bentley said, "So, you were called by Mr. Arden Greyson to check on his dog. And you didn't see anything unusual until you were leaving, at which point you saw an erratic woman dressed in rags running across the street."

Fatima asked nervously, "Did she say I hit her?"

Bentley took out his notepad, licked his finger, and turned through the pages slowly.

"I didn't hit her," Fatima said. She turned to me and repeated, "I didn't hit her."

"That's not actually what brings me here today," Bentley said, his voice low and hypnotically calm. "There was another incident this morning. A separate one. I wonder if you could close your eyes for a moment and try to recall if you saw anything unusual on Beacon Street. Perhaps when you were returning to your aunt's vehicle?" He fixed her with his steely gaze. "Close your eyes, take a deep breath, travel back to this morning in your mind, and tell me what you saw."

She looked at me as though seeking a second opinion. I gave her an encouraging smile. Sure. I would vouch for Bentley.

Fatima drew in a deep breath and closed her eyes, exactly as he'd suggested. "I'm there now," she said. "I'm noticing that all the lawns are brown, because of the hot weather." She coughed once. "And it's smoky. The air quality won't be good today."

"Is the door to Ishmael Greyson's apartment open or closed?"

"Closed," she said without hesitation.

"Do you hear any people?"

She frowned. "I hear rustling. Something's behind me."

"What's behind you?"

"I... I can't see it. When I turn my head to look, it's gone, behind the bushes." Her eyes suddenly flew open. "That's why I was driving so fast when I pulled away. I can't believe I forgot until now. I was scared of the thing in the shadows."

"Some sort of animal?"

She leaned forward and whispered, "Do you believe in demons?"

Bentley replied, "Do you?"

Her eyes widened behind the thick lenses. "Of course not. It was probably just a stray cat." She stared up at him steadily. "But isn't it funny how your mind can play tricks on you?"

Bentley pressed on. "This thing in the bushes, did it move on four feet or two?"

"Two," she said without hesitation. The she pulled back and wrinkled her nose. "Which means it probably wasn't a cat, after all."

"Not a cat," he said, making a note in his little book.

Bentley thanked Fatima for her insight, and handed her a card. "Call me if you remember anything else."

She asked sweetly, "What happened, anyway?"

"A homicide," he said off-handedly. "A grisly, senseless act of violence."

Her jaw dropped.

He observed her for a moment, then said, "Miss Nix, please keep that information under your hat until such time as the details are officially released."

Her eyes glistened, and soon tears were streaming down both cheeks. Her lower lip trembled as she asked, "Wh-wh-who? Who was killed?"

"I believe you already know."

She turned her teary gaze on me, then Bentley, then me again. Her voice a hoarse whisper, she asked, "Ishmael? Is that why you asked if his door was open?"

Bentley made a gesture, as though tipping an invisible hat. "Ma'am, that information hasn't yet been released. I'm not at liberty to say." Then he turned and strode toward the front door. He pushed open the door without a backward glance and left. The door closed behind him, and somewhere deep in the vet clinic a chime sounded.

I stood at the counter, dumbfounded. Fatima continued crying. My heart broke for her. Bentley had practically destroyed the young woman, who'd been nothing but sweet and kind and compassionate to me, my family members, and my pets.

"It's going to be okay," I said to her soothingly. "Detective Bentley is one of the best. He's going to find whoever did that, and keep us safe."

She sniffed and got control of her breathing. "Zara," she said softly. "I want to show you something."

I nodded toward the door. "I should get going."

She held both of her small hands up in front of her face. A rainbow of light arced between her palms.

"Oh," I said. "Oh!" And then, because nothing more clever came to mind, I said it a third time. "Oh!"

Fatima Nix was a witch.

Hoarsely, she said, "I didn't see anything in the bushes, but I felt it." The rainbow sputtered out like a guttering candle. "Something horrible and nasty and evil. Do you know about that sort of thing?"

"Horrible and nasty and evil? You'll have to be more specific. Did it have wings? Glowing eyes?"

"It was angry," she said. "That's all I know. So angry."

"Okay. I'll pass that along to the detective." I held my own hands up, palms a few inches apart. "What about the, uh, rainbow thing? Should we meet again and talk about that?"

She shook her head. "Don't tell anyone I told you."

"I won't," I promised. "Did you show me that because you know something about me?"

She clamped her lips shut and kept them that way. Her eyes, however, said yes. Yes, she'd known about me for ages, possibly even before I knew about me. Being a witch, that was.

I thanked her for her help and headed for the door.

CHAPTER 15

When I got to Bentley's car, the engine was running and the air conditioning was on. I leaned toward the vents and let the cool air dry the sweat on my temples.

After a strangely quiet moment, Bentley said, "Young Fatima Nix must have told you something. Something big."

"What makes you say that?"

"Your face."

I rolled my eyes and continued using the vents while I lifted the hair at the back of my neck. I'd only had a few minutes on the way back to the car to think about the news I'd just learned. I had barely processed it, let alone come to a decision about whether or not to tell Bentley. Did he have any right to know the young veterinary assistant was a witch? She had a valid reason for being at the scene of the crime, and likely was off the suspect list. Her powers weren't necessarily any of his business.

But, on the other hand, if he knew about her abilities, he could be an ally. He might even protect her from those who sought to abuse her and her powers. Fatima had figured out we were partners. Had she shown me her magic with the expectation I would tell him?

Bentley continued with his line of interrogation. "Specifically, it was the mouth part of your face," he said.

"By which I mean you got into the car and didn't say anything for a full thirty seconds. I counted."

For the second time that morning, I thought about how nice it would be to blast his butt with the butt-chomping spell.

He continued to stare at me expectantly.

I adjusted the cooling vents and asked, "What happens to any confidential information I give you? Does it go into a big database that everyone at the DWM has access to?"

Bentley pointed to his own temple, which, unlike mine, wasn't glistening with sweat. "The information goes up here, and then it only goes into reports if it's relevant to the case. What were you two talking about in there?"

I could tell him part of the truth. "Fatima swears something was watching her when she went to her car this morning."

"I know that. I was there when she told us."

"She wanted me to know it was something evil and angry. She didn't see it, but she felt it."

"And?" He raised an eyebrow.

I didn't want to tell him Fatima was a witch. I'd only had the information myself for less than five minutes. It was way too soon to consider breaking the young witch's confidence.

And yet, Fatima must have expected I would tell the detective about her rainbow demonstration. She wasn't the brightest girl, but she must have figured out we were working together on the case.

Bentley shifted impatiently in the driver's seat, making the leather squeak. "Did she admit to being a witch?"

Reluctantly, I nodded, even though I didn't like his choice of verb. She hadn't *admitted* anything. Did he go around *admitting* to being a detective? No. It wasn't fair that being a witch came with so much baggage. Thousands of years of persecution will do that for a group of people.

The steely-eyed detective didn't smile, but the crow's feet around his eyes disappeared. He looked like a person who'd just placed five difficult jigsaw puzzle pieces in a row. He was pleased at the results of his observational skills combined with a dose of good luck.

"Are you happy now?" I asked, my voice tinged with the same defeated bitterness that every person uttering that phrase uses. *Are you happy now? Now that you've gotten your way while everything I hold dear has been compromised?*

The pleasure spread across Bentley's face, pulling up the corners of his mouth. "Since it runs in families, there's a good chance my hunch about her aunt, Maisy, is correct. Both of the Nix women must be witches." He reached into his jacket pocket, but then seemed to change his mind, resting his hands instead on the steering wheel. "How exactly did she tell you?"

"She actually showed me. Like this." I raised my hands, palms facing each other, leaving a four-inch gap. I didn't have the foggiest idea how to make a rainbow, so I substituted, pulsing a flash of blue plasma between my hands. It blinked brighter than I expected. The air crackled. The interior of the vehicle dramatically pressurized and then released, as though we'd been plunged underwater and then popped. The blue plasma went supernova, blindingly bright.

Bentley, who'd been leaning forward to see what I was doing, yelped and pulled away so quickly he banged the back of his head on the driver's side window. By the sound of the impact, it would leave a bump.

"Oops," I said, blinking away the dark spots in my eyes. "That's not such a smart thing to do in confined spaces."

He rubbed the back of his head. "You think?"

"Fatima did a different spell. It was a pretty rainbow, and it didn't have the same bite as my defensive magic." I reached a hand toward him. "Want me to heal that bump on your noggin? It'll only take a minute."

He pulled back from my hand, repeating the bump. "Don't you dare touch my noggin, thank you." He rubbed his head again. "I take full responsibility for myself," he said. "I should have known better than to lean in. Those magical guns of yours are always loaded."

I clasped my hands together tightly. "You would have liked the rainbow," I said.

"I'm not so sure I would."

"I'd sure like to know how that rainbow spell of hers works. I can't imagine what good it would do a witch, but it was very pretty."

"Perhaps you two could team up and shoot rainbows at this evil, angry thing that chops off heads. Why does that make me think of a Saturday morning cartoon?"

"Don't tease," I said.

He sighed and rubbed his head some more. "Maybe I'm onto something. Weaponized rainbows might be exactly what's needed."

"We could try that on our monster, but first we need to locate it." I fastened my seatbelt. "Where are we off to next? An interview with Arden Greyson? To confirm Fatima's story and find out what he knows?"

"I believe Mr. Greyson is still at the station, where they brought him from the marina."

"Great. Let's get him while he's fresh."

He gave me a wary look. "That's not the best idea."

"I promise I won't zap you again. I won't zap anyone."

"Zara, it's one thing for me to bring you with me in the field, but there are a lot of people at the station who'd be suspicious if I showed up with my own personal... librarian in tow."

"Every detective should be so lucky as to have a personal librarian."

"I'll drop you off at your house. That is, unless you'd prefer to be dropped off somewhere else."

"You're done with me already? I've outed two witches for you today. I've betrayed my own kind, and my only reward is that I'm being dumped?"

"You aren't being dumped."

"But you're dropping me off the case. With not even a thank-you."

"You did get a coffee," he deadpanned, pointing to the takeout cup in the center console.

I gave him my fiercest librarian glare. The one reserved for the naughtiest patrons who smuggled in food and ate it while using the computers to access porn.

Bentley ate up my fierce look without even flinching. He waved at the vet clinic bag on my lap. "Also, you picked up some cat food. Now you can cross that particular errand off your to-do list."

"Bentley, your sense of humor is so dry it's amazing I'm not completely dehydrated from sitting in this car with you."

"Thank you," he said. "Not many people appreciate it."

He shoulder-checked, then pulled the car out onto the street. At the intersection, he turned in the direction of my neighborhood. He really was taking me home.

"I do appreciate your help on the case," he said. "Thank you."

"You're welcome."

"I'll thank you again with a nice dinner once the case is solved."

"Assuming you can solve it without me."

"You may be a powerful witch, but I assure you, I'm not some bumbling fool."

"No comment," I said.

We drove in silence until I broke it. "Whether you take me with you or not, I'm still on this case. I'm your only contact with the ghost."

"I know." He kept one hand on the steering wheel while he reached up with the other one and thumbed something under his shirt collar.

A few minutes later, he reached up and touched the lump again.

As much as I wanted to give him the silent treatment curiosity got the better of me. "Bentley, are you wearing some sort of talisman?"

"What? No!" He adjusted his shoulders and posture, then touched the thing at his throat a third time.

"What are you wearing under there? Is it a locket?"

"It's none of your business."

Now I *needed* to know. "Come on, Bentley. What have you got? A St. Christopher medallion? A lucky rabbit's paw?"

"It's nothing."

"Then why do you keep touching it?"

He sighed. Then he propped one elbow on the steering wheel and used both hands to unbutton his shirt collar.

"You tell me what you see," he said, angling his upper body so I could see what hung at his throat.

A flash of sunshine glinting off a passing car blinded me temporarily. I blinked the bright spots from my eyes and focused on Bentley's neck. The first thing I saw was a few strands of chest hair, and a few square inches of Bentley that I hadn't seen before. I felt a twinge of guilt for badgering him into revealing himself to me, but not so much that I turned away.

He wore a thick gold chain, and hanging on the chain was something long and narrow. It looked like nothing. Nothing at all. I blinked. And then it was something. A bullet.

A bullet?

"You tell me what you see," he repeated.

"You're wearing a bullet around your neck," I said. "That can't be safe. Is it a rimfire bullet?"

"It's not what it appears to be," he said in a calm, soothing tone. "There's no gunpowder, I assure you."

"So, it's an artistic replica sort of thing?"

"You could say that." He held the steering wheel with his elbow again as he did up his collar.

"But why? Why are you wearing a fake bullet?"

He patted the lump under his shirt. "I don't expect you to understand this, but I'm going to need it some day."

"Okay." I rested my head back on the headrest of the passenger seat. "That's cute that you're superstitious. It gives you another dimension."

"What about you? Do you wear any talismans?"

"Not really." I touched the groove at my throat, imagining what it might feel like to have a round of ammunition there, even if it was a replica.

A bullet.

I'd done so many things that day. I'd worn a bunny suit at a crime scene, met the local medical examiner, partnered with a detective, identified another family of witches, learned that Bentley had some sort of weird death-wish-superstition thing, and I'd managed to pick up extra cat food before we ran out—for a change.

CHAPTER 16

It was 2:30 when Bentley dropped me off at my house. My car, Foxy Pumpkin, was parked in her usual spot on the street, so I expected to find my daughter inside the house. Thinking about seeing Zoey helped me shake off the grumpiness I felt about getting booted off the case.

I walked in the house, kicked off my shoes, and called up the stairs, "Hi, Honey! I'm home!"

There was a pattering of tiny feet. A red fox appeared at the top of the stair. Zoey-Fox took the steps down, transitioning into human form almost seamlessly. There was an awkward moment where she was hunched forward with her fingers on a step below herself. She nearly tripped, but didn't. She straightened up and reached the bottom step in fully human form. Her clothes had made the transition smoothly, with not a button out of place. She wore a triumphant expression on her face.

I did what any good mother would do. I clapped and cheered like her number one fan, which I was.

"That was so smooth," I gushed. "From four legs to two, while descending the stairs. You're my hero!"

She shrugged and tried to pretend it was no big deal. "I almost tripped over my hand and went down in a ball."

"But you didn't," I said. "And you'll get better. Practice makes perfect. At least that's what Aunt Zinnia nto my head whenever I complain about

s like the egg-peeling thing."

1 down to pet Boa, who was circling the

all the divine smells from the veterinary

ing her tail in pleasure.

"You were running errands?" Zoey asked. "You ditched me at the museum to run errands?"

"It's not how it looks." I grabbed the cat food and took it back to the kitchen. I was suddenly inside the kitchen much sooner than I expected. Something was different. I rotated slowly, scanning the room.

"Zoey, is it my imagination, or has the walk to the kitchen gotten shorter? The kitchen's bigger now, isn't it?"

Zoey pursed her lips and looked around, nodding. "I think it is," she said. "About fifteen percent bigger."

"When did this happen? I swear it was the usual size before we left for the museum."

She scrunched her face. "When I got back from the museum, I was listening to music in my room. I heard some noise, but I thought it was just Ribbons or Boa jumping around. I didn't think to check if our magical house was remodeling itself."

I patted one of the walls. "Thanks, house. That was very thoughtful of you. We have been spending a lot more time in the kitchen lately."

The house didn't reply. It never had—not in words, anyway.

I hadn't known the house was magic when I bought it. When I'd first toured the place, I'd fallen in love at first sight. I'd adored it for what it appeared to be: a lovely old three-storey Victorian Gothic, the exterior painted a heart-racing shade of red and the interior needing a few decorating ideas. Upstairs were three bedrooms, which had magically turned into two bedrooms plus a linen closet before I'd moved in. The house had a funny way of changing itself to suit our needs—or to suit what it thought were our needs. A basement lair had appeared at the same time my new wyvern friend found himself looking for underground accommodations. Sometimes I wondered where the house's true loyalty lay. It had been all too happy to literally squeeze me out of my own bedroom when my father had stayed with us in a temporary third bedroom. Ever since then, I'd been extra careful to show gratitude for any and all of the house's self-remodeling decisions, whether I liked them or not. Truth be told, I liked the change to the kitchen, so showering the house with compliments wasn't difficult.

Zoey chimed in with a few compliments about the larger space, and helped put away Boa's food.

I mentally prepared to fill her in on the morning's activities. I used to try to keep my adventures from her, but she was too clever and saw through my lies anyway.

"Did you have lunch?" I asked.

"I could eat," she replied.

"Well, obviously. You are a Riddle."

We pulled some leftover Thai takeout from the fridge and pulled up to the new kitchen island, which now had a brighter laminate surface, in addition to being nearly twice the square footage.

"Nice choice on the island," I said loudly while offering two thumbs up at the ceiling.

"Enough about the reconfiguration," Zoey said. "What did you do with Detective Bentley after you ditched me at the museum?"

"We began our adventure with a no-holds-barred tour of the murder house. I mean, uh, the crime scene."

"Was it super-gross?"

"Yes. I would definitely describe the scene of the crime as *super-gross*. I believe that's what Bentley wrote in his official report."

"Did they find the head?"

"It was in a trophy case."

Her hazel eyes widened. "Cool."

I pointed at her. "Not the reaction I was expecting."

She ran a hand through her shiny red hair casually. "I think I could help the police someday. I've got a really good sense of smell, especially in fox form." She gave me a serious look. "I could have sniffed out that severed head in no time."

I leaned forward, gave her a pat on the head, and continued telling her about my day. After touring the crime scene, I'd had my conversation with Dr. Jerry Lund, the medical examiner, who was one of the key people in the know about the town's supernatural secrets.

From there, Bentley and I had gone to see the victim's sister, Carrot Greyson, the tattoo artist. She was likely in shock from the news, but managed to give us a lead when she mentioned the feud her brother had with the owner of Dreamland Coffee, Maisy Nix. When we found out Maisy's car had been on Beacon Street that morning, it seemed we were closing in on our chief suspect.

Zoey listened without interrupting. If I paused too long to chew my Thai food, she waved impatiently for me to keep talking, even with my mouth full.

I explained how the visit with Maisy Nix would have been a dead end, except I'd detected a counterspell at work, deflecting my threat detection spell. That, combined with Bentley's suspicions about the woman, pointed toward her being a witch. Then Maisy told us her niece Fatima had borrowed her car, so our next logical step was to visit the younger Nix.

Unfortunately, Fatima Nix hadn't noticed much at the Greyson residence. She'd detected an angry, evil presence as she was leaving, but that wasn't big news, since I'd felt it at the crime scene myself.

However, she had revealed to me a pretty big secret. I described the rainbow light to Zoey, and what it all meant.

"They're witches," I said. "The Nix family. Aunt and niece, just like Zinnia and yours truly. How do ya like them apples?"

"Wow," she said. "More witches."

"Like us," I said.

"Like you," she corrected.

When I was done telling my sixteen-year-old fox-shifter daughter everything there was to know about the Greyson homicide investigation thus far, she was quiet for a long time.

"Hey." I poked her with a chopstick. "I haven't broken you, have I? Should I have kept this to myself? It's all pretty heavy for a teenager."

She forced a smile. "I'm not broken. Just thinking." She rubbed her forehead and frowned. "Since magic runs in families, that means that everyone who knows you're a witch must think I have powers, too."

"Or at least suspect you do," I said.

"And everyone who knows about Auntie Z must know about us."

I nodded. "Which is why Fatima Nix knew she could show me a magical rainbow without me passing out in terror."

She shook her head. "It's not fair," she said.

"Life's not fair."

She crossed her arms and stuck out her lower lip. It was a childish pout I hadn't seen her do lately.

"This sucks," she said without elaborating.

"So what if a few supernatural people know about us? We're getting to know them all, too."

"It should be private."

"Should it? Really? I mean, aren't we stronger if we all pull together, like a community?"

Her pout increased.

"Zoey, if you keep sticking out that lower lip, a bird is going to come along and poop on it."

"This isn't funny," she huffed.

If it wasn't funny, why was she making such a ridiculous pouting face? I probably shouldn't have teased her, but I couldn't help myself. That pout!

"Zoey, I think I hear Marzipants flying around the living room, looking for you. I didn't tell you, did I? Old Mrs. Pinkman wanted us to have her budgie, so she sent him here by bus."

"Even less funny," she huffed.

"It would be pretty funny if a budgie flew in here right now and pooped on that giant lower lip you have sticking out like a please-bomb-me target." I rubbed my chin. "I wonder if the house takes requests. Maybe if you say 'I wish' and then you wish for something, it delivers. I wish... I wish a budgie would—"

Zoey clamped her hand over my mouth. The new island was larger, but not too large for her to reach across to shut me up in the nick of time. With a hand-muffled voice, I promised to behave myself. She released my mouth and let out a huge sigh.

"I'm over it now," she said. "I always suspected that the people around here knew about our secrets, even though we don't know theirs. On some level, I've always known, but it's different to hear you say it out loud. It's weird that the short girl we buy Boa's cat food from knows about our family."

"You have to admit it's a little closer to being fair now. Now that you know she's a witch."

Zoey brightened. "Plus, she only *thinks* she knows. I'm actually a shifter, not a witch."

"Not so fast. That was the same clinic who stitched up Pawpaw. Fatima didn't say as much, but she might know the fox was a family member."

"Right," she said, her brightness fading.

And then I opened my big, dumb mouth and said something I shouldn't have. "But Fatima doesn't know about your birth father."

My daughter narrowed her eyes at me. "What do you mean?"

Zoey, your father's a genie! A demon!

The truth burned in my throat. Oh, how I wanted to tell her the truth. Except I didn't. I wanted someone else to tell her. What could I do? How could I stifle the burning in my throat?

I grabbed a wonton and stuffed it in my mouth.

She repeated herself. "What do you mean?"

With wonton crumbs spraying everywhere, I started rambling. "All I mean is that nobody knows *everything* about a person. There's always a bit of mystery. For example, today I discovered that Bentley has a sense of humor. It's very dry, or at least I think it's dry. Is dry what you call it when it's more cruel than funny? I mean, does anyone find sarcasm funny when they're the target of it? People say puns are the lowest form of humor, but maybe it's sarcasm."

Zoey continued to stare at me with narrowed eyes. She saw through my rambling as easily as she saw through my lies.

I kept going. When in doubt, double down! "Oh, speaking of Bentley, I learned today that he is a very generous tipper, at least when it comes to coffee."

In a low, level tone, she said, "You sure like to talk about Bentley a lot."

"Never mind about Bentley. Who do you think killed Ishmael Greyson?"

Her expression relaxed, and she glanced up at the ceiling the way she did when she encountered an intriguing logic puzzle. Ziggity! I had successfully engaged her intellect and steered her away from the taboo topic of her birth father.

She considered my question for a while before replying carefully, "Based on what you've told me so far, it sounds like the aunt who owns the coffee shop has a weak alibi. Who stays up all night roasting coffee when it could be done any time of day?"

I gasped. "You're right. That is very suspicious." I'd been so distracted by the counterspell, I hadn't seen the obvious.

Zoey beamed. "See? I could be very helpful on investigations." She touched her finger to the tip of her nose. "And not just with my sniffer."

I nodded. "The criminal masterminds of Wisteria need to think up better alibis if they want to get away with murder in our town."

Her smile faded. "I hope it wasn't Maisy Nix, though. It would be nice for you to have some witch friends besides Auntie Z."

I rested my elbows on the counter and my chin in my hands. "I feel the same way. I mean, she scares me in a mean cheerleader way, but I also want to be part of her posse. You can take the girl out of high school, but you can't take the high school out of the girl."

"I wonder if there's one coven in town or more than one. Whenever I ask Auntie Z, she pretends she doesn't hear me."

"Speaking of Auntie Z, I forgot to tell you the big news."

"Is she coming back early?"

"Not that I know of. The big news is I found out where she works. Would you believe she has an actual job?"

"I might believe it. What kind of job?"

"She works for City Hall. In the permits department."

Zoey shook her head. "I don't believe it. That's just... so... ordinary."

"Observe." I pulled out my phone, put it on speakerphone, and called the number for her department. Zinnia was on vacation, so she wouldn't answer, and besides, it was Saturday, so there was no danger of anyone in the office answering the call.

A recorded voice came over my phone speaker: *This is Zinnia Riddle. You have reached the Special Buildings Division of the Wisteria Permits Department. I'm out of the country right now, but if you'd like to leave a message, please do so, as this inbox is being monitored. Thank you.*

After the beep, I said into the receiver, "Busted. This is your niece, Zara. Call me when you get this." I ended the call and set the phone on the counter between us.

Zoey's mouth was agape.

I asked innocently, "Should I have been more subtle?"

"You sure couldn't have been *less* subtle."

"Oh, come on. I didn't say anything about figuring out Maisy and Fatima are witches." I reached for the phone. "I'll call back and leave a second message."

Zoey yanked my phone out of reach. "Don't you dare. Auntie Z is on vacation. You'll stress her out and make her do that thing where she pulls on her thumb."

"She pulls on her thumb? Is it part of casting a spell?"

"It's a nervous thing she does when you push her too far. You haven't noticed?" Zoey set down my phone and tugged on her own thumb in a gesture that suddenly did strike me as familiar. "She does this. Like she's making sure her thumb's still attached."

"You're right! She does do that, usually while she's giving me a lecture about being careful."

"For all the good it does," Zoey said teasingly.

"She's right that I should be more careful, but she's wrong about keeping all her secrets to herself. How am I supposed to know who to be careful around if I don't know who's got what powers?"

Zoey shook her head. "Don't try to twist this around. I think you should let Auntie Z tell you things herself, when she's ready." She paused for emphasis. "Even if it takes a few more months. Be patient."

"You may not have noticed this before, but your mother doesn't sit on things for long." My eye twitched. That wasn't entirely true. "I would only keep secrets from my loved ones if I felt it was absolutely necessary for their own protection."

"Such as?"

"When you were just a wee little girl, I never told you the Boob Fairy wasn't real. In fact, I kept up the ruse by sneaking into your room at night and leaving training bras under your pillow." I paused thoughtfully. "It's funny. You never believed in Santa Claus, not for a hot minute, but you believed in the Boob Fairy right up until she blessed you with your first bumps."

Zoey rolled her eyes. "That's not quite how I remember it."

"You don't remember our long conversations about how the Boob Fairy would have to use the fire escape to visit us since our apartment didn't have a chimney?"

She flattened her lips and gave me a humorless look. But I'd spent the last three hours riding around with Bentley, so I was immune to humorless looks and shrugged it off easily.

The doorbell rang, interrupting whatever might have come next.

"Doorbell," I said to my daughter.

"Doorbell?" She gave me a fake confused look. "Do you mean that funny little sound that goes ding-dong? Could that be the doorbell?"

I gave her a pointed look. Answering the door was her job and hers alone. "Doorbell."

"I don't hear anything," she said. "Have you checked your ears? Auntie Z said brainweevils can cause auditory hallucinations before they eat your brains."

Whoever was at the door rang the bell again.

I pointed to the air. "Doorbell."

She cupped her hand to her ear. "Is that an ice cream truck I hear? Does an ice cream truck go *ding-dong*?"

I rubbed my hands together and blasted her buttocks with the spell that mimicked a nip by a toothy animal.

She jumped off the stool, shrieking. She twirled in a circle, looking to see what had bit her. When she realized it had been my new spell, she gave me a wide-eyed, indignant look. "Oh, no, you didn't," she breathed.

"That was nothing," I said. "That was the Teacup Chihuahua level. Barely any tooth in it. And besides, you deserved it." I pointed to the air, as though the ding-dong of the doorbell still hung there above us. "You have one job, Zoey."

"You're such a mom," she said huffily.

I twitched one finger threateningly. "The next level is Toy Poodle."

She ran toward the front door making a sound halfway between terror and delight, just as I knew she would.

CHAPTER 17

Zoey returned to the kitchen, ashen-faced. She said in a hushed town, "Mom, there's a man at the front door. It's the guy from the murder house."

I whispered back, "What does he want?"

"He asked for Winona Vander Zalm." Winona Vander Zalm was the former owner of our home. She'd been dead for close to a year, which was how I'd come to be in possession of her magical house.

"That's odd," I said.

"I know, right? I didn't want to tell him she's dead. He's had a rough day."

"But he already knows Winona's dead. He's the one who told me how she went." I shook away the thought and patted my daughter on the shoulder. "That was kind of you to spare his feelings, Zoey. I'll go talk to him." I gave her a kiss on the forehead. "You're a good kid."

She grabbed Boa, huddled the white fluffball in her arms, and ran upstairs to her room. I went to the front door, checking my outfit as I did. I was still wearing the morning's gray wool suit, and felt grateful I hadn't changed into sweatpants yet. Heaven forbid I wear comfortable clothes and not have my hair perfectly in place, or Arden was liable to mistake me for a homeless person like Fatima had.

I reached the front door, which stood ajar. Standing patiently in the shade of my front porch was Arden Greyson. He wore jeans and a plaid short-sleeved shirt. In one hand, he carried a fishing tackle box. His dog, a chocolate-brown Labradoodle, sat not-so-patiently at his side. When Doodles saw me, she pranced on the spot and wagged her tail so hard that her whole butt swung back and forth.

"Mr. Greyson," I said.

He gave me a double take, as though he truly had been expecting the elegant and well-preserved Winona Vander Zalm.

He squinted at me. "Zara, is it? Zara Riddle?" He switched the tackle box to his left hand and offered me his right to shake.

"That's right." I shook his hand, which felt weak and boneless. "I moved in here with my daughter back in March. We've met a few times. I bought this house after Ms. Vander Zalm passed away earlier this year."

He limply withdrew his hand from mine and slapped it against his forehead. "Darn my spotty memory. I knew that." He shook his head. "Was that your daughter who answered the door just now?"

"Yes. My daughter, Zoey."

"The poor girl must think I'm crazy, ringing your doorbell and asking to see a dead woman." Another head shake and a sheepish smile. "Please apologize to her on my behalf. I've had a difficult day, and I suppose it slipped my mind that Ms. Vander Zalm was no longer with us."

I leaned to the side and glanced past him down the street. Most of the crime scene vehicles had moved on from in front of his place. Only a single unmarked van remained.

Arden Greyson followed my gaze. "I suppose you already heard the news." His voice was gritty with pain. The crime scene flashed in my mind. The red streaks on the walls. The headless body. The blood congealing on the black leather of the sofa.

"I've heard," I agreed.

"Bad news travels like wildfire," he said.

I took a step back, inviting him to come in. My manners were not perfect, but I knew better than to make a person discuss their loved one's recent homicide on my front porch.

"People will talk," I said. "Would you like to join me for a cup of tea?"

"Why, thank you for the kind offer, but I wouldn't want to impose." His words said no, yet he didn't turn to leave.

"I insist." I waved him in. It was what Winona would have wanted.

Doodles trotted in confidently. She didn't need a third invitation. Her owner followed, muttering apologies for interrupting my day. The dog barked sharply and trotted to the base of the stairs. She stood up on her hind legs and sniffed the railing—the railing that Ribbons slid down regularly.

Arden stared mutely at his dog, who was attempting to climb the stairs on two feet so she didn't have to take her moist brown nose off the tantalizing smells of the railing.

Arden asked Doodles, "What is it, girl?" He asked me, "You don't have peanut butter smeared on the railing, do you?"

"She must be smelling our cat," I said.

Arden frowned. "It must be a real special cat."

"Not as special as she thinks she is," I said.

He chuckled. "That's cats for you."

I waved for him to follow me back to my extra-spacious kitchen. He set the tackle box on the ample island's counter and scanned the room. His wrinkles melted and his eyes grew wider as he scanned.

"It's real nice, what you've done with Winona's place," he said. "Funny. The kitchen is smaller than I recall. That's memory for you."

"Really? I swear it's bigger than it was yesterday."

His eyebrows knitted. "Beg your pardon?"

I waved a hand. "Just a joke about my housekeeping skills." I filled the kettle and listed the selection of teas available. He chose a Rooibos blend, and took a seat at the island. Doodles came in just long enough to whimper at her owner before she trotted out again—presumably to sniff around for the wyvern. *Good luck*, I thought. I could never find Ribbons if he didn't want to be found, and I doubted the dog would do any better no matter how keen her nose.

Arden didn't speak until after he'd taken his first sip of tea.

"There was an accident," he said. "Or I suppose it wasn't an accident. My great-nephew was killed last night. He's the one who was renting the apartment above my garage." He stared into the honey-colored tea. "It's a real mess up there. They gave me some cards for the people who clean things like that. Did you know there are people whose jobs are to clean things like that?"

"Yes." I took a sip of my own tea. "I've never used those services before, but I understand it's a special type of job."

"You're a librarian, isn't that right?"

"I am."

"You must know all sorts of things."

"I have picked up a fair bit of information over the years. Some of it useful, some of it not so much." Doodles entered the kitchen and came to my side for some reassuring pets. Her coiled fur was impossibly soft. I wanted to bury my face in her silky ears. How could terrible things like beheadings happen in the same world that also had soft Labradoodles?

After a stretch of silence, I said, "Mr. Greyson, I'm very sorry for your loss. If there's anything I can do for you, please let me know. I guess when things like this happen, neighbors bring over casseroles. I'm not much of a cook, but I've learned you can use the potato chip crumbs at the bottom of the bag for a great casserole topping, and I can always give it a shot."

"That's mighty kind of you," he said. "There must be something about this house, that it only attracts good women. Winona was an odd bird, but she had a good heart. I suppose the reason you found me on your porch today is because there's still something of Winona left behind here in this house."

Little did he know!

He brought his gaze up to meet mine. "Do you believe in that sort of thing? People leaving behind a sort of energy?"

"I can't say that I don't." I gave him a gentle smile. "I have a very open mind."

He turned toward the kitchen's only window, a faraway look in his eyes. "I swear I saw Ishmael walking through my house this morning, right when I was heading out fishing. I figured he'd snuck into my place to grab some coffee. Typical bachelor, he was always short on some thing or another. I started talking to him like he was there, except when I followed him into the kitchen, he wasn't there." His eyes flicked from the window to mine. "Must have been his ghost."

He stared at me, unwavering.

I answered slowly. "Plenty of people have reported seeing ghosts. You wouldn't be the first."

"I'm not crazy. Forgetful, yes. And eccentric." He grinned. "Maybe too eccentric for my own good."

"Nothing wrong with a little eccentricity."

"I knew you'd understand," he said, sounding relieved. "Now, I'd like to ask you a question. If it's none of my business, just say so, and I'll leave it be."

"Sure. I mean, ask away."

He leaned back and rubbed his chin as he gave me a long look.

Finally, he spoke. "Now, what is it that makes a beautiful, smart woman such as yourself want to become a librarian?"

I let out a surprised laugh. I'd been expecting something a lot more personal.

"A woman like you could have been anything, I imagine," he said. "Why did you want to spend your days with a bunch of musty old books?"

Still laughing, I struck a finger in the air. "First of all, the materials in a well-run library should never be musty."

I went on to tell him about the cleaning and preservation systems used by modern libraries.

He asked another question, and then another, becoming more interested with each answer.

Rarely had I enjoyed such an enthusiastic grilling about my profession.

The time passed, as it always does in these rare magical moments, quickly and without friction.

* * *

Arden Greyson and I talked our way through three cups of tea each. We talked about libraries, then the educational system, then everything that was right and wrong with generations not our own, and then we finally moved on to politics, both national and local.

Arden had some interesting theories about Mayor Paula Paladini. He believed she was part of some Illuminati-like secret organization. I found this both scandalous and hilarious. He thanked me for humoring his eccentricities, and we moved on to a discussion of home renovations, and what type of landscaping gave the biggest boost to a home's resale value.

Doodles eventually wore herself out sniffing for wyverns. She rested on the kitchen floor at her master's feet, perking up when he slipped her the occasional ladyfinger cookie from the plate on the table.

When Zoey wandered into the kitchen, smacking her lips and eyeballing the remaining ladyfingers, it was nearly five o'clock. Arden Greyson and I had been talking for hours, and not about the recent tragedy. Since his mention of Ishmael appearing as a ghost in the house, the topic hadn't come back around to the homicide.

Zoey poured herself a big glass of water and joined us at the kitchen island. She reached for the tackle box Arden had brought with him and lightly ran her fingers over the rusty buckles.

"You can go ahead and open that," Arden said good-naturedly. "Do you have an interest in fishing lures, young lady?"

She flipped up the buckles and opened the lid with a rusty creak. "Some of the girls at school use these kind of feathers for earrings," she said.

"They sure do." He chuckled. "There was a time, not long ago, when you couldn't get the feathers because the teenagers kept buying out the stock."

I asked, "Did you catch anything this morning? You were out fishing, right?"

"Didn't even get a nibble," he said.

"That's too bad."

Zoey lifted the top tray out of the tackle box and peered into the darkness. "Ooh," she exclaimed. "What's that?"

He followed her gaze and his face lit up. "That," he said proudly, "is a karambit."

"A karambit," Zoey repeated. She reached in and pulled out the knife. It had a carved bone handle and a long curved blade, like the letter C. Unlike the metal of the fishing tackle box, the blade on the unusual knife was fresh and new. It gleamed under the kitchen light, appearing almost white.

"It's so light, and the grip is perfect for my hand," Zoey said. She used the blade to swish the air in front of her in a very un-Zoey-like motion.

Something in the air shifted, as though agitated by the slashing of the sharp blade. My skin prickled, and my senses sharpened.

I silently noted that the curved blade was the perfect shape to wrap around a human's neck. In fact, if applied with enough force, it might be used for decapitation. Were we looking at the murder weapon? Had Arden walked it right into my house, under my nose?

I met Zoey's gaze and sent her a look. *Be careful.* She acknowledged my unspoken warning with the smallest of blinks—a gesture that would likely go unnoticed by the owner of the knife who was sitting with us.

"What's it for?" Zoey asked brightly, still swishing the knife.

"Oh, this and that," Arden said casually. "I understand they use them in the Philippines for farming. You could use it to rake roots and gather threshing."

"Neat," Zoey said. "It's like a sickle."

"I found it in the trash," he said.

Zoey and I exchanged a look.

"When?" I asked. Had it been that morning?

"A few weeks back," he said casually, not picking up on the tension in my voice. "I don't know why my nephew was throwing out a perfectly good knife. Funny thing is, it's so sharp that it cut its way out of the bag, almost like it didn't want to be thrown out."

Zoey and I exchanged another look. The knife had its own intentions?

Arden went on. "I figured I might put it to use gutting fish, but I haven't had the chance yet."

He continued talking about fishing in the local waters, and how things went with the various seasons. His voice blurred in the background.

Arden Greyson claimed he hadn't used the knife, but what if someone else had? What if it was the weapon that had been used on Ishmael? There had to be a reason it was now inside my house. Ghosts had their ways of affecting the living. It was possible Ishmael had used his ghostly hands to influence his great-uncle into walking across the street and dropping the murder weapon practically at my feet.

Zoey continued to play with the knife, switching it from one hand to the other. *Better it's in her hands than his*, I thought.

Arden met my eyes and gave me a questioning look. "The young one is comfortable with a blade," he remarked.

I chuckled and said, "My daughter, the weapons expert."

Arden said to her, "Careful. It's awfully sharp."

How would he know if was sharp if he hadn't used it yet?

She carefully returned it to the tackle box. "That was fun," she said.

I put my hands on my hips and playfully said, "Really? *That was fun?* Who are you and what have you done to my daughter?" I smiled as I explained to Arden, "My daughter is normally afraid of knives, or so she claims whenever you ask her to chop vegetables."

"Kids outgrow their childish fears eventually," he said sagely.

"So they do."

I kept smiling, and at the same time, I cast a mild camouflage spell over his fishing tackle box. The spell was, from what I could gather, designed to keep unexpected guests from noticing messes. My aunt had taught me how to cast it over piles of unfolded laundry and a whole variety of things that I just happened to have examples of in my house. It didn't make things invisible, but it did cause them to blend with their environment to avoid detection by visitors. If my hastily cast spell worked, Arden might forget his tackle box on my counter.

I got up from my chair and glanced around theatrically.

"Speaking of chopping vegetables, we should probably get dinner started," I said.

Arden squinted at the window. "Is it that time already?"

Zoey chimed in, "Time flies when you're having fun." She shot me a wide-eyed, now-what look.

I said to Arden, who was still gazing at the window, "Mr. Greyson, would you like to stay for dinner?" *Please say no.*

He immediately got to his feet. "No," he said softly. "I've already taken up more than my fair share of your hospitality." His dog jumped up and smelled Arden's outstretched fingers for cookies. Arden turned, swept his gaze through the area where his tackle box sat under the camouflage spell, pressed his lips together briefly, then proceeded toward the door. The spell had worked.

Zoey trailed along behind us as I walked Arden and Doodles to the front door. Zoey caught my eye, nodded toward the kitchen, and raised an eyebrow. I gave her a quick eye flash to let her know that getting the tackle box was part of my plan. All the better for me to get the karambit tested as evidence.

Arden walked out the front door and paused on the porch. "Ms. Riddle," he said slowly.

In unison, Zoey and I chirped, "Yes?"

He glanced back over his shoulder just long enough to say, "If you do happen to make one of those casseroles with the potato chips on top, I wouldn't say no to such a thing."

I pointed a finger at him. "Your wish is my command."

Doodles trotted down the stairs and led Arden Greyson away.

CHAPTER 18

As soon as Arden was gone, Zoey followed me into the kitchen where we both took another look at the knife.

She asked, "How can something so pretty be used to murder?" She took it by the handle again and swished it through the air.

"I'd tell you not to touch it, but I guess you already got your DNA all over it when Arden was here."

"Not my DNA," she corrected. "But it probably is coated with my epithelial cells, which *might* contain my DNA."

"My daughter, the weapons expert and also the crime scene investigator."

She made an excited sound. "Can you test for DNA with magic?"

"I believe that's a job for science. However, I can do this." I cast a threat detection spell over both the karambit and the tackle box. This time, the spell didn't splash back in my face like used toothpaste, but it didn't reveal anything helpful, either.

Zoey balanced the knife on one finger. "What type of metal is this? It feels a lot lighter than it looks."

"Maybe it's hollow." I got an idea and snapped my fingers. "Hold that thought! Your great-aunt gave me something before she went on vacation." I grabbed my purse and pulled out a tube of ordinary-looking lipstick. I removed the lid with a flourish, revealing a ravishing shade of red lipstick.

"Ooh," Zoey said. "I like that color."

"Me, too." I applied the lipstick to my lips, and blotted it with a kitchen napkin.

Zoey gave me a skeptical look. "How does red lipstick help you analyze metal content? Does it make you able to taste it?"

"Good guess, but this is actually just regular lipstick. What we want is under here."

I put the cap back on the tube, turned it over, and unscrewed the bottom. Inside was a compartment that held an odorless white powder. I gestured for Zoey to set the curved knife on the counter. She did so, and I sprinkled both the blade and the handle with a small amount of the powder.

I didn't need to cast a spell. This was a magical compound, so the spell was already baked in, so to speak. There was a slight ozone spell as the powder analyzed the composition.

The spell did its magic, then returned the results as words spoken softly in my head. *One karambit. Handle composition: Sixty percent hydroxyapatite with collagen fibers. Common name: Bone. Origin: Unknown.*

"Bone," I said to Zoey. "The handle is carved bone, but I don't know what animal it's from."

"What about the blade?"

I focused my eyes on the gleaming blade and waited. The spell played on-hold music inside my head. Soft jazz. I had just started tapping my food in time with the music when the words returned. *Blade composition: Unknown. Origin: Insufficient data.*

"The spell doesn't know," I reported to Zoey. "Either that or I'm not using the powder right. What a waste." I frowned at the tiny amount remaining in the hidden compartment. My aunt had given me the powder as a reward for learning a tricky bit of magic—peeling the shell off an uncooked egg while keeping it levitating and intact. I had actually enjoyed the task, though I pretended it was excruciating because I could tell it pleased Aunt Zinnia to torture me a little. I had planned to use the powder to find out exactly what kind of raw fish the local sushi place was using in its suspiciously inexpensive sashimi, but now a third of the powder was gone.

"It wasn't a total waste," Zoey said in her usual cheerful way, the way she always sounded right before pointing out the bright side of any situation.

"You're just trying to cheer me up."

She studied my face carefully before saying, "That lipstick suits you. I bet Detective Bentley will notice how pretty you look when he comes to pick up the knife for more testing."

I snorted. "He doesn't see me that way."

"Why not?"

"I don't know. He just doesn't. Besides, he was dating your grandmother."

"I think they were more like friends. They weren't in love, according to her."

"Ew." I made a face. "Either way, I'm not interested in dating that va—" I still couldn't say the word, thanks to her magic, but I did have a new substitution that she would hate. "I'm not interested in that *upgraded zombie's* used-up leftovers. She probably drained out whatever sense of humor he had along with half his blood."

"Gigi doesn't drink from humans."

"So she claims."

"She wouldn't lie to her family."

I pulled my head back. "Are you serious? For one third of your young life, she did nothing *but* lie to the family. She let us think she was dead. For five long years."

Zoey couldn't argue with that. Her grandmother—my mother—had made the choice at a young age to curse away her own witchcraft. Later in life, she'd suffered an illness that could only be cured by her dying and then being brought back to life. Well, *sort of* back to life. I called her an upgraded zombie. She was a creature of the grave, thinner and more beautiful than ever, with her sleek, black hair. A person couldn't blame a man like Bentley for being attracted to the woman, no matter what she was. Riddle women did have their charms, even after death.

I used my magic to grab my phone and put in a call to Bentley.

Zoey listened to my side of the conversation, watching me like I was must-see TV.

* * *

Twenty minutes later, my doorbell rang again. This time it was Bentley. He wasted no time in getting to the knife.

He stood staring at it on the kitchen island's counter for a long time. The detective scowled at the karambit so hard, I could have sworn I saw a brand-new vertical wrinkle form on his forehead.

"You shouldn't have stolen this," he said gruffly.

"I didn't steal it," I said heavily. "Arden Greyson wandered over here of his own free will. I made him some tea, and he was so dazzled by my skills as a conversationalist that he left his whole tackle box behind by accident."

Bentley attempted to bag the knife in an evidence bag, but the curved edge was so sharp it snagged the plastic, sliced through, and fell out. I caught the falling karambit with my magic so it didn't scratch the floor.

Bentley stared at me with round eyes. He'd been caught off guard by my levitation.

"You get used to it," I said. "By which I mean seeing household objects defy the laws of physics. Did I ever tell you the first time I used levitation, it was to catch a falling glass, right over there by that sink?"

He scratched his head. "Is that so?"

The knife wavered in the air between us.

Bentley looked down at his feet. "I don't know if a guy can ever get used to witchcraft, but thanks. You saved my shoes." He swished his mouth from side to side. "And possibly a toe."

I held both hands to my chest and pretended to swoon. "He finds me handy! Oh, be still my beating heart."

Bentley retrieved a new plastic evidence bag, gingerly wrapped it around the floating karambit, then carefully held it by the handle so it couldn't escape again.

"You certainly are handy," he said gruffly without looking at me. "It was cunning of you to entertain Mr. Greyson and gain his trust."

"Cunning? I was being neighborly."

"How about stealing the man's tackle box? Was that neighborly?"

"I can't think of anything more neighborly than protecting the neighborhood from a killer."

The detective nodded. "Very well, then. I can't say I would have thought of the same thing, even if I had your powers. It may not have been cunning, but it was clever."

I swooned again. "He finds me clever!"

Bentley looked around the kitchen. "Who are you talking to?"

I shrugged. Didn't everyone have an imaginary audience who followed them around to laugh at their crazy antics? Other than those folks, Bentley and I were alone in the kitchen. My daughter had returned to her bedroom after answering the door.

He shook his head. "I swear, whenever I'm around you, I feel like I'm on some hidden-camera TV show. You're always saying the strangest things. What's that all about?"

"It's called having a personality."

"Oh," he said flatly. "Is that what it is? I suppose I wouldn't know. I'm only a detective. When I'm not working on a homicide case or eating donuts, I park myself in a dark closet, like a robot."

I stared at him for a moment. I hadn't given much thought to Bentley's personal life until now. I tried to picture him doing regular things. Picking up milk and bread at the store. Taking his car in for an oil change. Frolicking on the beach with a kite on a windy day. Nope. Couldn't picture any of those things, and yet, I could easily imagine him parked in a dark closet like a robot.

"Stop it," he said. "Stop imagining me standing in a dark closet."

I let out a burst of laughter. "Bentley! You can read minds! You have supernatural powers after all."

"It's not mind reading," he said. "Well, not exactly. It's called *theory of mind*. I observe a person's facial expressions and body language, then use my empathy to imagine what I'd be thinking if I was that person."

"Is that so? What am I thinking right now?"

He rubbed his chin and studied me thoughtfully. "You're trying to think of something that would embarrass me."

I flashed my eyes and looked him over. "Such as...?" I licked my lips suggestively.

He sighed. "Stop undressing me with your eyes."

"I was doing no such thing," I said indignantly. Technically, I'd only been *pretending* to undress him with my eyes. For a laugh. I didn't want to picture his tanned skin extending below his shirt collar across a taut, muscular chest. Or the narrow line of dark hair that might run below his belly button. Or the way his muscular thighs might look sticking out from the bottom of cotton boxers. How was I so certain he wore boxers? And why was I picturing them as gray with black stripes?

"Zara," he said.

My throat felt thick. "What?" I'd gotten trapped in my imagination and was finding it difficult to extract myself.

He sniffed the air. "Did you eat dinner already?"

I was glad for the topic change. "Yes. I ate with Zoey. We had nuked leftovers."

He gave the air another sniff.

I waited for him to make a comment about my lack of cooking skills, but he didn't say anything.

His stomach broke the silence with a growl.

I suddenly caught his subtle hint. I jumped toward the refrigerator with a speed that startled Bentley into take a step backward, bumping into one of the kitchen island's chairs, making it scrape on the floor.

"You must be starving," I said. "You've been working on this case since dawn, and you probably haven't had anything to eat, have you?"

"I had coffee," he said. "I can go a day or two without eating."

"Crazy talk!" I yanked open the fridge and started pulling out containers and jars. "Let me whip up something for you. It won't take a minute."

"No need. I'll be heading straight back to the office with this weapon. I can stop by the cafeteria if I get hungry."

"By the sound of that stomach, you're well past hungry."

"I know my limits."

I paused in my fridge raiding and gave him an over-the-glasses look. I didn't wear glasses, but thanks to my librarian training, under the most esteemed of long-timers, I'd learned my over-the-glasses look from the best in the business. Bentley received the look and gave me a sheepish one in return.

"Sure, you do," I said. "Your mouth says you're leaving, but your butt's trying to make friends with that chair." I waved for him to sit down. "You bought the coffee today, so dinner's on me."

He set the bagged knife on the counter without making a sound. "If you insist," he said. "Where might I wash my hands?"

I nodded at the hallway. "There's a powder room on the main floor, or you can use the kitchen sink if you can't bear to be away from me."

He raised an eyebrow at me as he took off his gray suit jacket and hung it on the back of a chair. "A wise man knows when he's being tested," he said as he walked over to the kitchen sink. He undid his cuff buttons and methodically rolled up his shirt sleeves. He washed his hands, with soap, and then held them dripping above the sink.

He said, "Paper towel?"

I realized I'd been standing motionless in front of the open refrigerator door watching him wash his hands. As though it were must-see TV. I ducked down into the fridge and called out, "On your left, behind the Darth Vader cookie jar."

He found the roll and dried his hands as he commented, "Interesting cookie jar."

"You like it? It reminds me of my mother."

"Because she used to make you cookies?"

"No." I closed the fridge door. "Because I saw her choke a person using her mind."

He cocked his head. "What?"

"Never mind." I dropped the assortment of takeout containers on the counter. "Tonight's special is a fusion dish. Lemon chicken with lasagna."

"Perfect. I'll make the salad."

I laughed. "Good one."

He was heading to the back door. "I'll use the lettuce and tomatoes from your back garden. Unless you were saving them for some other occasion?"

"Uh, no. Not at all. Now is the perfect occasion to use the lettuce and tomatoes and whatever else is growing back there."

He walked out to the back yard. I peered after him in semi-disbelief. I'd completely forgotten about the small vegetable garden I'd planted while under the influence of a ghost with two green thumbs.

What a day of surprises this was turning out to be.

* * *

After dinner, Bentley insisted he couldn't possibly eat another bite, but then I showed him my method for making ice cream sandwiches using miniature chocolate chip cookies.

He ate three.

"I'll just waddle my way out the door," he joked.

"One for the road?" I sent another ice cream sandwich orbiting around his head like a satellite.

He sighed and then opened his mouth.

I sailed the flying vessel into port.

He pushed his chair back, unrolled his shirt sleeves, straightened his tie, and pulled on his suit jacket. He was Bentley, as before, but also not as before. He looked different now. Not as monochrome. There was color in his cheeks.

"I should be getting back to the office," he said.

"Are you done for the day, or will you stick around while they do testing on the knife?"

He snorted, as though finding the idea of being done for the day amusing. "I'm not done by a long shot," he said heavily. He took a step toward the door and paused. "What sort of things do you have planned for this evening?"

"I've got a few books I was going to look through to see what there is about beheadings."

"Research is always good." He nodded and adjusted the sleeves of his jacket.

"But I already had a quick scan through my books this morning, and there wasn't much."

"Ah." He rubbed his chin. "If you're not sick to death of me, you could come along with me to the medical examiner's. Your perspective thus far has been rather helpful."

I snapped my fingers and held out my arm for my purse. "The morgue on Saturday night? Now that's a date!"

He blinked. "You really are a witch, aren't you?"

"I really am." I walked ahead of him toward the front door, stopped at the stairwell, and called up to my daughter, "Bentley's taking me on a date to the morgue! Don't wait up!"

Her disembodied voice replied, "Don't do anything Auntie Z wouldn't do!"

"You know, when you say something like that, you're just egging me on!"

She giggled. "Have fun at the morgue!"

Bentley joined me at the stairwell and called up, "I'll take excellent care of your mother, Zoey."

There was a thump, and footsteps, then Zoey appeared at the top of the stairs. Her hazel eyes were wide. "Are you really going to the morgue? I thought you were joking."

"This is what happens when you joke all the time," Bentley said to me. "You become the boy who cried wolf."

I held up my hand, sassy style. "Excuse me? The boy who cried wolf was doing it to get attention. He wasn't very funny. I'm hilarious."

Bentley gave me a smug look. "My point stands."

"He does make a good point," Zoey said.

I put my hands on my hips and glared up the stairs. "*Et tu*, daughter?"

"Mom, this morning when you tossed me the keys at the museum and said you were going to help Detective Bentley solve a homicide, I thought you were just going to the bathroom or something. I waited around like a dummy for an hour before I realized you weren't coming back."

My hands were still on my hips, and I was starting to feel the exasperation I'd been pretending to feel. "Now you're pulling my leg."

"I'm not." She sighed. "Sometimes when you run off, I feel like I've been..." She mumbled something under her breath.

"What?"

"Abandoned," she said. The word stung.

My daughter felt abandoned? Because I tossed her the car keys and didn't get into a lengthy discussion about homicide investigation in the middle of a crowded museum? That didn't seem fair.

Her cheeks were flushed. Softly, she repeated, "Sometimes I feel abandoned. I'm not saying it's your fault. It's just... how I feel."

My own cheeks felt hot. She was calling me a bad mother, right in front of the detective?

I should have calmly reflected back her feelings and promised to discuss it in detail at a more appropriate time.

However, being me, I volleyed back with what seemed like humor. "Is there anything else you'd like to discuss right now? How about the fact I don't turn down your bed and put a chocolate mint on the pillow every night?" As soon as I said it, I regretted it. But there was no spell that could pull back words.

She said nothing.

I felt Bentley's hand on my shoulder. "You've had a long day," he said. "I shouldn't take you away from—"

I wheeled around on him. "Don't you dare ditch me now, partner. You promised me the morgue, and we're going to the morgue."

He raised his eyebrows and gave a wide-eyed look to the floor beneath our feet. "All right, then."

I turned to my daughter. I'd had a few seconds to calm down. Barely. I softened my voice as much as I could manage. "Sweetie, I'm sorry it felt like you were abandoned at the museum today. I should have taken more time to talk to you." I swallowed, and then the words I should have said in the first place came to me. "I'm sorry I abandoned you."

Bentley, wisely, said nothing.

After a long pause, Zoey took three slow steps down the stairs toward us and ducked her head. "Oh, Mom. I was fine. It all worked out."

"I just wasn't thinking. I'm really sorry."

"I know."

"You're my everything, kid."

Her cheeks flushed again, this time probably with embarrassment. "I'm okay, I swear."

And she was. The thing about teenagers was they could go from okay to not-okay in a heartbeat, but they could go the other way almost as quickly, too. And my beautiful, sweet, kind daughter was more resilient than most. She really did deserve a better mother than the one she got. But I would keep trying, anyway.

She waved me toward the front door with a limp arm. "Go on your date to the morgue."

"I don't have to go."

"You should go."

"I should probably stick around close to home. For your safety."

"Mom, just go." She sighed and flashed her eyes at me. "I promise not to get in any trouble."

I shook a finger at her. "No potions."

She shuffled down a few more steps and gave me an exasperated look. "No potions," she promised.

I put my hands on my hips. "I'd make you do that my-word-is-a-bond thing, but you're not old enough." I shook my head. "It's rather convenient that it doesn't work on people under twenty-four."

She gave me an innocent look. "It's because our brains are still forming."

I turned to explain the whole thing to the detective, but judging by the look on his face, he already knew.

"It's true about brain development," Bentley said in agreement. "We don't see a drop-off in risk-taking behavior until after that age."

Risk-taking behavior. Like hunting? I asked the detective, "How old was Ishmael? Twenty-six? He was barely an adult."

"Barely. You're right about that, and it may have been a factor." He gestured toward the door. "Shall we?"

I took his elbow playfully. "Let's go to the morgue."

He looked down at my fingers on his suit jacket, then up at my face with an amused expression. "Ah, but it gets better," he said, waggling his eyebrows. "The morgue is located in the underground headquarters of a secret organization."

I gasped. "The DWM? I'm so excited-slash-terrified!"

CHAPTER 19

I'd been to the underground headquarters of the Department of Water and Magic a few times. Each time, I'd gone in through a different secret entrance. It was only logical that the place had a few access points—all the better to hide a stream of people and creatures coming in and out—but it was nevertheless dizzying.

For this visit, we entered the Wisteria Police Department, then ducked through a service door, which brought us to an elevator with the expected high-tech security panel. There was a palm and eye scan for Bentley, and then, weirdly enough, a brief interrogation by a disembodied female voice.

"Welcome back, Zara Riddle," the voice said, managing to sound both robotic and breathily sexy at the same time. "We hope you enjoy your visit to our headquarters."

"Thank you, disembodied voice," I said.

"You may call me Codex," she said, sounding husky along with breathy.

Bentley muttered under his breath, "That's new."

"I am new," she replied. "Thank you for noticing, Detective. Allow me to introduce myself. I am Codex. I am the voice of this building's automated systems."

I peered up at the glowing red dot on the video screen. "Are you a robot?"

"Thank you for asking, Ms. Riddle. I am not a robot. I am the voice of this building's automated systems."

"You're software?"

"Thank you for asking, Ms. Riddle. I am not software. Software is a program used by a computer. Let me see if I can explain by using an example. You and Detective Bentley use the language English, yet you are not English."

Bentley frowned. "My ancestors are English."

"A wonderful observation," cooed the voice. "My ancestors are software."

Bentley muttered something unintelligible.

The light on the display screen turned amber. The voice—Codex—continued, "We have now exceeded our allotted time allowance for pleasantries. Please proceed to your destination at once."

The doors slid open faster than I'd ever seen elevator doors open. Bentley and I hopped in immediately. We exchanged a look but didn't dare speak until we we'd ridden down multiple stories, then exited the elevator.

"That was new," Bentley said again, once the doors had closed between us.

I gave him a bemused look. "We are currently ten or twenty stories beneath street level, inside a labyrinth of secret tunnels, filled with monsters. Does the fact that the exits are guarded by a flirty artificial intelligence make you feel more safe or less safe?"

He squeezed his chin thoughtfully. "With some things, it's best not to ask questions or examine too closely."

"I hear you. It's like when you're getting on an airplane, and you recognize the pilot from the fast food pit at the airport, where you noticed he had trouble getting his straw into his drink container." I mimed clumsy repeated stabbing. "And he kept going like this, over and over, poke, poke, poke, not hitting the little patch of foil over the hole, until finally the straw gave up and crumpled in on itself."

"That's a rather specific example."

I squeezed my own chin thoughtfully. "It wasn't a perfect simile. How about this? It's like when you're donating blood, and you—"

"Blood?" His eyes widened.

"Yeah. It's like when you're donating blood, and you recognize the *nurse* from the fast food pit at the mall, where you noticed she couldn't get her straw into her drink container." I mimed more futile stabbing.

"Enough with the blood talk, and all the poking." Bentley waved a hand to stop me. "You're very good at examples."

"I can do better. How about this one? It's like when you're getting on the roller coaster, and there's a safety announcement, except it's not done by a person. The announcer is actually an insane computer who talks in riddles."

Bentley gave me two weary thumbs up. "Perfect." He started walking down a concrete-walled corridor. "Right this way. We're actually meeting with someone from legal before we head down to the morgue."

"Someone from legal? Why?"

"He knew the victim personally, so I'd like to ask a few questions. He's actually—"

I whooped excitedly as a sign caught my eye. "The cafeteria?" I asked. "Are we meeting this guy from legal in the cafeteria?"

"Yes."

"Great." I put a skip in my step. "I could eat."

"Didn't you just eat?"

"I didn't say I was hungry. I said I could eat." I fell in step with the detective. "I hear the cherry cheesecake is to die for."

"Cherry cheesecake," Bentley said, his voice sounding more dreamy than weary. He licked his lips. "Dark, red cherry syrup." He reached up and touched the bullet talisman that formed a lump under the collar of his shirt.

"See? You're not hungry, but you could eat."

His voice low and gritty, he said, "I could eat."

CHAPTER 20

The cafeteria at the DWM looked like the kind you'd find within the building of any corporation large enough to have a dedicated foodservice area, yet not gigantic enough to have multiple cafeterias, all with different themes.

The time was 8:30 pm, well past dinner, plus it was a Saturday. The place was understandably quiet. Nobody was seated on the gleaming white chairs. A lone janitor in dark-blue overalls barely glanced our way as he dragged his pine-scented mop back and forth across the polished concrete floors. Over at the food stations, the buffet had been closed for the day. There wasn't any hot food on offer, but there was a long row of refrigerated compartments offering sandwiches, salads, and—most importantly—cherry cheesecake.

I was yabbering away about cheesecake and headed toward it when Bentley grabbed my arm. He squeezed my bicep in what felt like urgency. I pulled myself away from the desserts, turned, and jerked to attention when I saw what he'd seen.

Walking in through the same door we had come was a creature from a fairy tale. Or a horror movie. It was the size of a pony, with the body of a lion and the head of an iguana. A *big* iguana.

I'd seen this creature before, during a visit to the underground offices. The beast had been walking down a hallway with a human, casually joking about eating a coworker's office chair. The beast was an iguammit, and *it* was a *him*. His name was Steve. He was the person we were there to meet with, except he wasn't in person form at all.

As the creature padded closer on its huge lion paws, I forced myself to blink a few times to break up the staring. The iguammit flicked its pink, forked tongue at us, then offered the iguana equivalent of a smile.

He spoke. "It has been a very long day for all of us, hasn't it?" Steve the Iguammit had a French-accented human voice despite his green, dry-looking iguana lips. If you closed your eyes, you'd swear his pleasant speech came from human lips. That was magic for you. Just a wee bit inconsistent at times. My daughter couldn't speak English at all when she was in fox form, yet this fantastical chimera, whose mouth wasn't even mammalian, could speak perfectly. Better than I could, some might say.

Bentley replied to the giant iguana face, his voice showing only a hint of terror. "It's been a very long day," he agreed. "And it's liable to be an even longer night."

Steve moved toward us with no hurry. He gave another flick of the forked tongue. His cone-shaped eye sockets rotated independently as he glanced around. He stopped in front of us, sat back on his lion haunches, and extended a front paw.

"Thank you for taking the long elevator ride down here," said the lizard-headed beast with an outstretched lion's paw.

Bentley offered his own hand with almost no hesitation.

As human hand touched iguammit paw, the air shimmered in a heat wave pattern. Powerful change magic passed through me in a hot burst, throwing off my balance the way a mild earthquake might. The chimera transformed. Bentley had begun shaking hands with a lion's paw, but now he was shaking hands with another human. A man. Also wearing a business suit.

Steve was dark-skinned, average height, with a slim build. He looked about thirty. His hair was black and tightly coiled to his head. He had an amiable, round face, with a cleft chin, clean shaven. Sliding down his short nose was a pair of round tortoiseshell glasses. The mottled brown and gold glasses emphasized his big, expressive brown eyes. He wore a stylish suit jacket over a tan-colored safari-style shirt with two buttons undone. No tie. The jacket and trousers were playfully mismatched in a youthful, fashion-forward way. Both garments were cut in a slimmer, more contemporary style than Bentley's conservative suit, yet not as feminine as my own gray suit. He looked exactly like the sort of sharp young man you'd trust with your legal documents, your taxes, your banking, or even your daughter. His posh, vaguely French accent certainly added to his charm.

The man continued his conversation with Bentley as though he hadn't just shifted form. "I deeply regret that we are not meeting under better circumstances." Steve's deep, rich voice as a human was exactly the same as it had been as an iguammit.

Bentley tilted his head back and offered the man a grim look. "Being a detective, these are the type of circumstances under which I meet most new people."

Steve nodded and shot me a shy look. He had the thickest eyelashes I'd ever seen. He said to Bentley, "I recognize your redheaded partner, yet we haven't been formally introduced."

Bentley opened his mouth to introduce me, but I beat him to it.

"Zara Riddle," I said, offering my hand. He shook it. I was mildly disappointed his hand didn't turn into a paw and then back again for me.

He gripped my hand like a man with no intention of releasing it. "You're a natural redhead," he said.

"Down to the last freckle," I replied.

"I do love the color red."

"That's right," I said. I knew that about his kind. "And you love red candy, too, right?"

He finally released my hand and gave me a coy look, batting his thick eyelashes behind the tortoiseshell-framed lenses. "Who told you?"

Nobody had told me. I'd read that particular fact in the book I called the DWM Monster Manual. Iguammits such as Steve were prone to periods of intense concentration during which they often forgot to eat. When famished, they would eat almost anything, but they loved red-colored candy the most. At the mention of red candy, something had started bubbling up in my memory. The glass jars of red candy at Carrot the tattoo artist's studio.

Two pieces of a puzzle snapped together. Carrot had red candy, and her boyfriend Sefu was sometimes called Steve. He was a potential suspect. And he was standing in front of me.

Steve seemed to catch something in my expression. "Have I offended you, Ms. Riddle? I do apologize if I've been rude in any way. It's been a very long day."

"You're Sefu," I said tentatively.

"I am. Most people call me Steve." He shuffled from one foot to the other, glancing down.

"You're a lawyer here, and you're also the person Carrot Greyson is dating?"

"Of course." He hunched his shoulders under his stylish suit jacket. "Am I to assume, by your question, that you were not made aware of that fact before now?"

"So it would seem."

Bentley broke in, "I apologize, Mr. Adebayo. I should have told Zara on the way over."

"No need to apologize." Sefu Adebayo, also known as Steve the Iguammit or Steve the Lawyer, fidgeted with his tan shirt where a tie might have been. "We are all on the same team. We can grieve for the loss of our late friend, Ishmael, another time. Right now, it's important we put all your resources toward catching whoever did that unspeakable deed."

He met my gaze with shining eyes.

"I'm sorry for your loss," I said.

He jerked his head downward. "Thank you, but I must admit that Ishmael and I weren't very close," Steve said. "My heart is breaking right now for his sister, of whom I'm very fond."

Of whom I'm very fond. For a young-looking guy, Steve had an old-fashioned way of speaking. Did the style came from his education? Or was he older than he appeared? Like maybe a century or two older?

Bentley cut in. "When we spoke on the phone earlier today, you said that Miss Carrot Greyson is unaware of the supernatural. Is that true, or were you reluctant to discuss such things over an unsecured line?"

Steve rubbed the base of his nose. "Carrot doesn't know what I am, and I'd prefer that she doesn't find out. Eventually, perhaps after we're married, I'll break the news. I'll start, of course, by revealing her own powers as a rune mage."

In unison, both Bentley and I said, "Rune mage?"

"Yes." Steve took off his glasses and began cleaning them with a square of blue cloth he took from his jacket pocket. "I believe Carrot has the ability to forge psychic connections with other beings, using symbols." His speech took on an instructive tone, aided by the professor-like cleaning of the glasses. "In the old days, the ancients drew runes upon their skin using charred wood and dark berries. They conducted rituals around fires and waterfalls, attempting to communicate with the spirit world or distant villages."

"Before the days of phones and telegrams," I said.

Steve shot me a pleased look. "Before language, even."

"You got me," I said. "I can't even imagine a time before language."

Bentley snorted.

Steve continued. "Carrot hasn't been indoctrinated with the ancient knowledge by a mentor, and yet, the magic has found a way to her. Without knowing it, Carrot has been channeling rune magic through the tattoos on her body."

Bentley asked, "How is it that she's unaware of this? A person should be able to tell if they're under the influence of magic."

Not necessarily, I thought. Bentley had no idea he'd been under a certain black-haired upgraded-zombie's spell.

"Carrot is not surprised by coincidences because she believes in superstition and magic the way many people do," Steve explained. "As a vague force that can be influenced by prayer or," he wrinkled his nose, "positive thinking."

Bentley asked, "Can she use this rune mage tattoo power to control people? To make others do her bidding?"

Steve paused before answering, "Anything is possible. She has been a suspect in a homicide case before. I was first alerted to her magical abilities when she awoke from a dream, ran to her car, and drove to a crime site." He smiled at the memory. "That case has since been closed. It was officially determined she was merely a witness to events. An innocent bystander, who was only involved because of a few foolish choices she made in her love life."

"Yup," I said. "I know that tune. Love makes you stupid."

Steve sighed and got a wistful look. "It certainly does."

Bentley cleared his throat. "No, it doesn't. The opposite is true. Love—actual love, not infatuation or lust—clarifies everything."

Steve and I both turned to the detective for further explanation. He offered none.

After it was clear Bentley didn't have more to say about love and its ability to make people the opposite of stupid, Steve continued talking about Carrot.

"It is really quite wondrous how intuitive Carrot is," Steve said. "Recently, she has been talking about getting another tattoo. Either a lion or an iguana." He raised his eyebrows emphatically. "Her idea entirely."

"A lion or an iguana," Bentley mused. "Sounds like your tattooed girlfriend knows more about you than she's letting on." He gave Steve a playful, brotherly punch on the shoulder.

Steve winced. His human form was apparently not very rugged.

"She knows without knowing," Steve said.

Bentley raised his eyebrows. "It could be the power of love that's allowing her to see the truth."

Steve held his cleaned glasses up to the cafeteria's bright windows and inspected them as he spoke. "But even if one sees the truth, how can one be certain it's not another wishful illusion? Surely you are both familiar with the expression *we see what we wish to see*."

Bentley followed the man's gaze past the eyeglasses to the bright windows.

"You mean like that pretty view," Bentley said. "We see what we wish to see. If we believe hard enough, the illusion becomes the truth."

I followed his gaze. Beyond the cafeteria's huge window panes there was what appeared to be a sunny courtyard. The courtyard had been lovingly landscaped with a variety of shrubs and bright flowers that bobbed in a light breeze. Except there were no flowers, and it wasn't a courtyard. It couldn't have been. We were at least ten stories—maybe twenty—below ground. They might have been able to grow plants, but they didn't have sunshine.

"Exactly," Steve said. "The view is a courtyard if you believe it is."

"What are those glass panels made of, anyway?" Bentley asked. "Television screens? A projection of some kind?"

Steve smiled, looking like a professor who was pleased by a student's astute questions. "It's not exactly my department, but I can tell you that it's hybrid technology. Magic and science."

I asked him, "Is that what Codex the Talking Elevator is made of? Magic and science?"

Steve's smile fell off his face immediately. "*Codex* is not my favorite innovation. The architects don't even know why they're making her. They simply are." He waved at the windows. "At least this window technology has an obvious end use. It offers a pretty view, and helps prevent Seasonal Affective Disorder. That's all. It's not going to one day..." He trailed off, shuddering.

Bentley shot me an uneasy look.

I gave him a that's-what-you-get look right back.

We'd come here for information, and we were getting plenty of it. Not necessarily the information we'd come for, but I was thrilled to learn more about both rune mages and the inner workings of the DWM.

Steve shook his head as though waking himself from a daydream. "We... are... standing in the cafeteria," he said uncertainly. He looked past us, in the direction of the refrigeration units. "We should get something from foodservices." He glanced upward briefly. "It will look suspicious on the surveillance feed if we stand here talking and don't partake of the amenities."

I swung my arms enthusiastically. "Hot diggity dog. We wouldn't want a security team to swarm in here and shoot us for looking suspicious. I guess we'd better get some cheesecake!"

CHAPTER 21

The three of us poured cups of hot coffee from the self-serve kiosk, then selected cold treats from the cooler.

Steve stared at the cold meatball sub, but didn't grab it.

"That sub looks good," I commented.

"Yes, but my girlfriend is vegetarian," Steve said. "She doesn't like kissing me if I have meat breath."

I clapped him on the shoulder. "You're a good boyfriend."

He gave me a wry smile. "A good boyfriend who'll be enjoying a kale salad."

I selected the cherry cheesecake, of course. I'd inherited a craving from a spirit, and while the spirit had been returned to its body, the craving had never left. I'd been thinking about cherry cheesecake ever since, and while I'd had it a few times, I hadn't been able to get the DWM cafeteria's version until now.

We sat at a table near the fake windows and dug in.

The cheesecake was exactly as delicious as I remembered, thanks to my borrowed memories. Pretty soon my wedge was gone, like magic.

Bentley had gotten the cheesecake as well, but he wasn't that hungry. He took only one bite, then poked it a few times while we talked to Steve about Ishmael.

When Bentley wasn't looking, I took his plate and ate his as well. The second slice was even better than the first, thanks to it being stolen.

I ate and listened while Bentley questioned Steve about Ishmael's work schedule, his relationship with his colleagues, and his relationships outside of work. Steve painted a picture of a young man who was pretty typical for a twenty-six-year-old. He had rubbed a few people the wrong way, particularly those further up the chain of command, because he didn't take well to direction. He was also a braggart who let everyone around him know about the most minor of achievements.

"Who brags about emptying their email inbox?" Steve asked rhetorically. "Some days he couldn't let an hour go by without letting people in the adjacent cubicles know he had successfully removed a sliver from his finger, or shot three crumpled pieces of paper in a row into the recycling basket across the room."

"That would be irritating," Bentley said. "But it's not behavior worthy of a beheading."

"Not in this country," Steve agreed.

Bentley tapped his notepad. "Thank you for your insight. And now it has come to the part of the interview where I must ask about your own whereabouts last night."

"That's easy." Steve took off his glasses and began cleaning them a second time. "I'm Carrot's alibi, and she is mine. I was at her apartment above the tattoo studio all night."

"How convenient," Bentley said.

Steve's hands paused mid-glasses-rub. "Oh? What might you mean by that?"

"With the two of you being each other's alibis, you might also be each other's accomplices. Kill him together, collect the inheritance."

"I see." The cleaning of the glasses resumed. "But surely you saw the state of his apartment. He spent all his savings on vacations and those ridiculous safaris. I suspect I'll have to pitch in from my own funds to pay for his funeral costs." He placed his glasses on his nose and pushed them up delicately. "Which I will do, of course. Anything for Carrot." He placed his elbows on the table and leaned forward. "Any idea when Dr. Lund will be finished with the body? I'd like to get to the cremation arrangements sooner rather than later." He looked from Bentley to me and added, "For Carrot's sake."

Right, I thought, suspicion bells ringing. *To give the victim's sister closure, not to destroy physical evidence. Righty-ho.*

The iguammit shifter's enthusiasm over cremation arrangements had suddenly roused my suspicions. On the true crime shows, the family member who was the most interested in getting the body cremated was always the killer, or protecting the killer. Was Steve protecting his girlfriend? *Anything for Carrot*, he'd said. *Anything?*

The two men returned to their discussion of the victim and the arrangements for his remains. Bentley stated that he remained hopeful for a swift resolution to the case so that everyone could have their closure.

I kept a close eye on Steve's face, watching for signs of deception. If he'd been a regular human, not a supernatural creature, I might have tried one of my spells on him. The bluffing spell, while technically not a lie detector, was a great one for getting people to open up. However, Aunt Zinnia had beaten a bit of good sense into me. I wouldn't risk casting magic. I could handle an angry Bentley, but I wasn't so sure about an iguammit.

My gaze drifted from Steve's face to the giant windows. The image of the sunny courtyard was perfect. No pixellation or flaws in color. And yet, what lay on the other side of the windows was no courtyard. It was probably just more offices.

My gaze remained on the fake courtyard, and a tickle of anxiety crept up my spine. I couldn't shake the uneasy feeling that someone or something was watching us from the other side. I felt like a caught critter in a glass box.

Codex is always watching, I thought. The absurdity almost made me laugh. I was worried about a computer! Just when you think you've seen all the weird stuff at the DWM, they pull a new, weirder rabbit out of their hat.

* * *

I was enjoying my third slice of cherry cheesecake when the interview finished up. Steve Adebayo received a message on his phone, and mentioned he was needed back in the legal department for something unrelated to the Greyson case.

"Please call if you think of anything," Bentley said, handing over a business card.

"Certainly." Steve stood, rolled his shoulders back, and coolly buttoned his body-hugging jacket. "I'll walk you to the nearest exit."

"No need." Bentley got to his feet and did the same shoulder-rolling and jacket-buttoning. "We'll be stopping by the morgue to see Dr. Lund with a possible murder weapon."

"It's our hot Saturday-night date," I interjected. I got to my feet, rolled back my shoulders, and then not-so-coolly flicked the cheesecake crust crumbs off my suit jacket.

Steve's eyes flashed with interest behind his round glasses. "A possible murder weapon? Do you have it with you?"

Bentley nodded to his suitcase, which had been sitting innocuously on the chair next to him the whole time. "Would you like to see it?"

Steve half-clapped and half-tented his hands together like a schoolboy supervillain. "Might I?"

Bentley glanced over at me as though seeking permission.

"He might as well have a look," I said. "Maybe he'll recognize it."

A frown flashed across Bentley's face, ever so briefly. I had the impression I'd given the incorrect answer, failing a test I didn't know I was taking.

The detective turned toward the suitcase, picked it up robotically, and held it over the cafeteria table without setting it down. "Zara, you've gotten crumbs everywhere," he said.

"Some of those crumbs were there when we sat down, I swear." I cast a simple spell to tidy away the crumbs. The air gave none of its usual resistance. The spell was a dud. The crumbs remained untouched.

I muttered under my breath and tried the spell again. Nothing. Then levitation, sweeping my hand above the table to guide the direction.

Bentley said, "I'd rather not dirty my suitcase with those crumbs."

"Hang on," I said. "I'm trying to clear them." Another hand sweep. Still nothing.

Steve cleared his throat. "Ms. Riddle, if you're attempting to use magic to remove the crumbs, you'll find it won't work."

I gave him a suspicious look. "Why's that?"

"Uh..." He grimaced and glanced around.

My mind made a paranoid leap. "Was there something in the cheesecake? Witchbane?" My tone was accusatory.

"No! Goodness, no!" He held one hand to his throat. "We don't poison people here. Not even witches."

He claimed there had been no witchbane, but even so, I silently admonished myself for not casting a threat detection spell over the food. The DWM was comprised of mostly shifters, and their kind had a natural distrust of witches. It wouldn't have surprised me at all if their standard cafeteria food was laced with witchbane, the plant that sapped witch powers.

Bentley asked, "What's going on?"

"There's a dampening field in place," Steve said with a tight smile. "Just a dampening spell. You haven't been altered or damaged, I assure you."

"A dampening field," Bentley said. "That seems logical."

"Sure," I said. "But I was only trying to sweep away crumbs. Is mild levitation really a security threat?"

"It's a potential threat if it's witchcraft," Steve said matter-of-factly.

"Hey, wait a minute," I said. "I've done magic down here before. Just simple stuff like opening locked doors, but it always worked before."

Steve raised his eyebrows. "That must have been before we had Codex."

"Codex." I shot Bentley a look. I did not like this new Codex system. Not one bit.

Bentley sighed. He was still holding the suitcase above the table.

I groaned, grabbed some napkins, and manually dusted the crumbs off the table. As disturbed as I was about having my powers dampened without my knowledge, there had been no real damage. I would know better the next time I ventured down there.

"Good enough," Bentley said when I was done. He set down the suitcase and unsnapped the buckles. He lifted the top to reveal the karambit inside, nestled in its multiple plastic bags.

Steve leaned over to look at the weapon, and then immediately pulled back, hurtling away as though being struck by an invisible force. Both of his hands flew to cover his mouth. He made a guttural noise.

Bentley and I stared at Steve. Was he afraid of knives? Why would he ask to see a weapon, then be so shocked?

Steve held up one hand and wriggled his fingers apologetically while he composed himself. With the other hand still over his mouth, he said, "I apologize for my reaction. I suppose my curiosity got the better of me, and I forgot how squeamish I am about knives. Plus, imagining it being used to harm poor Ishmael. It's all just too much."

Bentley said, "Perfectly understandable. Most civilians aren't prepared to see the things I deal with every day."

Steve kept retreating, putting a few more feet between himself and the suitcase. With a forced chuckle, he said, "There's a reason I got into the law side of law and order."

I squinted at him. Something wasn't adding up. I asked, "You're squeamish, and yet you're dating a tattoo artist?"

Steve wiped a bead of sweat from the side of his face. "You've met her," he said shakily. "Carrot is the most beautiful girl in the world."

"She is... a lovely girl," Bentley said hesitantly.

We exchanged a look. Carrot Greyson was cute, in her own way, but it was hard to swallow the idea of her being the most beautiful girl in the world. Had she cast some kind of enchantment over her boyfriend?

"Again, I do apologize for my reaction," Steve said. "I'm sure Dr. Lund will be much more helpful than I've been."

Bentley closed the suitcase and snapped it shut. "There we go," he said calmly. "You can breathe easy. The big, scary knife can't hurt you."

Steve used his glasses-cleaning cloth to mop the side of his face. "Thank you for being so understanding. If you don't mind me asking, where did you find this weapon?"

"Around," Bentley said cryptically.

Steve's eyes twitched. "Are there more of them, do you think?"

"Why?" Bentley cocked his head.

Steve took a deep breath to compose himself, then curled his index fingers into C shapes. Using the curved fingers, he made a scissoring gesture. "Two blades working together would act as scissors," he said. "That would explain the twin blood spatters on the wall."

"You saw the blood spatters on the wall?"

Steve nodded, then brought both hands up to partially cover his eyes with his fingers, like a kid watching a scary movie. "I had a look at the crime scene photos on my computer, like this. I didn't want to, but if the other people in Ishmael's family are in danger, I felt I had to look. We need to know what we're dealing with."

"I'm glad you did take a peek," Bentley said. "That's a very keen observation you've made about two of these blades working together like scissors." Bentley made a scissoring gesture. "Chop, chop, and off goes the head."

Steve swallowed audibly, then burped. "Oh, no," he said. "I might be sick."

Bentley waved a hand in the direction of the cafeteria's exit. "Don't let us keep you another minute. You've been a great help in the case, Mr. Adebayo."

"Any time," Steve muttered as he half-walked, half-jogged away.

CHAPTER 22

After Steve left, Bentley said, "What an odd man."

"Is he still a suspect?"

"I don't know," the detective said slowly. "He does give the impression he's hiding something, or covering for someone."

"You mean his girlfriend? The most beautiful girl in the world?"

Bentley frowned. "Love is blind," he said.

I pointed at him. "I'm glad you said it and not me. I try not to judge people by their looks, but..."

"Say no more." He nodded. "She'd only make the top ten list," he said. "Not the number one spot."

"Exactly." I looked down, plucked a stray cheesecake crumb from my suit jacket, and popped it in my mouth. "Where to next? Is it time for the morgue?"

"That depends. Are you feeling up to it?"

I shrugged. "It's why we came."

He waved one hand. "What about the dampener field? You have no power down here."

"No, but I've got you, Bentley. My personal bodyguard. What more does a girl need?" I fluttered my eyelashes at him.

"I do have my service revolver," he agreed. "You don't suppose the dampener field affects guns, do you?"

"Let's hope we don't have to find out."

* * *

After a few wrong turns in the underground labyrinth, we finally reached the morgue.

Dr. Jerry Lund, the medical examiner, had left a note on the door for Bentley: *Back in five minutes.*

The door was unlocked, so we entered.

Despite being in a secret organization's underground headquarters, the morgue looked exactly like all the morgues I'd seen on TV. There was a big wall of metal drawers, rolling steel tables, hanging scales, a workstation full of glass vials, microscopes, and computer equipment. All of it was lit with bright overhead lamps. The only thing unusual about this morgue was the large arched picture window. It was the same height and shape as the ones I'd seen earlier that day at Dreamland Coffee. Unlike Dreamland, which showed the Wisteria street outside, this huge window showed an alpine meadow view.

At the sight of the lovely meadow, I forgot all about the wall of huge drawers. For an instant, I forgot I was in a morgue. As I stared, a Jersey cow meandered into view, the bell on its collar tinkling with its slow, ambling movements.

Bentley and I exchanged a look. We were deep underground, so the window was just another illusion, probably a high-resolution screen. As for the sound of the tinkling bell, it must have been transmitted through speakers. Even so, knowing the cow was an illusion didn't take away the wonder. I went to the window and looked left and right. To my surprise, I was able to see more of the alpine meadow view.

"This isn't flat," I said in astonishment to Bentley. "It's not a screen at all. Come over here and look."

He begrudgingly joined me at the window and took a look for himself. There was an audible click as his jaw dropped open.

Bentley composed himself to say, "Magic?"

"They prefer high tech down here over magic, but maybe." I sniffed the air. The morgue had smelled of disinfectant when we entered, but over here by the window, the air was as sweet as a summer meadow.

Bentley said, "I swear I feel a breeze."

"And I swear I can smell those flowers." Over on the alpine meadow, the cow's ears pricked up, as though she'd heard me. She lifted her tail and let out a pile of road apples. A different scent hit my nostrils. I turned to Bentley with wide eyes.

"Yup," he said. "I smell it, too."

"I can understand the flowers, but why would they program in cow plops?"

Bentley glanced over at the stainless steel tables. "Morgues do have certain odors," he said.

"Ah," I said, catching on. "If you're working on a body and you catch a whiff of something, you'd rather believe it's coming from the adorable cow outside your window than from a human corpse."

Bentley made a fist and reached up to rap on the glass. His knuckles passed through the plane and kept going. When his fist had been submerged to the wrist, he finally struck a solid surface. There was a dull thump that matched the movement of his arm.

The cow, who'd been watching us, twitched an ear as though irritated. She stared at us a moment, then went back to cropping a mouthful of yellow wildflowers.

Dr. Jerry Lund, who must have entered the room on tiptoe, spoke behind us. "I see Bessy has been keeping you entertained in my absence."

We both whirled around to face the short doctor.

"Is she real?" I asked.

"There is a Bessy," Lund said enigmatically.

I took another look at the view over my shoulder, and then checked the time. "Switzerland is nine hours ahead of us. Sunrise would be around six-thirty this time of year.

Judging by the angle of the sun, I'd say this is a live view."

Lund chuckled. "Close. Daybreak is shortly after six o'clock this time of year."

Bentley, who still had his hand submerged in the view, said nothing.

Lund clapped his hands. "I understand you've brought me a possible murder weapon?"

Bentley pulled his hand from the view and slowly turned away from Bessy on her mountain meadow. He put his suitcase on a rolling steel table, opened it again, and cautiously withdrew the weapon.

The medical examiner got to work. He unwrapped the knife with gloved hands, and set it under a trio of tools similar to magnifying glasses. Next, he placed it in a steel compartment, closed a hatch, pressed some buttons, and watched a monitor.

After a moment he said, "No blood. If this was used to slice off Ishmael Greyson's head, it was impeccably cleaned." The monitor flashed. The medical examiner wheeled around to face me. "But there is residue from a magical powder on the blade."

"That's my fault," I said sheepishly. I explained how I'd used my aunt's powder to determine the materials in the blade, only to turn up no answers. "The powder is supposed to disappear completely after the test runs."

The doctor bounced his eyebrows. "Things that are supposed to disappear completely rarely do." His bullfrog lips formed a wide, knowing smile.

I apologized for sullying the potential evidence.

He waved it off with one gloved hand. "No harm done, Zara. I'm just giving you a hard time." He clasped his hands together. "Now, we get to do the fun part."

The fun part?

He excused himself, went through a door, and returned a moment later. He was wheeling a cart, on which was a life-sized human bust made from what appeared to be Jell-O. It was green and jiggled.

"You'll see why this is the fun part," the doctor explained.

He grasped the handle of the karambit with both hands, checked to see that nothing was behind him, then wound up and sliced the blade through the air with surprising speed. He chopped off the green Jell-O head.

Beside me, Bentley made a low, guttural sound. The bust wasn't Jell-O through and through. The interior contained both bones and meat, anatomically similar to that of a human.

"Cool," I said.

"Uhh," Bentley said, grimacing. "That's a new one."

I took a closer look without touching the material. "It's like those jellied salads people made in the fifties," I said. "Aspic. Or head cheese."

"Very much so," Lund said, grinning. He set down the karambit, then picked up the severed head with the enthusiasm of a kid grabbing his new toy on Christmas morning. "I've got to run the next test in the lab next door," he said breathlessly. "But based on a quick visual of the striation pattern, I'd say we have our murder weapon."

Bentley and I exchanged a look.

We had our murder weapon?

"But what about the blood?" I asked. "You said it was clean."

The doctor blinked at me. "I said it must have been thoroughly cleaned. But the striation pattern tells a story, and that story is that this karambit, or one like it, was used to chop off the victim's head. I'll be able to prepare a thorough report after I run some more tests."

Bentley asked, "How long will these tests take?"

"A few hours," Lund said. "You can wait here, if you'd like." He glanced around. "I've misplaced the remote control for the window view, but if you can find it, you can switch Bessy's channel to something more entertaining."

There was a distinctively cow-like snort that came over the speakers. I turned to see Bessy standing a mere three feet from the window, chewing her cud and seemingly staring directly at us.

Bentley asked in a whisper, "Can she see us?"

"Not exactly," Lund said. "I'd love to stay and chat, but time's ticking." He waved the severed jelly head emphatically.

"See you in a few hours," I said.

"No," Bentley said to me. To Lund, he said, "We'll show ourselves out. You have my number. You can call me with the test results."

"Will do, Detective." Lund used his hip to push a big red button next to a door. The door opened, and he passed through with the green severed head in his hands. "Oh," he said, and he came back into the room again. "If you're looking for the victim, he's around here somewhere."

He was? Bentley and I must have had the same thought, because we both looked over at the wall of drawers.

Lund chuckled. "Yes, his body's in there. We put the head back on and we're waiting to see if he comes back to life. Nothing yet."

"Good?" Bentley said, half statement and half question.

"What I meant was his *ghost* is around," Lund clarified. "There have been some sightings around Greyson's former desk. We have a few members on staff who are sensitive to such things. Not witches, exactly, but similarly afflicted."

"Ishmael's spirit is here?" I asked. "Down here, underground?"

"You're the witch," Lund said. "Go check his office, and then you tell me!"

CHAPTER 23

After stopping a few different DWM employees to ask for directions, we finally reached Greyson's office.

We opened the door. The ghost was there, sitting on a chair, probably looking the same as he had when alive.

The office itself was tiny, but private. The workspace was a nondescript L-shaped desk that wasn't huge yet was still too big for the room. In addition to the desk and chair, there was also one chair for visitors, and a brass coat rack. A navy-blue windbreaker hung on the coat rack, its limp fabric making a bat-like shape.

I didn't have to imagine how Ishmael Greyson had looked in his office environment, since he was there now, albeit slightly translucent. He glanced over at the two of us standing in his doorway, then went back to work, flexing his ghostly fingers over his computer keyboard.

Bentley was first to enter the office. "It smells sweet and rotten," he said. "Do ghosts have a smell?"

I hadn't told him about the ghost sitting on the chair. I probably should have, but I was curious to see if the detective could sense the spirit in other ways.

Bentley had detected one thing, for sure. The office did have an odor. "Check the garbage bin under the desk," I said.

Bentley stooped down and did so. "Banana peels," he reported. "That explains the smell." He sighed and took a seat on the chair.

Ishmael, who'd been sitting on the chair, jumped backward, through the chair. He stood behind it, indignantly waving his arms and frowning at the man in the gray suit who now occupied his chair.

"Brrr," Bentley said, rubbing his arms. "Did you do something to the air conditioning?"

"Nope," I said, still watching him closely. "Do you sense something?"

Bentley ran his hands over the surface of the desk, then abruptly wheeled the chair around to face me. "We're not alone," he said, eyes wide.

"We are not," I confirmed.

Bentley's eyes narrowed to their regular steeliness. He rotated his head, slowly surveying the office. "He's standing right here," Bentley said, gesturing to an area next to where Ishmael stood.

"Close. You're about two feet to the left of him."

Bentley snorted. "But not bad for a regular guy."

"Your guesses are limited by the fact that it's a pretty small office. You couldn't swing a cat in here." The expression made me think of Boa, so I quickly added, "Not that I'd swing a cat. What a horrible saying."

Bentley stared through the ghost, squinting. "What's he doing now? Is he still there?"

"He's just standing there, probably trying to figure out why two strangers are inside his office."

"He doesn't know what happened to him, does he?" Bentley shook his head. "Poor bastard." More head shaking. "He had a rough morning, and he didn't even get to take the day off. He's down here at this sad little office of his, working away in this glorified hamster cage. That's not very fair, is it? He should be moving on to some better place."

"They do move on after their..." *Don't talk about homicide in front of the ghost who doesn't know he's dead!* "After their earthly business is done. Once we find out who chopped off his, uh, cabbage, he can..." I was going to say *take early retirement*, but Ishmael had turned his attention to me. Judging by the changes in his facial expression, it seemed he could understand some of what I was saying.

"Something's happening." Bentley got to his feet and edged along the interior of the L-shaped desk to come stand next to me. He murmured in my ear, "You take the lead, ghost whisperer. Tell me what to do and I'll do it."

Ishmael, still staring into my eyes, took three steps toward me. He stopped right in front of me, inches away. The air he occupied was chilly. Being this close to an honest-to-goodness spirit would send most people running to the hills, but most people aren't witches. I wasn't frightened. Even so, a couple of my wimpier hair follicles were frightened, judging by the goose bumps. Ishmael took a mini step closer. His chin was practically overlapping the tip of my nose.

Bentley demanded, "What's happening? I can't see him, Zara. You have to tell me what you see. Be my eyes."

I whispered out of the corner of my mouth, "Ishmael Greyson is now standing directly in front of me. His face is right in my face."

There was a snap, a click, and movement at my side. Bentley had his revolver drawn. He pointed the muzzle at Ishmael's temple.

Ishmael noticed the gun. His bulging eyes protruded even more than seemed possible. Could a ghost's eyes pop right out? I hoped not. He didn't move, except for his bugged-out eyes, which flicked between Bentley's face and mine.

"Put the gun away," I said out of the corner of my mouth. "What good do you think it will do shooting a you-know-what? It's all concrete down here. You'll probably kill one of us with the ricochet."

"A gun does plenty of good, even if you don't fire it," Bentley replied defensively. "Follow my logic: If he doesn't know he's a you-know-what, then he'll respect the threat." Bentley shook the gun and continued in a commanding voice. "Talk to us, Ishmael. Give us the names of anyone who might want to hurt you."

To my surprise, Ishmael seemed to comprehend the question. He mouthed something. *Who'd want to hurt me? I'm nobody.*

I relayed my interpretation of Ishmael's lip movements to the detective.

Bentley slowly lowered the gun and put it away resignedly. "So much for getting a helpful answer." He waved his now-empty hand. "Do your witch thing. Get him to possess your body. I can at least try to interview him once he's inside you."

"Do my witch thing?"

"Any time," Bentley said impatiently.

I would have given him some more sass, but he had a point. I was there for a reason, and that reason was to channel the ghost. No point bickering about what I'd already agreed to do.

"Hold your horses," I said. "I'm trying." I tilted my head back and sniffed.

Bentley gave me a raised eyebrow. "Are you planning to sneeze him into talking?"

"They travel in on the breath," I explained. I sniffed again. My sinuses tickled from the influx of chilly ghost air.

"Is it working yet? You don't look any different." Bentley was many things, but being patient about Spirit Charming wasn't one of them.

I sniffed again, then reported, "It doesn't seem to be working."

"Ah." Bentley nodded knowingly. "A watched pot doesn't boil. I'll turn away." He rotated so he was facing the corner with the coat rack and the bat-like hanging windbreaker.

I sniffed yet again, harder than ever. Ishmael didn't turn to smoke and travel up my nostrils on my breath. Instead, he took a step backward and regarded me with suspicion. His buggy eyes narrowed to the point where they looked nearly as steely as the detective's. I sniffed, and huffed, and puffed, and wheezed, and even sneezed.

Nothing.

I felt like the big bad wolf, trying to blow down three straw houses to eat the little piggies. I sounded like him, too.

Still nothing but wary looks from Ishmael.

Spirit Charmed though I might be, this spirit didn't find me charming at all.

The rezoning spell.

My recent experiment with transforming myself had to be the reason this ghost was behaving so different from the other ghosts I'd encountered. If only there was some way I could know for sure. If only...

The room tone in the small office changed, and a female voice came through hidden speakers. "I am Codex. I am at your service. Do you require assistance?"

Bentley jumped at the sound of the voice and took a fighter's stance, not that it would do much good against a computer.

He frowned at me and asked, "You heard that too, right?"

I nodded. "I may have accidentally summoned her. I think I pressed a psychic call button."

"You what?"

"I was just thinking about how I wished I could run some diagnostics."

"I see," he said. "That's actually a good idea."

"Why, thank you, Detective."

He tilted his face up toward the ceiling, to where the speakers seemed to be situated. "Hello again, Codex," he said. "We were wondering if you could help us with something."

"Please state your request, Detective."

Bentley waved for me to ask. I waved for him to go ahead.

Bentley said, "Can you confirm for us who is inside this office?"

"Scanning now." The bright overhead lights abruptly blinked off. A wave of green light in a grid pattern washed over the room. The lights flickered on again almost immediately.

Bentley muttered, "Witches and ghosts, and now we've got the holo deck from *Star Trek*."

Codex replied matter-of-factly, "The holo deck is on a different floor, Detective Bentley."

"Just tell us who's in this office," I said.

Codex responded in her robotic yet sultry voice. "Detective Theodore Bentley, on a visitor's pass with restricted access. Registered Witch Zara Riddle, also on a visitor's pass with restricted access. And Junior Agent Ishmael Greyson." There was a very human-like pause. "That's odd." Another pause. "Ishmael Greyson's vital signs indicate that he is clinically dead. His body is located in the morgue, in the care of Dr. Jerry Lund. Therefore, because Junior Agent Ishmael Greyson is deceased, the presence within his office must be of spectral origin. Shall I scan again?"

"No need," Bentley said curtly. I detected a note of claustrophobic panic in his voice, but I didn't check his face because my attention was now focused on Ishmael Greyson.

Ishmael, who had just been informed of his *clinical deadness* by an artificial intelligence, was taking the news poorly. He flickered, bright and dim, like a light bulb with a loose connection. His lips trembled as they moved. He mouthed the word*deceased.*

I reached a hand out to steady the young man, but my hand passed right through his shoulder. He looked at my hand and grimaced horribly. My attempt at comforting him had upset him nearly as much as the announcement by Codex.

The air changed. The zone near him lost its chill. The air neutralized, and then rapidly heated. It was getting hot in the tiny office.

Ishmael's mouth opened in a silent howl. He turned white hot, then orange, as though being consumed by flames. And then, just when I was going to warn Bentley to take cover, the ghost was gone. The temperature was comfortable, and the office was quiet.

I turned to find Bentley reaching for his gun again.

"No need," I said gently, laying my hand on his shoulder. "Greyson has left the room." I flicked my eyes up at the ceiling. "I guess he was upset when *someone* broke the news about his death the way she did."

Through gritted teeth, Bentley said, "You mean *something*, not *someone*."

Codex spoke again, a hint of amusement in her computerized voice. "Junior Agent Ishmael Greyson is no longer on the premises."

"Thanks for your help," I said dryly.

"My algorithms detect sarcasm," Codex replied. "Is there some other way I can offer assistance?"

"You've done enough," Bentley said.

"More sarcasm," Codex noted.

He put his hands on his hips and growled up at the ceiling, "Did you have to tell the ghost he was dead? You scared him off."

"Detective, I was complying with your request."

He sighed and dropped his arms limply at his sides. "Yes, I suppose you were. What else did you pick up on that scan of yours?"

"I detected that Zara Riddle's witch powers have been restricted."

"We know about the dampening field," I said, nodding. "I found out in the cafeteria. I guess your shifter bosses don't like us witches and our witcher-i-doo."

"That's not the restriction I'm referring to," Codex said. "You have been altered."

Bentley gave me a quizzical look. "What's she talking about?"

"Uh..." I was reluctant to admit I might have messed up my own powers.

Codex said, "Zara Riddle, you have been significantly altered recently. There is a rezoning spell in effect."

"Oh, that." I waved a hand casually. I could feel Bentley's eyes on me. And Codex's. Assuming she even had eyes. I tugged at the back of my collar to let out some steam that was forming. "Yeah, there might be a rezoning spell in effect. I was kind of, um, trying something."

Bentley's eyes bore into me. "You were trying something?"

I felt my cheeks flushing with embarrassment. "Just a wee little transformation spell. It was supposed to help me get control over my powers. Nothing too crazy."

Codex said, "On the contrary. The rezoning spell you have cast upon yourself is, by your own definition, crazy. It is unadvisable for supernatural beings to take such measures. The suppression of powers may lead to permanent injury, or death."

I waved my hand again in the air. "Yeah, yeah. Lots of things lead to permanent injury and death." I coughed into my hand. Sniffing the ghost had given me a dry throat. I desperately wanted to change the subject. Anything to get Bentley to stop staring at me that way.

I coughed again, then asked, "Codex, do you have any idea where Greyson went after he flashed out of here?"

She replied calmly, "My sensors are restricted to this facility."

Hearing that she was limited to the facility did offer me some small comfort.

"Thanks anyway," I said. "I guess we'll show ourselves out now." I turned to leave Greyson's tiny, claustrophobic office.

Bentley stretched out an arm and barred my exit. "Is it true? What she said about you doing something dangerous to yourself?"

"She's just a computer built by shifters. What does she know about witchcraft?"

Codex said, "I am Codex. I contain the collected works of millennia. I know more about witchcraft than any witch, alive or dead."

I snorted. "Good thing you're not full of yourself," I said.

"My sensors detect sarcasm," Codex replied, almost playfully.

Bentley hadn't taken his eyes off me. "Zara, it's probably not my business what spells you cast on yourself, but as your friend, I'm concerned."

"I'll take that under advisement." I crossed my arms. "And you're right about it not being any of your business."

He winced. "Don't be so sure of that. If you've done something to yourself, and you're unable to communicate with ghosts, then I have no use for you."

My cheeks, which had been hot from embarrassment, suddenly burned with rage. "You have no use for me?"

He dropped his arm from the doorway and took a half step back into the hallway. "I misspoke," he said. "What I mean is, the department has no use for you."

"Just like that?"

"Don't get nippy."

"Nippy? You're lucky there's a dampening spell on this facility, or I'd show you nippy. I have just the spell to show you nippy."

"Zara," Bentley said in what he probably felt was a very reasonable tone. "We don't involve civilians in investigations without good reason."

"No. You just like partnering with them so you can dump them. Twice in one day."

"I haven't dumped you once, let alone twice."

"Check your math, Detective."

"I'm not dumping you. I just need to know more about —"

I lurched past him and stomped down the hallway.

If I'd had better control over my emotions, I might have explained to him that I *didn't* have control over my emotions.

Close proximity to ghosts who were upset tended to stir up my own feelings. When Ishmael had gone all ghost-inferno before leaving, a part of me had caught fire as well.

But, since I didn't have control over myself, I didn't explain any of that to Detective Bentley. What I did do was call him a few bad names and threaten to cast a whole bunch of painful spells on him as soon as we were topside.

CHAPTER 24

Ice cream. I needed ice cream. What do you do when you feel like you're an erupting volcano? Cool the lava. With ice cream.

"Mom?"

I looked up from my sundae to find my daughter, in her pajamas, staring at me. Her hair was tangled on one side from sleep.

"Did I wake you?" I asked.

"Not at all," she said. "Technically, it was the doors that woke me. The front door. The cupboard door. The freezer door."

I winced. "Sorry about that. Will you accept half of this delicious sundae as an apology?" I used magic to open the utensil drawer across the kitchen and lift out a long-handled sundae spoon. After having my powers dampened underground, even the smallest touches felt luxurious.

My sleepy-eyed daughter looked down at the sweet peace offering. "Are those gummy bears in your sundae?"

"You bet. I love how they get extra firm when the ice cream partly freezes them."

"Ooh. That is nice." She plucked the floating spoon from the air and joined me at the kitchen island. "Apology accepted."

We excavated our way through a third of the sundae, reaching the ladyfingers and jam layer, before she spoke again.

"How did date night at the morgue go?"

"As you may have guessed by the girth of this planet-sized sundae, it did not go well."

She smirked. "No kiss goodnight?"

"Bentley didn't even drive me home. He passed me off on Persephone Rose."

"Who?"

"Persephone Rose."

"I heard you the first time. Who is he or she?"

"Persephone Rose is a silly young woman from the Wisteria Police Department who has a giant schoolgirl crush on Bentley. She did nothing but talk about how wonderful and brilliant he is the whole way home."

Zoey's eyes twinkled. "Now I understand the door slamming. You're jealous."

I snorted. "She can have him. If he has any *use* for her. He has no *use* for me, apparently." I stabbed through the ladyfinger and jam layer, into the granola. "Can you believe that? I spent my entire Saturday helping him with his homicide case, and just because I didn't do the witcher-i-doo song and dance at his command, he dismissed me! Not once, but twice. Like I didn't have anything else to offer!"

She gave me a puzzled look. "Song and dance?"

"The ghost thing." I waved my spoon, dropping chunks of granola and beheaded gummy bears on the counter. "The whole Spirit Charmed thing." I took another bite. "You know, there's a lot more to me than my ravishing good looks and my wicher-i-doo."

"Mom, I love this thing where you start at the end of the story and rant like a crazy person, but it's two o'clock in the morning. I have no idea what you're talking about, but I think we should go to bed and talk about this tomorrow, when you've calmed down."

"I'll never calm down. Never."

She raised her eyebrows.

I sighed. "Okay. I've already calmed down a bit."

"What happened? Did Bentley really kick you off the case again?"

I growled. "Now I'm riled up again! How dare he take up my whole Saturday, then give me the bum's rush out of there just when it gets good?!"

"Start at the beginning," she said. "You seemed happy enough when you left here tonight for your date at the morgue. Start there."

"Good idea." I wiped my mouth with a napkin. "You're such a brilliant kid. So logical and thoughtful."

"You left here with Bentley. Then what?"

"We drove to the WPD, where we used a secret elevator to go underground to the DWM."

Zoey cocked her head. "It's underneath the police department, too? Wow. It must be enormous. It must run underneath half the town." She looked down as she dug through striated layers of sundae. "Like an ant colony. Or a mole burrow." She met my gaze, her hazel eyes twinkling. "Did you know that animals that burrow underground are called *fossorial*?"

"Fossorial. I feel like I should know that word, but I don't."

She beamed. Zoey loved springing new vocabulary on me as much as she loved beating me at Scrabble. I used to think she was the reigning champion at the game because she dominated the board spatially, but I was starting to think she also knew more words than I did.

Fossorial, I thought. *Now use it in a sentence.* "After we left here, Bentley I went down into the DWM's *fossorial lair*."

"Burrow," she corrected.

"If you saw it, you'd agree it's more of a lair than a burrow. Concrete walls, not dirt."

"Lair it is. Keep talking."

"So, we went down there, only to be given a hard time by a computer. A computer! Its name is Codex. Well, *her* name."

Her eyes widened. "Artificial intelligence?"

I nodded.

"Keep talking," she said. "Keep talking and don't stop."

I grinned. "Sweeter words have never been spoken."

I did as requested. I told her all about the underground building's new security system, the spell-dampening measures, the interview with Carrot's lawyer boyfriend Steve, and my visit to the morgue. Zoey was just as fascinated by the bell-wearing cow in the alpine meadow as she was about the medical examiner using the karambit to behead a dummy made of headcheese.

When I got to what happened in Ishmael's tiny office, she found the encounter both spooky and fascinating. She giggled at the image of Bentley drawing his gun and blindly aiming it at a ghost's temple—for all the good that did. But when I relayed the very worst part, the part about me getting booted off the case for the second undignified time, she only shrugged.

"Bentley does have a point," she said. "If you can't charm the victim's ghost into communicating with you, you're basically just a civilian."

"But we did communicate! I could see Ishmael when nobody else could. Plus, we had a bit of a dialog. He mouthed some words at me."

"Sure, but only enough to make it clear he doesn't know who murdered him."

"True."

"The killer must have snuck up behind him and done it... lickety-split," she said.

"So to speak."

"That means the killer must have skipped that whole speech-from-the-villain thing. That's when the bad guy in a James Bond movie explains his whole evil plan."

I gasped. "People actually do that in real life," I said. I had witnessed it myself, at least once. "I guess, deep down, everyone wants the world to know they're good at stuff. Even killers."

Zoey nodded. "But poor Ishmael Greyson doesn't know who killed him, so whether you can sniff him into your head or not, you're not much use to Bentley, the WPD, or the DWM."

"What you're saying makes perfect sense. I agree with your logic. But answer me this, smart child of mine. If Bentley was only doing the logical thing by dismissing me, why do I still feel like slamming doors?"

"Maybe it was *the way* he said it to you."

"He did eventually come around and thank me." I wrinkled my nose. "Probably out of self-preservation, due to all the spells I threatened to cast on him once we got above ground."

"Oh, Mom."

"And he even apologized before he shipped me off with Persephone. He was actually quite apologetic, now that I think about it."

"Then you must feel all door-slammy because of the ghost." She gave me a pointed look. "And not out of any romantic jealousy over young Persephone."

I struck the air with my finger. "You're right. It was entirely from Ishmael. I've settled down, but his emotions are still affecting me."

She studied me thoughtfully. "Auntie Z says ghosts can have powerful tantrums." She lowered her voice. "She told me a story about something that happened to a friend of hers. There was once a ghost who used its own cremated ashes to form a body, and take revenge."

I shivered. The massive quantities of ice cream combined with the passing of time spent with a sympathetic listener had cooled off my rage.

"That's disturbing," I said. "The ghost made itself a body out of ashes?"

Zoey nodded. "And I don't think it happened to Auntie Z's *friend*, if you know what I mean."

I did know what she meant. "Your great-aunt has more secrets than a librarian has unread books on her nightstand."

Zoey got up from her chair and went to the cupboard. "I'll make you some coffee," she said.

I yawned and checked the time. "It's too early. I can still get a few hours of sleep before the next thing goes wrong."

"No. You need to go downstairs with your spell notes. You need to set things back to normal." She quickly added, "And by normal, I mean normal for you. Not normal-normal. You need to reverse that library rezoning spell that you shouldn't have cast in the first place."

"You think?" I gave her a defiant look.

"Don't you?" She measured coffee grounds into the filter compartment. "A highly advanced computer intelligence was able to scan you and detect that something was wrong. What more evidence do you need that what you did was wrong? I don't want you to get sick and die like Gigi did. I don't want to lose you."

I bit my tongue. We hadn't lost Gigi, technically.

"I think you should see Gigi's friend, Dr. Ankh, for a consultation," Zoey said. "Gigi says she knows a lot about witches."

I gasped in horror. "Since when do you trust the opinion of the woman who turned your grandmother into a you-know-what?"

"You don't have to do what Dr. Ankh says, but it might help to get a medical opinion." She turned on the coffee maker. "Or you could just reverse the spell tonight. The coffee will be ready in a few minutes."

"Even if I wanted to reverse the spell, it might take me a few days to work through the counterspell."

"I could call Gigi and get Dr. Ankh's phone number?"

"No way. You haven't met her yourself, but if you did, you'd agree with me that Dr. Ankh has a strong evil vibe. She's always talking about the purity of bloodlines." I gave Zoey a mother-knows-best look. "Throughout history, that sort of talk is rarely associated with good things. For example, the royal families kept marrying their own cousins to produce their pureblood offspring."

"They wouldn't have, if they'd known what we do nowadays about DNA."

I pulled a face, sticking out my tongue. "Some of them even married siblings."

Zoey shrugged. "Maybe with genetic engineering, they can eventually get right back to it."

"How can you be so calm and logical about it? Cousins getting married. Siblings having babies together!"

She rubbed her chin with her index finger. "I think because I don't have any cousins, let alone siblings, I haven't experienced the feelings associated with that taboo personally."

"Just because you haven't met them doesn't mean you don't have tons of..." I realized what I was saying only after it was too late to stop myself.

Zoey pounced. She was on me like white lightning. Like Boa on unguarded deli ham. "I have siblings? Do you mean I have half-siblings, on my father's side?"

My throat tightened. Now I'd done it. *Zara tries to be a good mother. Zara tries not to blurt out family secrets in the wee hours of the morning.*

If only we could get back to trashing on Bentley or arguing about my rezoning spell. But it was too late.

I tried to play it off casually. "We can't really know for sure that you *don't* have any half-siblings. But, I assure you, the possibility of you bumping into one of these theoretical half-siblings, out of all the billions of people in the world, is highly unlikely." I tilted my chin up and proclaimed, "Please feel free to date whomever you want."

She gave me a deadly serious glare. "You said my father died a long time ago. That's what you told me. But now you're saying he's been around, having kids?"

"He did disappear," I said. "That's as good as dead. Basically. After enough years missing, a person can be declared legally dead."

Her voice became quieter and colder. "That's not what you told me."

"You were just a little girl," I said. "You already had enough things working against you, by which of course I mean being raised by me." I forced a laugh. "Not that there's anything wrong with you, in spite of having me for a single parent. You're brilliant, and strong, and healthy, and—"

"Mom."

I blinked repeatedly and took another angle. "So I told a little white lie. What sort of mother would I be if I let you grow up feeling abandoned? Forgotten? You know how hard that was for me. I only saw my father one day a year. I know from personal experience what it feels like to mean so little to your father."

Zoey shook her head. She opened her mouth and then closed it.

"What?" I asked.

Another head shake, and then finally the words poured out. "Pawpaw loves you, Mom. He only saw you once a year because that was all Gigi and the family would allow. They had something on him, Mom. He tried to fight them, but he didn't have the resources, and they threatened to take away his one day. That's why he tried to cram so much into the times he saw you. He was trying to make up for a whole year of missing you."

To say I was stunned by this revelation would be an understatement.

For an instant, my heart rose. I wanted to believe what she was saying was true. But then the wise part of me took over and punched down my stupid, weak heart. It wasn't true. My daughter had been brainwashed. Clearly.

Through clenched teeth, I said, "You can't believe what that man says. He's a trickster. He's a foxy trickster."

"Not all men are bad, Mom. I know you've had a few bad experiences."

I snorted. "A few?"

"I know Mr. Moore tricked you and lied to you, but not all guys are like that."

"This?" I sputtered, trying to get the feelings out in words. "*This* from the girl who wanted to cast an anti-love spell on herself? Suddenly you're on Team Men?"

"Mom."

"What's changed? It must be love. Love has made your head soft." I crossed my arms. "After I abandoned you at the museum today, that young man in the caveman costume must have shown you around his cave."

She shook her finger at me. "Don't try to change the subject. Don't smoke me out. We were talking about my half-siblings."

Don't smoke me out? What an excellent idea. Witches had many ways to change the topic of conversation. Violence was one way, but sometimes the simplest parlor tricks worked best.

I twirled my tongue and cast a spell. I didn't use that particular spell frequently, but it was easy enough to cast without accidentally inverting, even under tense circumstances. The Witch Tongue flew from my mouth effortlessly. The air around us glittered. It was working. Billowing plumes of pink smoke rose from the floor all around us.

Zoey made a startled noise.

Brightly, I said, "Hey, did I ever show you how good I've gotten at the pink fog?"

"Don't you dare fog me out!"

It was too late. The foggy pink clouds filled the entire kitchen, including the space between us. I could no longer see her face, or her accusing expression. I could barely see the tip of my own nose.

Zoey's voice was muffled by the pink clouds. "We need to talk about this eventually, Mom. If I have brothers and sisters, I have a right to know."

"Do you? Really? What about your right to privacy? What about theirs?" The pink clouds ebbed, and the fog thinned enough for me to be able to see her face. It wasn't a pretty sight. I quickly doubled the pink clouds in the room, then doubled the spell again.

"Screw privacy," she said.

"Honestly, Zoey, I don't even know for sure if you have any siblings. It's all theoretical. That's the truth."

She made a grumbling, displeased noise.

I paused to take in the situation as calmly as I could.

Mother-daughter relations were at an all-time low.

I should have cleared the fog and made things better. But, for whatever reason, I didn't. Was it the lingering effects of Ishmael's tantrum or just my own stupidity? I'd never know for sure.

What I did next was truly shameful.

If I'd been in the running for Mother of the Year, this certainly would have disqualified me.

I used my telekinesis to grab a mug, plus the nearly full pot of coffee, and floated both over to me. I silently climbed off my chair and edged my way blindly toward the door to the basement.

"Thanks for the coffee," I said through the pink haze. "Now get some sleep. We'll talk in the morning."

I didn't wait for a response. I slipped through the door to the basement with the coffee, locked the door behind me, and retreated to my basement lair.

I reached the bottom step. My daughter was stomping around the kitchen, cursing me.

In the basement, there was a whipping sound, the movement of bat-like wings, and then the scrape of talons on stone. Ribbons landed on the stone ledge over my desk. Orange light flared. He used his wyvern fire to light the candles above my desk. I had plenty of electric lamps, but the flickering of candles helped me do my best work.

"You must have heard everything," I said. "What a day, huh?"

"Poor Zed," he said, his Count Chocula voice echoing telepathically in my head. "You have had a very long day."

"I sure have."

"And, worst of all, Zed, I'm afraid you are no longer in the running for the Mother of the Year Award."

CHAPTER 25

Ribbons let out a sigh that was much louder and longer than his tiny wyvern lungs should have allowed. "You're being *so* boring, Zed."

I looked up from my spell notes, which I'd been focused on despite the constant interruptions. An hour earlier, I'd had to unlock the basement door for the cat before she scratched a hole in the door. Since then, she'd been chasing an insect around the basement and yowling pitifully about her failure to make the kill.

"So terribly boring," Ribbons reiterated.

The wyvern was slouching, hunchbacked, on the stone shelf above my desk. With that posture, he looked less like a tiny dragon and more like a gargoyle. A bored gargoyle.

I tapped the eraser of my pencil on my chin thoughtfully. "If I'm so boring, why do you hang out with me?"

Ribbons sighed again, his nostrils flaring as he emitted the pretty orange ribbons he'd been named after.

"I am what you humans call a *homebody*," he said.

"A homewyvern?"

He reached down with his arm, flapping out the attached bat-like wing, and snatched the pencil from my hand.

"Tell Zoey who her father is," he said. "I want to see what she does when she finds out." He gnawed on the pencil eraser tentatively, then bit it off and began chewing. "Tell her, Zed."

I gave him an oh-really look. "Tell her what, exactly?" I leaned forward, so I was eye to eye with his glossy black wyvern eyes. His breath smelled of sweet peppermint and chewed pencil eraser. "What is it you think you know, Half-Pint?"

"I know what I know, Giraffe Pants."

"You're bluffing."

Ribbons dropped the eraser-less pencil on the desk and drew himself up to his full height, which, excluding the tail, was slightly taller than a single-serving soda bottle. He tended to puff up like that when he had nothing to back up his claims. I grabbed my coffee mug and took a sip while I waited for him to admit he was bluffing.

His green scaly eyelids changed shape, giving him a malevolent, evil expression. He spat the words into my mind. "Oh, but I do know, Zed."

"Sure, you do."

"You fornicated with a demon, Zed."

I was so shocked, I choked and spewed out my coffee, spraying the desk.

Ribbons was faster than my volley of coffee spray. He jumped in the air, unfurled his wings, and flew straight up like a rocket. He rotated and stuck a landing on the ceiling. The wooden ceiling beam creaked as his talons dug in.

He continued, his voice taunting. "You fornicated with a demon, and I don't mean last month at the castle when you almost did, but didn't. It was years ago, Zed. You know it. I know it. Are you going to make me say the rest of it?"

"Say it," I managed.

"I know that the genie who calls himself Archer Caine is Zoey's father."

The basement was quiet. Even Boa had settled down. There was a wet, smacking sound as the white cat noisily consumed the insect she'd finally captured.

Ribbons' telepathic voice rested. He used his throat to make a chittering sound similar to a squirrel's warning chatter. It was how he laughed.

I craned my neck and looked up at his upside-down face. "You knew? This whole time?"

He flicked out his purple tongue and licked one beady black eye and then the other. Eye-licking was one of his many smugness indicators.

"I've known for a while," he said. "Let's tell her right now, Zed."

"It's late."

"She's not sleeping. I can hear her tossing and turning in bed." He swung from side to side hypnotically. "Let's go upstairs and tell your daughter that you fornicated with a demon, Zed."

"Would you please stop saying *fornicated*? What a horrible word." Accurate, but horrible.

"What term would you prefer? Making the beast with two backs? Dancing the Paphian jig? Shooting 'twixt wind and water? Shaking the sheets? Groping for trout in a peculiar river? That last one's Shakespeare, by the way."

"You are a vile little creature. I can't believe I let you talk to me this way. I can't believe I let you live here rent free."

He stretched out his wings. "But you like meeeeeeee. You like Ribbons." His beady black eyes seemed to double in size.

"I suppose I do appreciate your knowledge and your honesty," I replied evenly.

"You looooove meeeee!"

I tapped the desk. "Get your skinny chicken butt down here. I'm getting a crick in my neck. Get down here, reheat what's left of my coffee, and tell me everything you know about demons."

"Demons? Or genies? All genies are demons, but not all demons are genies."

I tapped the desk again. "You know darn well what I mean. If I'm going to tell Zoey, assuming there's ever a time that feels right, I'd like to know something about genies. She is half genie, after all."

Ribbons descended to the desk soundlessly, like a drop of sparkling green sap falling from a tall tree. He waddled, duck-like, over to my half-full coffee mug. The wyvern was as ungainly on solid ground as he was graceful in the air. He dropped the muzzle of his seahorse-shaped head into my coffee, steamed it, then returned to his usual perch on the shelf above my desk.

"Genies," I prompted him.

He used one of the green, claw-like hands connected to his wings to stroke an imaginary beard. "The first thing you should know about genies is their kind don't belong in this world, Zed."

"Really? I'll skip that part when I break the news to Zoey. Teenagers have a hard enough time fitting in without being told their kind aren't welcome in this world."

"My word choice was inaccurate. What I meant is they're not *from* this world."

"Are they from Hell?" I leaned forward. "Hell is a real place?"

More stroking of the nonexistent beard. All he needed was a pair of round spectacles, and he'd be Professor Wyvern.

"Any place can be Hell, or Heaven," he said playfully. The ridges above his eyes waggled like sparkly eyebrows.

I leaned back again. "I'm not interested in discussing the power of positive thinking right now, my beady-eyed barista." I took a sip of the reheated coffee. The cheeky wyvern's saliva added a mint flavor I'd more than gotten accustomed to. I waved for him to get to the point.

"Genies," Ribbons said, as though announcing the topic of his presentation before a large crowd. "Once upon a time, humans and demons and half-gods all lived together. This was known as the Time of the Four Eves. Do you know about the Four Eves?"

"Morganna Faire told me a pretty crazy story about four ladies who were created for the first man, Adam. Although he wasn't technically the first man, just the one the gods didn't destroy and reboot. Was that story true?"

"As true as any of the Old Tales, Zed. As true as the stories they tell today on the television and the internet."

"Hmm." I took another sip of the coffee. *As true as today's news* wasn't saying much for the hairdresser-genie's veracity.

Ribbons elaborated on his opening theme and went on with the story.

To summarize, long ago, humans and magical creatures lived together, not just on Earth, but on multiple worlds. They traveled between these worlds through space-time tunnels formed by burrowing creatures called timewyrms. From Ribbon's description, the timewyrms resembled the sandworms of science fiction. The wyvern went on for quite some time about the timewyrms, which I thought was a random tangent until he got to the part where timewyrms were instrumental in separating the humans from the magical creatures, sequestering them to just one world. "For their own protection," Ribbons said.

I held up a hand. "Wait. For whose protection? The timewyrms, or the demons, or the humans?"

Ribbons let fly one of his chittering laughs. "Oh, Zed. You do know how to amuse me. It was for the protection of the puny humans, of course."

"Right. The puny humans." I rolled my eyes.

"Remember, at that time, humans were many, many years away from inventing their weapons of mass destruction. They were easy pickings for the other predators."

"Blood-sucking ones?"

Ribbons nodded. "That kind, and more. The humans would have died out, but the gods favored them for some reason. The gods took no pleasure in watching their favorite pets be enslaved, tortured, and eaten—by anyone but themselves, of course. And back in those old days, the timewyrms served the gods." He looked down at his torso and smoothed some sparkling green scales along his belly. "The timewyrms only serve themselves these days, ever since the gods abandoned us." There was a weighty sadness to his telepathic voice.

"Ribbons, how old are you?"

He gave me a coy look. "The age of a creature is of no importance, only the length of its memory."

"Fine. I'll bite. How long is your memory?"

"My memory stretches back to the First Days. All wyverns are one. We share a common memory. It's the equivalent of an oral history." He looked down and ruffled the scales he'd just smoothed. "Unfortunately, our memories are far from complete. They're not at all like your human libraries. I must admit you puny humans have outdone us with your technology, with your books."

"Two points for the puny humans," I said.

There was a flash of white fluff as Boa jumped on my lap and bunted my hand for chin scratches.

"So, let me see if I've got this straight," I said. "The timewyrms burrowed tunnels through time and space, and dropped all the humans on Earth, and all the other creatures in other places. Other planets."

"Same planet," he said. "But in different dimensions, with other astral configurations. My own home world has two moons. Or so I recall through the shared memories. I was hatched here, in this world. Like you."

"You must be pretty old, because red wyverns, the female ones, are extinct."

He didn't reply, but a neon sign in my head flashed NO COMMENT.

"No way!" I slapped the surface of the desk, startling Boa enough to cease her purring. "Red wyverns aren't extinct? Ribbons! Do you have a girlfriend?"

Another flashing sign: NO COMMENT.

"Naughty boy," I said. "Though Aunt Zinnia suspected as much. She said the only potion that would be powerful enough to melt a genie like Morganna would be one made with venom from a female." I leaned forward, elbows on the desk. "So? Where'd you meet her? Is it a cute story?"

The neon sign flashed a third time, this time also accompanied by a horrible squealing, like feedback over a PA system. I yelped and covered my ears—not that it did any good keeping out a telepathic signal.

"Genies," Ribbons said in the ringing quiet following the squelch. "I'll tell you what I know, and no more." He yawned. "Then I need my beauty sleep."

I chucked back the remainder of my coffee and nodded for him to keep talking.

"Their powers in the other worlds are nearly as limitless as those of the half-gods. They are the rulers in many kingdoms. But here on Earth, this *particular* Earth, their powers are limited. They can put humans into trances, and they can put lesser beings into stasis fields. But they are mortal, and live in borrowed bodies that age rapidly."

I felt a surge of concern for Archer Caine. Was he in hiding somewhere right now, dying of old age before Zoey could meet him?

I interrupted to ask, "How rapidly?"

"I misspoke. When I say rapidly, I mean at the same rate as humans. To a wyvern, that's rapid."

"How do they borrow bodies? Do they always make cloned copies of other humans, like Archer did with Chet Moore?" The genie had split a second body off the DWM shifter when he was transitioning into his wolf form.

"That was a new development," Ribbons said. "Made possible only because the genie had infected the shifter's blood during Morganna's first experiment that went awry."

I scoffed. Chet Moore had nearly been killed by a flesh-machine monstrosity. It had been a bit more dramatic than an experiment "gone awry."

"The point of the Erasure Machine was to allow the genies to use fully grown bodies," Ribbons said. "Previous to this recent development, they had to respawn from life to life as infants. They had to wait until they were eighteen, or even in their early twenties, before their collective genie memories kicked in."

Something about what Ribbons said tickled away in my brain, unfurling ribbons of thoughts. The wyvern seemed to be aware of my reaction and paused his story. I chased the unfurling ribbons through my mind.

If genies had human lifespans, and respawned as babies who didn't know they were genies until they were over eighteen...

"That's right," Ribbons said, responding to what he'd read in my mind. "Archer didn't know he was a genie when he fornicated, I mean, made a child with you."

A new, horrifying thought struck me. If genies respawned as babies who didn't know they were...

"No," Ribbons said. "Zoey is not a genie."

I sighed in relief. What an emotional roller coaster the whole day had been—and the night hadn't gotten any less bumpy.

"But she's not *not* a genie," Ribbons said.

"She's not *not* a genie?"

"We don't know what she is." He brought his claw-like hands together and rubbed them. "Which is why you need to tell her. Then she can tell us what she is."

I snorted. "Good luck with that. Have you met a teenager? They're the last people who know what they are."

Ribbons didn't seem rattled. "With my kind, there is a story about a special kind of being."

"What kind?"

"A creature of mixed origin."

"Do you mean one who is half genie, one quarter witch, and one quarter shifter?"

"The story doesn't say so much about her pedigree, but I can tell you she is called the Soul Eater."

The Soul Eater. That sounded an awful lot like the Soul Catcher.

I waved for Ribbons to keep talking.

"The Soul Eater will reunite the worlds," Ribbons said. "Or destroy them all."

I got goose bumps all over. I immediately blocked my mind from the wyvern before he could read my next thoughts.

I had also heard such a story. Only it had been called a prophecy. My daughter had been named in the text of some ancient scrolls that had been dug up from the bottom of the sea. In the translation, she was called a Soul Catcher, not a Soul Eater. However, even with the more neutral term, the prophecy hadn't exactly filled me with gleeful anticipation about my daughter's future.

My mind was reeling. The prophecy had seemed like such a ridiculous thing. Who believed in prophecies anymore? Probably the same people who believed the Earth was flat or the moon landing was faked. But now that the wyvern was talking about his kind's version of the prophecy, it didn't seem so ridiculous.

In the dead of night, it was much easier to believe the unbelievable.

My goose bumps were growing more goose bumps.

Boa, who'd been purring away in my lap, suddenly went from a soft noodle consistency to rigid muscle tension. She hissed at something behind me, then licked her lips and transitioned into a low, guttural howl.

I turned my head slowly. I already knew what I was going to see before I saw it.

A ghost.

Ishmael Greyson stood near the foot of the stairs, looking lost, his neck faintly glowing where it had been chopped by a curved blade or two.

With all the family drama, all the talk about genies and other worlds and prophecies, I'd actually forgotten about the poor fellow.

CHAPTER 26

My ghostly drop-in visitor put an end to my discussion of genies with Ribbons.

Boa continued making horrible noises, her white tail twitching in agitation.

"I'm getting a ghastly headache," Ribbons announced. "You've got to do something about that ghost, Zed."

"What do you think I've been trying to do all day?"

"Try harder." He launched himself into the air above my desk. The beating of his wings sent my hair flying, blinding me. By the time my hair settled back down, the pint-size wyvern had already disappeared. Where had he gone? I squinted at the inky blackness along the edges of the basement. I really had to get a decent lighting system installed down there. Or hire a decorator. It was a shame that whenever my magical house spontaneously remodeled itself, it didn't provide the same cozy comforts that a good interior designer would.

Boa hissed once more, then jumped off my lap and high-tailed it up the stairs.

Ishmael stood where he'd appeared, still looking lost and confused.

"Sorry about the chilly reception from my pets," I said to Ishmael. "But you're welcome to hang out with me for a bit."

He gave me a glum nod.

* * *

For the next hour, I tried to gently prod Ishmael into communicating with me. I hoped he'd tell me who or what he was involved with that might have gotten him killed. It was slow going, without much progress. He seemed to know he was deceased, but not understand what that meant.

After a while, I was frustrated nearly to the point of crying. His sadness was affecting me. He seemed like a nice enough young man, and it really was a tragedy that his life had been cut short. Also, I was worn out by a lack of sleep and a lack of progress.

Was the real problem coming from my foolish attempt to improve my powers? I was on the verge of caving in, of admitting Zoey was right. Casting the rezoning spell on myself had been a mistake. I was not a tidy, well-organized library for ghosts. I was Zara Riddle. I was a witch. I was a woman, and my life was messy.

I took out my notes, looked them over, and considered how I might reverse the spell. The markings on the page swam before my eyes. My head began to throb with the same ghastly headache Ribbons had complained of.

I snapped my journal shut and tucked it back into the hidden drawer.

Now was not the time to make big life decisions. I was too emotional, too exhausted.

Also, perhaps I was giving up on my transformation too easily. The homicide was barely a day old. A very long day, but still just one day. Had I ever resolved anything thorny in just one day?

Nope.

My briefest ghost possession had been by the Pressman girl. And even with the help of several DWM agents, solving that apparent homicide had still taken me a few days. Complicated things took time to unravel.

"Let's get some fresh air," I said to the ghost. "Wanna go for a walk?"

He brightened up at once. If he'd had puppy ears, they would have pricked up eagerly. He didn't quite understand that he was dead or even that I was a witch, but there was enough humanity left in the guy that he knew a walk outside was a good idea.

I led him up from the basement, and through the house. The sun was rising, and the rooms were filled with eerie orange light that wasn't as bright as it should have been. The sun was red again, glowing like an ember. The smoke from the nearby forest fires still hadn't cleared away.

The house was quiet.

"Shh," I told Ishmael. "Be very quiet. Don't wake my daughter."

I was kidding, of course. Ghosts didn't make noises without great effort. But poor goofy-looking Ishmael didn't know that. He hunched his shoulders, held his finger to his semitransparent lips, and tiptoed along behind me. He tiptoed all the way out the front door.

"The air smells smoky," I said to him as we walked down the sidewalk.

He sniffed the air and gave me a puzzled look. He didn't seem to detect the smoke.

"Your nose might not be working the way it used to," I said. "Since you don't have any olfactory cells, you can't pick up on smells." I tilted my head. "Then again, by the same rule, you don't have any retinas or optical nerves, yet you can see me."

He continued giving me a puzzled look as we walked.

"Maybe it's a type of radar," I said. "Sonar. Like what bats use."

He shrugged, put his hands in his pockets, and kicked a pine cone off the sidewalk. The pine cone bounced into the street.

Ghost, I thought. The movie, not the noun. In the classic nineties movie *Ghost*, starring Patrick Swayze and Demi Moore—no relation to the Moores next door, according to them—the fictional ghosts could move objects in the real world if they knew how to focus their energy. There had been a touching scene where Swayze's character had floated a penny over to a tearful Moore.

I shivered. It was eerie how often movies got the details about magic right.

* * *

For the next hour, as the red sun rose overhead, I walked around Wisteria with my new ghost pal at my side.

I hoped we might walk past something or someone that triggered a reaction from him, but he remained calm and amiable. As far as ghosts went, he was pleasant company. As long as someone or something—like Codex —didn't drop the truth bombs hard enough to ignite him into a volcano of rage.

We wound up in front of Dreamland Coffee—the same downtown location I'd visited the day before with Bentley. Because I hadn't been to bed in the meantime, my sense of time wasn't working right, and being there again gave me a strong feeling of déjà vu.

The door opened, and customers came out, along with the scent of freshly roasted coffee. When the heavenly smell hit my olfactory cells—which were very real and working perfectly, unlike Ishmael's—my very real mouth watered. I'd never wanted coffee more.

I turned to Ishmael. "Do you happen to have any cash on you? We left the house so quietly that I forgot to grab my purse."

Ishmael reached into his pockets and turned them inside out. A couple of people in exercise clothes jogged by. All but one of them jogged straight through my ghost friend. The one person who dodged around the ghost, a man, slowed down and looked back at me over his shoulder, puzzled.

Another group of joggers rounded the corner and came through. This time not one of the group bothered avoiding Ishmael. They all jogged right through like he wasn't there.

Ishmael patted himself and gave me a hurt look. Further up the street were even more joggers heading our way. In the other direction, the man who'd dodged Ishmael was now standing still, drinking from a bottle of water while watching us.

"We need to get you off the street," I told the ghost.

The coffee shop smelled great, and it was also the nearest shelter. I could see through the windows that Maisy Nix was at the counter. How was she feeling toward me now? Had she talked to her niece, Fatima, and received the report that I knew about her family's secret? Would she welcome me to the coven with open arms and show me how to make that neat rainbow?

Or would she fly into a witch rage and hit me with hot, sparking plasma?

Time to find out.

I pushed open the door and pretended to fuss with my jacket button, pausing long enough to let Ishmael come inside as well. He could have walked through the door, but it probably didn't help his self-esteem to do so.

"Zara Riddle," Maisy called out with a cheery tone. She looked as tall and gorgeous as I felt rumpled and sleep-deprived. Her ebony hair was swept up in a topknot, all the better to feature the length of her neck and her perfect, medium-brown skin. She gave me a quick smile that emphasized the sharp planes of her face and broadened her strong jaw. She wore an orange Dreamland Coffee apron, this time with a hot-pink blouse underneath. The orange and pink, almost tertiary on the color wheel, looked so wrong together they were right, vibrating with energy. She wasn't yawning today.

Upon receiving her cheerful greeting, I smiled with relief. She wasn't going to char me with lightning on the spot.

"Two times in two days," she exclaimed loudly. "I haven't seen you this much since good ol' Tansy Wick's ghost was in possession of your taste buds! Get in here and get a coffee, you silly ol' witch, you!"

I stopped in my tracks, horrified. So much for subtlety. The coffee shop was crowded, full of people enjoying their first cups of the morning in small groups. A few of them had sweaty hair and wore jogging shoes. This was evidently where the Sunday morning jogging crew wound up after their run.

I backtracked toward the door. The joggers weren't looking my way yet. If I ducked out quick enough, they might not connect my face to Maisy's proclamation of *witch!*

But the door wouldn't open for me. It was stuck tight, by magic.

"Oh, Zara! The look on your face!" Maisy cackled.

I raised both of my hands, palms-up, in a gesture of *what's-your-problem*?

"Calm down," the other witch said. "I'm speaking to you through a sound focus." She waved at the seated customers. "None of them can hear us. Look."

I glanced around. Sure enough, none of the coffee drinkers were even looking my way, let alone showing interest in Maisy's talk of ghostly possession.

"You got me," I said. "You totally got me."

Maisy replied, "It's a pretty simple spell. I can show you sometime."

I walked up to the counter and asked—quietly, because I didn't know if the sound focus went both ways, "Is it the sound bubble spell, modified in shape to form a tunnel?"

"No." She drew her head back and twisted her lips. "But that's a good idea. One could approach a sound focus that way." She looked me up and down. "Zara, you're not modifying spells, are you? Don't tell me you're into dangerous home brew!"

"Home brew?" I'd never heard it called that before. "That wouldn't be a very wise thing for a novice such as myself to do."

She watched me, her expression frozen. "No. It wouldn't be wise for someone such as yourself to attempt. As a novice, you really should be under constant supervision by a mentor."

"Are you offering?" I grinned. "My aunt's out of town at the moment, as I'm guessing you already know."

Through a tight mouth, she said, "I've got my hands full with my niece, but I might be available for the occasional lesson or question."

"Great! I have two questions. First, can you see the ghost standing next to me?"

"No." Her mouth contorted into a tight frown. "Sadly, I do not possess that type of sight."

"Second question, then. Can I run a tab? I'd love to get one of your amazing coffees, but I left my house in a hurry and forgot my purse."

Her frown changed into a smile of bemusement. "A witch need not beg for money."

"So, you'll loan it to me? Sort of a witch-to-witch thing?"

"That's not what I meant."

"What did you mean?"

"Just that a witch need never beg for money. Haven't you figured that out?"

"Oh, I'm sure I could pickpocket like a professional if I wanted to, but a life of crime is not the life for me."

"Probably for the best." She shook her head and moved over to the coffee machine. "What would you like?"

"Vanilla latte."

"That was Ishmael Greyson's favorite drink. Are you here about him again?"

"Sort of. I'm here *with* him."

"Then I'll make two vanilla lattes," she said. "One for him and one for you."

"That's not nece—" My attention was drawn by the sight of Ishmael nodding his head. He'd been leaning against the counter next to me, watching my conversation with Maisy with great interest.

"Actually, that's perfect," I said. "He's currently smiling and looking forward to it."

"I always liked Ishmael," she said. "I can't be bothered to give people a hard time unless I like them. You do understand what I mean, don't you?"

"I think so. My coworker at the library, Frank Wonder, is always pulling elaborate pranks on me. He's a good friend, in spite of that."

"On the contrary. That's how you know he's a good friend."

"Okay. I do see what you mean."

"Frank. He's the flamingo?"

I pressed my lips together to give my brain time to catch up with my mouth. She'd casually asked me to confirm a friend's powers. Was this a trap? A test?

I answered slowly, "Frank does have bright pink hair, like a flamingo, if that's what you mean."

She winked at me. "Of course that's what I mean. I would never expect you to divulge anyone else's secrets."

"Maybe. You did suggest I might pick people's pockets for coffee money."

Her chin dipped down, and she fumbled the silver mini-pitcher she'd been using to catch the machine's espresso.

She quickly recovered and said, "Oh, Zara. I was only teasing you. It's what we witches do. Even the good ones can be naughty sometimes."

"I have a lot to learn. I guess your niece told you about my visit to the vet clinic yesterday afternoon?"

"She's talked about nothing but." The machine whirred as the brown elixir dripped into the silver mini-pitchers. "I understand there's a new menace on the loose. One who chops off heads."

I gave a sidelong glance over to Ishmael to check on the ghost. He was staring at the coffee and smiling, seemingly not connecting the idea of heads being chopped off with his own situation.

"I'm glad you're up to speed," I said. "Perhaps you can help. Two heads are better than one."

Her coffee-black eyes twinkled. "Two witches are better than one."

I nodded in agreement.

After she'd made the vanilla lattes, as well as an espresso for herself, Maisy said, "Let's take these coffees and sit in the back room. It's not very pretty to look at, but it's quiet and private, so I don't have to keep up the sound spell."

"Sure," I said, and she led me and my ghost buddy into the coffee shop's back office and storage room. She was right about it not being very pretty to look at.

CHAPTER 27

The three of us—Maisy Nix, Ishmael Greyson, and myself—sat around a small table in the storage area at the back of Dreamland Coffee.

Ishmael tentatively touched the rim of his coffee mug, wrapped his fingers around the handle, then left his hand there. His expression was serene. He didn't appear to be bothered that he couldn't pick up the mug or sip any of the vanilla latte. He simply sat there, quietly as always, as though waiting for something to happen.

"This table is unbalanced," I said to Maisy, noting the angle of my latte inside my cup. "That must be why it got sent away from the other tables in the front."

"Things around witches do have a tendency to become unbalanced." She kicked the base. To my surprise, the surface became more level and my latte evened out in the mug. There was no way kicking the table made it level. It had to have been magic.

"Fixed it," I said.

"This table is particularly jinxed," she said. "We've cast a lot of big spells on top of the old gal." She gave it a loving rub.

I leaned forward and touched a dark spot. "Is this a burn mark?"

Maisy raised an eyebrow. "You should ask Zinnia about that burn. She nearly set the whole place on fire."

"Oh?" I gave her my good-listener face—the one I used at the library when I suspected a patron with multiple late fees was about to tell me a whale of a tale that was well worth the equivalent of their late fees.

"Zinnia wouldn't like me discussing her business in her absence," Maisy said.

"She would not," I agreed.

"But we can talk about spells," she said. "Have you found the secret to peeling the raw egg?"

"There's a secret?"

She nodded. "Imagine you're holding the egg inside your mouth. Let your jaw drop down and forward, and cup your tongue. It gives focus to the oval form."

"My aunt never told me about that."

"She wants you to figure it out yourself, the hard way. She's actually a very good teacher, considering she doesn't have much experience as a mentor. Actually, her methods would be more than adequate... if you were the typical sixteen-year-old novice."

"Was that how old you were when...?"

"Yes." She tossed back her espresso and set the tiny cup down with a clink. "Is our friend still with us?"

I looked over the empty chair where Ishmael had been. "He's gone," I reported. "I didn't even see him go."

"Our girl talk must have bored him into the next dimension."

"Or he suddenly remembered he had other pressing business."

"Ishmael's pressing business days are over." She pursed her lips. "Lucky guy."

"If you say so."

She took his vanilla latte and set it before herself. "I don't like to see good coffee go to waste."

* * *

Maisy and I continued to talk shop—spells and potions and magical creatures. In what seemed like no time at all, an hour had passed.

"Sounds like it's getting busy out there," Maisy said, pushing her chair back. "Sundays start late, but the place can really fill up, between the joggers and the church crowd."

I smirked. "The church crowd comes here?"

She smirked back. "If they only knew their delicious coffee was roasted by a witch!"

"Oh, they might not even care. Half of them are probably shifters and gnomes, knowing this town."

She got to her feet. "Zara, as much as I would love to continue this long overdue meeting of ours, I do need to supervise my employees."

I got to my feet as well. "Thank you for letting me take up your Sunday morning," I said. "We should do this again some time."

"We should," she agreed.

I was about to make a joke about joining her "book club," if that was indeed what they called their coven, when I spotted something on the shelf behind Maisy. It was the karambit. The curved blade I'd dropped off the night before at the DWM. Or at least a very similar one.

A tiny croak came out of my throat.

"Zara?" She followed my gaze to the knife. She turned and picked it up.

I sucked in air and took a step back reflexively.

Tension filled the air. My senses tingled and time slowed.

Maisy narrowed her coffee-black eyes and took a step toward me. I took another step back.

"Zara, you seem upset about something," she said, brandishing the blade casually. "Are you afraid of knives?"

"Maybe a little bit," I said. It wasn't a lie. My daughter and I both had a powerful dislike for TV scenes where a character is shown chopping vegetables. Not quite a phobia, but definitely something.

Maisy was no dummy. She knew something was up. Slowly, as though tasting each word, she said, "But there's something about this knife in particular that you're reacting to." She swished it from side to side, watching my eyes as I tracked the blade. "Talk to me."

Her mouth blurred, the air around us crackled, and she cast a spell. It was fast and complicated, and something I'd never heard before.

I felt a buoyancy form, like a bubble in the pit of my stomach, and then words spilled from my mouth. "Ishmael Greyson was beheaded by a knife like that." The spell made me talk! I swallowed hard, but doing so couldn't stop the words from coming. "That must be why Ishmael led me here today. We were walking aimlessly, or so I thought, but then we ended up here. With the weapon that killed him." As the last words left my lips, I felt an immense sense of relief. It had to be a side effect of the spell.

"And you actually think I killed him," she said flatly. "Thanks a lot."

Whatever she'd cast on me was short in duration. The buoyancy in my stomach was gone. I felt no more unnatural compulsion to speak, and yet I did. I had questions.

"You have to admit it's an unusual blade," I said.

"I admit nothing. It's a pretty knife. That's why I have it."

"What do you use it for?"

She stared at me with narrowed eyes for a long moment. The coffee shop was getting busy. A din of laughter spilled into the cool back room.

Finally, she said, "Okay. I'll tell you what the knife is for, but you need to keep both of your hands where I can see them." She nodded at the round cafe table that stood between us. "Place both of your hands on the table."

I considered my options. Maisy Nix and the karambit were between me and the only exit. To my sides and behind me, the walls were all concrete blocks. If I was getting out of that storage room, it would be through Maisy Nix.

She made an impatient tsk sound. "Zara, just put your hands on the table. I'm not going to hurt you." She held one long-fingered hand to her chest. "I'm more worried about you getting excited and shooting me by accident. So, would you put your hands on the table, *please*?"

I didn't want to, but I placed my hands on the table anyway, of my own free will. The table's burnt and scarred surface was warm. Warmer than it should have been, given the temperature of the storage room.

Maisy's fingers twitched, her lips moved almost imperceptibly, and I felt the familiar tug in the air of a powerful spell being cast. Another one. This was stronger than the spell that had compelled me to speak. The table beneath my hands became hotter. Not hot enough to burn, but enough to make me want to pull away. I pulled away, but only jerked my shoulders. My hands were stuck. Magically glued to the table!

I used my telekinetic powers to reach for the nearest thing—a big bag of coffee. It would be perfect for knocking over Maisy while I made my escape, dragging the jinxed table with me if I had to.

But the bag of coffee didn't even budge. Those particular powers of mine weren't working. It was as though I'd been dosed with witchbane again. Had there been something in my vanilla latte? I tried casting the pink fog spell. No fog.

"Relax, Zara. It's only temporary."

I gave her a bewildered look. "Did you dose me with witchbane?"

She gave me a horrified look. "I'm not a monster," she said.

"If it wasn't witchbane, what did you do? Was it a spell, or the table?"

"It was all me." She grinned. "Although... that old table has been jinxed so many times over the years, I wouldn't be surprised if it got a few ideas of its own. Zinnia has told you about Animata, right?"

"Animata? Is that why you killed Ishmael Greyson?"

The grin fell off her face. "I didn't kill anyone, you silly witch."

"Not recently," I said.

She snorted.

I tried wiggling my fingers, then sliding my hands, then lifting up slowly, then quickly. With each attempt, I could swear I felt the table letting go and my hands wriggling or pulling away, but when I looked down, my hands hadn't moved at all.

"What is this magic?" I asked.

"A steadfast spell." She frowned. "Zinnia is right. You haven't been paying enough attention to your novice lessons. You should be able to identify spells being cast on you. And you should have known better than to put your hands on the table." She shook her head. "You shouldn't have let me block the only exit."

"I might not know everything, but I do know that witches aren't supposed to cast spells on each other, except in the event of an emergency."

She raised an eyebrow. "Such as pushing another witch out of the way of an oncoming bus?" Her eyes twinkled. "Lesson one: Witches aren't supposed to cast spells on each other. That is exactly what we tell the novices. For their own protection." She pursed her lips. "But how is a witch supposed to learn combat magic if she's never given the opportunity to duel?"

I stopped struggling against the table, adopted a relaxed pose, and gave the tall, dark-haired witch a polite smile. "Are you saying that this, right here, is a teaching moment? I love it. Teach me. What's the counter to a steadfast spell? I swear I'm a quick study if you give me a chance."

"Not so fast. First, don't you want to know what this pretty knife is for?" She floated the karambit in front of herself. The sharp, curved blade glinted as it rotated through the air languidly.

"If it's all the same to you, I'd rather you told me than, uh, demonstrated."

She shook her head. "If I was going to kill you, Zara, you'd already be dead."

I swallowed hard. "Hearing you say that is not as reassuring as you might think."

She used magic to grab the same bag of coffee beans I'd tried to lift. She floated the bag to herself easily, and then, in one swift movement, used the karambit to slice open the burlap bag. A handful of dark brown beans fell to the floor and scattered noisily, punctuating the tension.

Maisy brushed her hands together, even though she had touched neither coffee bag nor karambit handle with anything but magic.

"And that's what I use the knife for," she said. "Our garbage collector gave it to me. He found it next to someone's trash and thought it would be perfect for opening bags of coffee."

"Whose trash?"

"How should I know? You can ask him yourself, if you want. He's an honest man, so I know it's the truth."

"An honest man who gives people knives from the garbage?"

"I ran it through the industrial dishwasher," she said. "And he was right about it being handy for opening coffee bags, as you've seen for yourself."

My scalp itched. I wanted to scratch it, but my hands were still locked down to the table.

"I believe you," I said calmly. "I guess that if you had used that blade to chop off someone's head, you wouldn't bring it back into work the next day and use it for opening bags of coffee." The table was cooling underneath my palms. "But you can't blame me for being suspicious."

"I suppose not."

She snapped her fingers.

My arms felt cool and light.

"You're free of the steadfast spell," she said. "Give yourself a moment to recover."

I shook my arms and edged toward the exit.

She said, "And please don't try to blast me with any of your novice magic and force me to teach you a real lesson. My employees don't know about my abilities. I'd hate to be put on spot, having to explain why I'm hauling your unconscious body out of here."

"I'd hate that, too." I twirled my tongue and cast an easy spell. Plumes of pink fog rose from the floor around me.

Maisy groaned. "Your aunt is right. You don't listen."

"Just testing," I said. "I'm not blasting you with anything, not unless you consider a few wisps of pink fog a threat."

She grumbled.

We stood where we were, neither of us moving as the fog dissipated.

Someone had to say something, so I did. "Well, that happened," I said flatly.

Maisy said, "This actually went pretty well for a first real meeting between two witches."

"Gosh. I'd hate to see a bad meeting."

"Power is a tricky thing," she said. "Having it doesn't make life any easier."

"If you say so. You weren't the one permanently high-fiving a table."

She glanced around, as though looking for a topic change. "I'd offer to team up with you and Bentley to help with the Greyson case, but... I don't want to."

"May I ask why? Aren't you worried about this evil menace that's on the loose in town?"

"That's not a fair assumption, Zara. I worry about a great many things. But a truly wise and powerful witch knows when to pitch in and when to mind her own business."

I looked around at the shelves of coffee beans. "Plus, you're probably busy running this place."

She snorted. "You think this is all I do? You have no idea what I do for the people of this town. No idea."

"How could I know? I didn't even know you were a witch until yesterday, when I tried casting that threat detection spell in here only to have it splash back in my face."

She shook her head. "I countered it by reflex before you'd even finished casting. Zinnia loves that spell, but it doesn't do much. Sometimes I wonder if she's an OCW."

"Obsessive Compulsive Wimp?"

"Overly Cautious Witch."

I pressed my lips together tightly to keep from laughing. Overly Cautious Witch? They say nothing's funnier than the truth. But I couldn't laugh. I didn't dare even smirk. Zinnia was my aunt, my family. I wasn't about to throw her under the bus for a moment of mean-girl bonding with Maisy Nix. *Zara tries to be a good niece.*

Maisy asked, "Do you know the punishment for being an OCW?"

"No. What?"

She deadpanned, "Old age."

I nodded. It was the truth, but the kind of truth that wasn't funny.

There was a scratching sound on the floor. Maisy was using magic to propel a broom to sweep up the fallen coffee beans. I was puzzled by this. It would have been easier and simpler to levitate the beans directly, but what did I know? The woman's skills far exceeded my own.

In the softest tone I'd heard her use that day, she asked, "Would you like to know what I was busy with the night Ishmael Greyson was killed?"

"Your alibi? No need. I'm crossing you off my suspect list. We're good."

"But wouldn't you like to know?"

I picked up on her second offer. She wanted me to want to know. "Yes," I said, as I imagined she wanted me to.

She reached out with one long arm and grabbed the broomstick mid-sweep. Her hair loosed itself from the high topknot and flew out, as though electrified by contact with the broom.

"I'd love to show you," she said, her voice as silky as the black hair settling around her shoulders. "Have you ever flown, Zara?"

"I'm guessing by the way you're holding that broom, you don't mean on an airplane." I took a second look at the broom now that it was in her hands. It did not look sturdy enough to hold one witch in the air, let alone two. Was she actually talking about flying on a broomstick?

"No," I said. "Not like that."

She closed the space between us in two easy strides, and grabbed my hand. A static charge passed through me, and my own hair whipped up as though swept by wind.

"Then let's fly, Zara. Let's fly."

"What about your Sunday crowd? What about...?"

She blinked her coffee-black eyes slowly. "Don't tell me you're worried about a handful of church ladies having to wait a few extra minutes to get their decaf dry cappuccinos."

"I suppose they can wait a few extra minutes."

"They can."

"How's your schedule?"

"I believe I have some time right now for a flight."

She hooted with excitement, making her hair and mine whip up again.

CHAPTER 28

Of all the days to wear a pencil skirt, I had to be wearing one the first time another witch invited me to fly on her broomstick.

"Just hike it up," Maisy Nix told me, tucking her long, black hair behind one ear confidently. "Nobody's going to see your underwear out here in the middle of nowhere."

We stood at the side of an old logging road, a few miles inland from the outskirts of Wisteria. We had gotten there in Maisy's car, with the broomstick in the back seat. She'd explained that while she could cast a sky glamour to disguise us in flight, and thus we could have taken off from the alley behind Dreamland Coffee, it wasn't worth the magical energy expenditure, not to mention the risk of being seen. The sky glamour was a sturdy spell, but not guaranteed to work on all beings and modern recording devices.

I used both palms to draw up my skirt. "Are you sure I can't ride side saddle?"

She used one elegant, long-fingered hand to wave along the length of the broomstick in her other hand. "Do you see any saddle on this thing? Let alone a side saddle?"

"About that," I said. "I have a question about ergonomics and comfort. Doesn't the broomstick ride up?"

"It would ride up if you sat on it with your full weight."

With my full weight. Did she mean...? In a flash, the solution hit me. There was a spell that subtracted most of a person's weight without affecting their size. I'd even seen it used, on my unconscious coworker, Frank.

"The body buoyancy spell," I said excitedly. "Is that what it's for? For witches to lighten themselves for flight?"

She gave me an appreciative look. "You *have* been learning!" She reached toward me. "Come closer and I'll cast yours. You can do mine. It lasts longer when another witch does it for you."

I couldn't help but take a step back.

Maisy stomped her boot impatiently, sending up a plume of dry dust from the old road. "Don't be such an OCW."

"Full disclosure," I said with an emphatic hand gesture. "The last time someone cast that spell on me, I died."

Maisy frowned. "That's not a known side effect of the body lightening spell. Did they make a mistake with the phrasing?"

"There was an unexpected interaction. I had been electrocuted shortly before they cast the spell. And by *they*, I mean Zinnia. You've probably figured that out, since she's the only witch I know, besides you."

"And Fatima."

"And Fatima," I agreed. How quickly I'd forgotten about Fatima. Poor girl. Something told me she was easily forgotten by others, too.

"Let me check something." Maisy looked down and kicked some pebbles. The pebbles scattered, but not naturally. They rolled as smoothly as glass marbles on smooth pavement despite being lumpy, random shapes on rutted dirt. The pebbles, about two dozen of them, surrounded me in a tidy circle and rolled to a stop.

I stared down at the pebble ring in wonder. I'd seen a lot of powerful magic in my short second life as a witch, but it was often the simplest things that surprised me the most.

"You are tired right now," Maisy said, her gaze fixed on the stones. She appeared to be reading them, like a witch in a fairy tale reading tea leaves or bones. "Your energy is low from lack of sleep and contact with a spirit's death rage. However, you have plenty of energy in reserve. More than you'll ever know." She looked up at me, her coffee-black eyes twinkling within her angular features. "Zara Riddle, I deem you safe for flight. Now get over here, and stop being an OCW."

Here goes nothing, I thought. I stepped over the ring of pebbles so as not to disturb them. Her diagnostic reading hadn't instilled me with much confidence, but it didn't need to. I really, really wanted to fly.

She talked me through a quick review of the body buoyancy spell, and then I cast it on her. Flawlessly, I might add. She took a test hop, soaring high in the air and whooping before floating down, landing with the grace of Mary Poppins, but without the umbrella. Seeing her float down jogged something in my memory. One time, I'd been falling from a bell tower window and in grave danger before I'd magically pushed out the skirt of my costume to cushion my descent. I should have used the body lightening spell! *Quel stupide*, as the French witches say.

Or perhaps not. It did take some time to work through the phrasing. Given the height of the bell tower and the limited descent time, I would have needed to have begun casting it before I went out the window. And if I'd known what was coming next in order to start casting, if I'd had such powers of reading the future, I might have made a few other different choices. So many different choices.

Maisy clapped her hands in front of my face.

"Focus," she barked. "No daydreaming on flights. Not unless you want to get intimate with the side of a mountain."

"Yes, sir," I said. "I mean, yes, ma'am." I held out my arms. "I'm ready to get buoyant." Holding out one's arms had nothing to do with the spell, yet it felt like the correct body language.

"It's already done," Maisy said with a smirk. "And, look. You're still alive." She turned toward the broomstick, which was hovering near us, at hip height and parallel to the ground. "Do you want front or back?"

"Uh..."

"I'm kidding." She threw one long leg over the broomstick. "Novices always ride the rear. Hop on!"

* * *

You'd think flying a broomstick would feel like riding a motorcycle, and in some ways it did.

As we banked left or right, I had to follow Maisy's lead, leaning my torso into the turn. Diving downward felt like barrelling down a roller coaster, and soaring upward made my insides—though lightened by the spell—feel heavier than the rest of me. But a motorcyle's movements are limited by the plane of the road surface. On the broomstick, there were no such limitations. Or so I quickly discovered when Maisy told me to hang on, then took us into a high Yo-Yo, an unloaded extension, rolling scissors, and finally, just when I'd relaxed my grip, a defensive spiral.

She called back over her shoulder, "Maneuvering is all about making trade-offs between airspeed, which is kinetic energy, and altitude, which is potential energy."

"Consider me impressed," I said, catching a mouthful of her silky black hair in my mouth. There was an anti-wind spell in effect that reduced our friction and kept the rushing air from affecting us, but a little wind came through, plus Maisy had a tendency to whip her head back and forth as she got more excited. I didn't know my fellow witch very well yet, but she was, without a doubt, a daredevil.

"You haven't seen anything yet," she said, whipping more silky black hair in my face.

"Is this what you were doing on Friday night? Practicing combat maneuvers? Is there someone else who can corroborate your alibi?"

"Look down," she said.

I leaned over and looked at the mountain we were cresting. The air here was ashy, and the ground was smoldering. The forest below us lay in charred ruins. Now I understood where she had been, and how she'd been of service to the community.

No words came to my lips. The devastation below was heartbreaking.

"I was with a team fighting the wildfire," she said.

The ruined land stretched out below us for miles. It must have been quite the battle to fight back the wildfire. I felt slightly ashamed. Now that I saw how much the mountainside had suffered, I wished I could take back my petty complaints about having a slightly dry throat from the smoke.

"Thank you for your service," I said in awe.

"It's hard work, but I have to admit it's fun, too."

"Fun?"

"Zara, I'm Flame Touched. The gift you have with spirits, I have it with one of the elements. Fire."

"What about water? Isn't that a better way to fight fire?" Even as I asked the question, I heard my mistake. Water wasn't the only way to fight fire. I knew that. But my brain wasn't working the way it would have been if I'd been standing at the Information Desk at the library.

"I was part of the squad doing a controlled burn," she explained. "My main job is to cast lines of fire downward, to prevent the spreading fire from picking up more fuel as it travels across the land. I also drop off some of the smokejumpers—the ones who are members of a special elite squad."

"That's incredible. You're a hero, Maisy. And not just because you make the world's best coffee."

She turned her head enough to look me in the eye. "And why do you think it's the world's best coffee?"

"No way! You use magic to roast the beans?"

"Every batch."

We suddenly dropped several feet. I gripped Maisy tighter. The broomstick shuddered like a motorcycle misfiring.

"We should land soon," Maisy said. "You're a drag on my resources."

"Sorry about that."

"Don't be. Once you get trained up, you'll be an asset. Every witch has got to start somewhere."

We took a slow, comfortable bank to change direction, and flew back toward the logging road from which we'd come. The ash in the air faded as we passed from smoking ruins to lush green forest once more.

There was a PING, not unlike the door-ajar warning of a land-based, normal vehicle.

"That's odd," Maisy said. "We're picking up something on the radar."

"You mean like an airplane?"

"Smaller. But it's not a bird." She leaned to the side to lift one hand, and pointed to the sky ahead. The broomstick immediately shuddered again and lurched under us. Maisy quickly placed her hand back on the stick and regained control. "Sometimes I forget I shouldn't try to point," she said. "The incoming object is at two o'clock."

A shape that was familiar—to me, anyway—came into view. Ribbons flapped his way toward us on glittering green wyvern wings.

"That's no incoming object, that's Ribbons," I said. "Have you met my wyvern friend before?"

"Not formally. And I don't see anything. I'll have to take your word for it, and the radar's."

Ribbons soared past us, did an impressive aeronautical maneuver there was no term for, and flew alongside us at shoulder height.

"Fancy meeting you here," he said coolly.

"Ribbons, meet Maisy Nix. Be polite and make yourself visible to her."

His appearance didn't change for me, but I could tell by the jolt of muscle tension that went through Maisy Nix when she was able to see him.

"A wyvern," she breathed. "How wonderful to meet you, sir."

He must have replied telepathically to her only, and it must have been something cheeky, because she giggled like a little girl. I tried very hard to not feel pangs of jealousy. He was *my* wyvern. I kept him in clean towels and maple syrup. How dare he flirt with some witch he didn't even know!

To me, Ribbons said, "You've got to come home, Zed."

"That's where I'm headed. More or less." A note of alarm might have registered in my nervous system. It was hard to tell on top of the adrenaline and magic of flying. "Is something wrong? Is it Zoey?"

"She's upset. You left the house without leaving a note, Zed. You're supposed to leave a note. You know the rules. You're the one who makes the rules, Zed."

"I know, I know," I said.

Maisy asked, "What's going on? Family emergency?"

"My daughter's upset with me."

"She's sixteen, right? If I know teenagers, that's got to be an everyday sort of problem."

"My teenager isn't like the regular ones." I leaned down and scanned for the road and the car. "Maisy, I appreciate you taking me for my first flight, but I should be getting home. When I left the house this morning, I forgot to leave a note."

"Why didn't you say so?" She clucked her tongue, like a rider asking her horse to speed up, and the broomstick nearly shot out from beneath of us. Ribbons used his throat to make a guttural sound similar to YEEEEHAW!

We soared past the logging road, Maisy's car, and over the outskirts of town.

"But what about your energy?" I asked. "And the risks of using the sky-cloaking glamour spell over town?"

"Hasn't your aunt taught you the greatest skill a witch can master? It's how to downplay your abilities so that everyone underestimates you."

She clucked her tongue again, and the broomstick sped up so quickly, the terrain below us actually stretched into smeared stripes.

Ribbons sent me a telepathic whimper. Even with his speedy wyvern wings, he couldn't match our new pace.

CHAPTER 29

We flew toward Beacon Street, Maisy steering the broom while I held on tightly, my forearms crossed over the witch's slim waist.

My house appeared as a red dot, then a triangle, a matchbook-sized miniature, an architectural model, a dollhouse, and, finally, it was as large as life. I'd only been away for a few hours, but approaching from the air in this unexpected way heightened my emotions. The lump in my throat had grown with our approach. As we circled the back yard, preparing for landing, I blinked tears from my eyes. Home! Home at last. Sweet solid ground.

We touched down, and my legs buckled under me unexpectedly. I landed on my butt. Hard.

Maisy tossed her hair over her shoulder as she turned to laugh at me.

"That darn gravity will get you, every time," the witch said merrily.

I groaned and pushed my pencil skirt down. It had been forming a thick belt instead of a skirt. Anyone looking would have seen my underwear. How undignified.

I gave Maisy a suspicious look as I wriggled on the ground like a beached fish. "Are you sure you didn't give me extra weight when you reversed the body buoyancy spell?"

"That's all you," she said, laughing again. "Don't blame me, Zara. Blame the ice cream."

"Ouch. You're kinda mean." I used my palms to press down the wrinkles on my skirt. "Now I understand why my aunt didn't introduce us. She was protecting me from you."

"Maybe so." She tilted her head to the side thoughtfully. "Maybe so," she repeated.

I glanced at the back door of my house, then back at Maisy. My concern for Zoey hadn't left my mind since Ribbons' appearance, but I did have a few more pressing questions for my new witch friend before she flew off.

"Who else is in the club?" I asked. "There's you, your niece, my aunt, and who else?"

She gave me a funny smile, her thick upper lip lifting to show her long teeth, so that she resembled a rodent. "Oh, I couldn't possibly say. It's against the rules." She gave me a coy look. "But don't let me stop you from guessing."

"How about Kathy Carmichael, the head librarian?"

Maisy's eye twitched. I was onto something.

I pressed on. "Kathy's always hinting that she knows things about magic, but she never comes out and says anything specific."

"Typical troll." Maisy rolled her eyes. "Always trolling for intel. She's as bad as Vincent Wick with his creepy little spy cameras."

"Did I hear you right? Kathy's a troll?"

"That may or may not be a rumor that may or may not hold some truth." She held one slim finger to her lips. "But you didn't hear it from me."

"Trolls are real?"

She waved a hand airily. "The preferred term is sprites. Apparently troll is a bad word. They get offended if you call them that." She made a tsk-tsk sound.

"Everyone gets so offended these days about labels. What next? Should we witches lobby to be called something different, like hag, or crone, or harpy, or she-devil?" Maisy wrinkled her nose. "Actually, I like she-devil."

Of course she would. The daredevil witch was a bit of a she-devil.

I circled back to the topic of Kathy's supernatural status.

"What can trolls do?" I asked, "I mean, um, *sprites*? What can sprites do?"

"Why don't you look it up in that Monster Manual of yours?" She bounced her eyebrows. "By the way, I'd love to borrow that book sometime."

A bargaining chip! "Any time. I'll trade you for a name. Another member of your coven."

"Nice try." Maisy waved a hand, then sighed. "I don't know why I'm being so careful. You probably know exactly who it is."

"I swear I don't. Kathy was my top guess, and my only guess."

"But you've probably heard plenty about our fourth member from your aunt. The two of them spend a lot of time together, especially now that..." She paused and pretended to zip her lips. "Never mind. It's not my place to say."

"That's not much of a hint," I growled. "Zinnia doesn't talk to me about her friends. She doesn't tell me anything juicy."

"Really? So she never told you about what happened with Fung?"

"Who? Do you mean the detective who was here before Bentley?"

Maisy's face registered disappointment. "What a shame. I was hoping to get the dirt from you. She won't tell me, either. She swears the two of them were just friends, but I can't shake the feeling there was more to it."

I held up both of my hands to show they were empty. "I've got no dirt, either. I'd never even heard of the guy until yesterday."

Maisy's dark eyes twinkled. "I think you *do* know something. You're toying with me right now, aren't you?"

I waved my empty palms. "All I know is Bentley got access to this guy Fung's full reports, and there's something in them about Zinnia being tough." I put my hands on my hips. "But that can't be news to anyone. We Riddle women are tougher than we look."

"Of course you are. Witch blood and shifter blood and heaven knows..." She paused and bared her long front teeth in what almost passed for a smile. "And heaven knows what else," she finished, her voice low and gritty.

A shudder passed through me, finishing with a tremble of both hands. I clasped my hands together, but they continued to tremble and twitch.

Maisy noticed my trembling and pointed at my hands. "You'll need plenty of rest before you're back up to power. That's technically my fault you're drained."

"What?"

She gave me a sheepish look. "I got the extra speed on the flight back by using you as a magical battery."

"A what?" I'd heard her perfectly, but it seemed like the right way to show one's rightful indignation when one has been used as a magical battery without her consent.

"You heard me," Maisy said coolly. "Zinnia should be teaching you about that."

Suddenly, I felt defensive of my aunt. "She's doing the best she can," I said. "I'm not the world's best student."

Maisy nodded and turned her head to survey my small patch of garden. "That's a nice crop of cucumbers and tomatoes," she said. "I can see that Tansy Wick's spirit did you some good."

"There are a few positive aspects to being Spirit Charmed."

"If you say so," she said flatly.

A quiet moment passed. A single Spotted Towhee landed on the fence and chirped at us.

Maisy waved an arm. "Enough chit chat," she said. "Now make with the hocus pocus. You've got enough juice left to cast a buoyancy spell for me." She stamped her foot impatiently. "Lighten me up, already. I gotta fly."

* * *

After Maisy took off, I stood for a moment staring after her. I couldn't see her, of course. Just the sky. Her cloaking glamour worked as well as the wyvern's. But I felt the urge to stare, all the same.

My hands were still trembling when I went inside the house through the back door. I found Zoey in her room, sitting cross-legged on her bed with a paperback in her hands. Boa was draped across her lap, fast asleep with her fangs showing.

Zoey gave me a guilty look. "Did Ribbons tattle on me?"

"Maybe," I said tentatively.

"Mom, I swear I only went down to your desk to get a pen, but then I couldn't find one, so I started poking around. And when I found those drawers that wouldn't open, I thought for sure you had something in there about..." She trailed off and stared at me. Her lower lip quivered. Not a pouting quiver, but something else. She was upset.

I understood. And I knew what I had to do.

"You were looking for something about your father," I said.

She looked down at the relaxed cat draped over her legs. "I broke a letter opener, and I chipped the drawer." She looked up again, her eyes tinged with red and glistening. "Do you hate me now?"

Ah. The mercurial moods of the teenager. Soon she would be facing problems I couldn't fix, but for now, for this one, I could help. This was a job for the truth. A hug plus the truth.

I crossed the threshold into her room, sat next to her on the bed, and wrapped my arms around my daughter. She sobbed as she buried her face in my hair.

"I don't hate you," I said. "I could never hate you."

She shook in my arms, which set off another round of post-flight trembling in my arms.

"I don't know what to do," she sobbed. "You're the person I go to when I need help, and you won't help me."

"I'm sorry I haven't been helpful."

She pulled back enough to glare at me. Another rapid mood change. "You made pink smoke, Mom. Pink smoke! And you snuck away like a thief!"

"I did do that, like a coward, and I'm sorry. If it's any consolation, I've withdrawn my nomination for Mother of the Year."

She pulled away as much as she could without uncrossing her legs. "I don't know why I'm so worried about you being mad at me. I'm mad at you. You treat me like I'm a baby, but I'm not. I deserve to know who I am." She fixed me with an angry pout so completely over the top it nearly made me giggle. "I deserve to know what I am," she spat out.

"You're half genie," I said.

She howled in outrage. "Don't make a joke out of this." She howled again. "You're so immature! For someone who's supposed to be the mother, you're so irritating!"

"Please stay calm," I said. "You're half genie, and I don't know what powers you might have. Please calm down. I don't want to get accidentally turned into smoke, or fire, or goo."

She started howling a third time, but abruptly cut herself off. She stared at me, unblinking, and brushed the tears from her red eyes.

"I'm what?"

"A quarter witch, a quarter shifter, and half genie. Your father had a different name when I knew him then, but these days he calls himself Archer Caine."

At the mention of his name, the door to the bedroom abruptly closed itself with a slam.

I looked around. "What was that?"

"Just the house," Zoey said.

"The house?"

She nodded. "The house is always listening in. It must be surprised. I think you caught it off guard."

I spoke up louder, intentionally. "*The house* shouldn't listen in to private conversations if it doesn't want to get caught off guard."

The house returned only a weary creak.

My daughter and I stared at each other.

"You're not surprised," I said.

She pursed her lips. "Well, when you didn't tell me, I figured it was bad."

"Being half genie is bad?"

She shrugged. "Good. Bad. Who knows?"

"It can't be bad. You're too good to be bad."

She looked down at the bedspread. "Mom, did he...?"

My arms trembled again. I was really feeling the depletion from the flight, and now this.

I took in a deep breath. Finally, I understood what she was asking.

If I'd been listening, truly listening, I would have heard it sooner.

Was it being drained of magic that made me finally understand? Was I a better mother without my powers? I couldn't think about that now.

All I could do was listen, feel what my daughter was feeling, and answer honestly.

"He didn't hurt me," I said softly. "Is that what you need to know?"

"Don't lie to me. I can take it."

My heart broke. Knowing that my cowardice had caused my daughter so much pain... It brought tears to my eyes. I blinked them back. This wasn't about me. This was about her.

"Zoey, I'm not lying. You were made with... well, not love, exactly, but you were made in a good way."

"You're not just saying that, are you?" She lifted her face and gave me a hopeful look.

I raised my hand. "My word is my bond. I'm not lying to you."

"What about that night?"

I frowned. "You don't really want those details, do you?"

"Not that," she said. " I mean, did you know? Did you know you were making a baby?"

"I knew I shouldn't have had so many Barberrian wine coolers."

She leaned forward, so her face was in mine. "You swore, Mom. You gave your word. You have to tell me the truth."

"Yes. That is how the swearing thing works."

"So, did you know?"

My throat was so tight. I didn't think the words would escape, even with the promise I'd made, but I heard the words pass hoarsely through my lips.

"Yes," I said. "I knew before. I knew during. And I knew after. I knew about you. It was no accident."

She stared at me a long moment, then whispered, "But you didn't love him." She sounded bitter.

My throat wouldn't let out any more words. If you don't know the truth, you can't tell it.

The cat had jumped off her lap when the door had slammed. Now Zoey uncrossed her legs and started to push away from me.

I caught her by both wrists and stopped her. I met her face again with mine, and I spoke the truth.

"Zolanda Daizy Cazzaundra Riddle, you were made with love, from my body. Every bone and pint of blood. Every hair on your head. Every freckle on your nose. You were made with love. By me."

She went limp and tossed herself into my arms.

CHAPTER 30

Once the secret of Zoey's paternity was out in the open, a weight I didn't know I'd been carrying lifted free of me. It felt similar to the body buoyancy spell I'd used for broomstick flying, but this magic was the regular kind that any person could experience.

I was unburdened now, and, like every person who's been unburdened, only after the load had been dropped could I appreciate how much I'd been carrying. Every muscle in my body relaxed. There was space within me, and air, and room for light and goodness.

As we sat together on Zoey's bed, talking about genies and what it all might mean for her, my head floated. Everything floated. I was helium inside. It seemed like the golden afternoon sunshine streaming in the window was the only thing holding me in place.

We talked about the night I met Archer. It had happened at a typical teen house party. The party had been full of people I didn't know. The house belonged to an older kid who was a buddy of Nathan Partridge's, a.k.a. Nash. He was my big-brother-like friend whose father rented a portion of the house my mother owned. Nash and his rock band were playing a cover song, not very well, when I slipped away with a cute boy who'd caught my eye.

"That's funny," Zoey said, interrupting the story. "I always thought Nash might be my father."

"Ew. Based on what?"

"You two were so close, and then you didn't see him anymore after you had me."

"He was like a brother."

She shrugged. "How can you say that? You never had a brother."

"No, but I've read books about siblings. Thanks to fiction, we've all lived countless other lives. As a fellow bookworm, you should know that."

"But you did drift apart after you had me." She sniffed. "It might have been nice to have an uncle around."

She had a good point, but there was a logical explanation. "I got cut off from Nash because he and his father still lived in your grandmother's house, and I was no longer welcome there."

Zoey stroked the tip of her nose carefully. "Look at the tip of this nose. Doesn't it look a bit like Nash's?"

"In the sense that it's a nose, sure."

"I swear I could see a clue when I looked at photos of Nash. The family resemblance." She touched her cheekbones lightly. "I thought I could see it in a few spots on my face."

"People see what they expect to see." I yawned and stretched in the sunbeam, feeling relaxed and cat-like. "Or what they *want* to see."

"I had this whole scenario in my head. Nash was going to get his big break and become a superstar. Then, one day he'd be giving an interview on TV, and he'd suddenly break down. It would be super-dramatic. He'd confess to the interviewer that no matter what he did in life, he'd never atone for abandoning his daughter."

I sucked in air through my teeth. "I'm sorry, kiddo. You'll never know how sorry I am you had to imagine those stories."

She looked down and tracked the ridges on her bed's blanket. "I imagine lots of scenarios. Sometimes I'll spend half an hour thinking about what I'd say if I bumped into some random famous person."

"I do that, too."

"But you're a witch, Mom. If you wanted to, you could meet anyone." She gave me a wide-eyed look. "Anyone!"

"Hmm." She had a point. There was no door in the world that was locked to a witch.

"Well, almost anyone." She wrinkled her nose. "I'm sure the Royal Family has supernatural people on their security team."

"You think so?"

"They must," she said. "Right?"

We both let the idea sink in. Imagine that! The Queen of England and her witches, shifters, and mages. *Her Majesty's Mages.* What a great book that would be.

I leaned back, and the bed rose up to meet me. My body felt so light and yet so heavy at the same time. I wanted to keep talking with my daughter, but I also wanted to feel her cool, cotton pillowcase against my cheek. It was both crisp and soft at once, like a good pillowcase should be. Being horizontal felt so right, so much better than being vertical. I pointed my toes and stretched out my legs.

The spell of sleep crept over me hungrily, like flames over dry wood. I muttered an apology to my daughter, about my battery being drained from flying on a broomstick all morning. She laughed and told me I was delirious. I hadn't told her about my first flight with Maisy Nix. Now I desperately wanted to tell her all about it, but no counterspell of conversation or coffee was going to keep sleep away.

* * *

I woke to find a wyvern's face hovering inches above mine. I started, but not as much as the first dozen times it had happened. They say you can get used to anything, and it's true. You can get used to peppermint breath and black eyes watching you sleep.

"That other witch stole your fire from you, Zed." Ribbons' green, scaly eyebrow ridges formed a deep V. "We must seek vengeance."

"Easy now. If Maisy had asked, I would have shared. Happily. I'm the one who wanted to get home fast."

"But she *didn't* ask." His frown deepened, and he repeated, "She. Did. Not. Ask."

I rolled away from the wyvern and rubbed my eyes. Judging by the amount of the light in the room, I'd been asleep on my daughter's bed for about four hours. Judging by the rumble in my stomach, it was time for dinner. Judging by the aroma of baking cheese in the air, leftover pizza was being reheated in the oven. Everything was right in the world. With the prospect of pizza on the horizon, how could I be upset about a little borrowed magic?

"We will teach her a lesson," Ribbons said.

"Actually, I'd prefer that we let this one go," I said. "You must have heard the expression 'Choose your battles wisely,' right?"

"Yes, but that's not how we say it, Zed."

"Okay. I'll bite." I jumped off the bed and cast the spell for the bed to make itself. "How do your people say it?"

Instead of answering in my head, Ribbons jumped in the air, unfurled his wings to their maximum span, and let out a fearsome roar.

"That's also good," I said. "I promise to jump up and roar at Maisy if she ever borrows my magic again without asking." I turned to the bed and finished straightening the blankets. My magic reserves were still low. The simple spell hadn't gone well. The pillow was circling underneath the covers like a restless, confused slug. I snapped my fingers to let the poor thing rest, then manually fluffed it and placed it at the head of the bed.

I turned to say something else to Ribbons, but he was already gone. I heard another scratch being added to the staircase's wooden handrail as he surfed his way downstairs, presumably drawn by the scent of leftover pizza.

* * *

We set the table in the formal dining room for dinner. Tonight we would dine in high style. It was Sunday, after all.

In addition to the reheated pizza, we would be eating fresh coleslaw that Zoey made with the food processor. Ever since we'd gotten the appliance as a belated housewarming gift, she'd become a bit of a coleslaw wizard.

While we placed the napkins, and then a dozen candles of various heights and scents, I caught her up on my day's activities.

Even with a big nap in the middle, my Sunday had been nearly as busy as Saturday. I was looking forward to getting to the library on Monday for some rest and relaxation!

First, I'd walked around town with Ishmael Greyson's ghost. He'd led me to Dreamland Coffee, where I'd had my first witch-to-witch meeting with Maisy. Everything had been going well enough, until I spotted a karambit exactly like the one used to kill him. After clearing up my "little misunderstanding" with Maisy, we'd moved on to more fun things. My first broomstick flight. From the air, I'd gotten a sense of her impressive work fighting the forest fires. Then Ribbons had located me, and Maisy had flown me home.

When I was done retelling the day's events, Zoey commented, "She witch-glued you to a table, then she sucked all the magic out of you?"

"When you say it like that, she sounds awful."

Zoey raised an eyebrow. "Maybe she *is* awful."

"She might be awful. But you know how I am. I give people a few chances. That's why I'm still friends with Charlize."

"Why do you do that? Aren't you worried people are going to take advantage of you?"

I looked down at the candles on the table and rearranged while I thought. I remembered a recent conversation with my mother, in which she had accused me of being too picky about friends. She felt I had a history of getting rid of people too easily. Zirconia Riddle had been wrong about many things, especially when it came to me. This was yet another example of how she'd never understood that her daughter wasn't the exact same person she was. Yes, I had ditched friends, but only after giving them about a million second chances. I could be incredibly forgiving... right up until I wasn't. I took a deep breath and answered my daughter's question truthfully.

"Zoey, at the end of the day, I'd rather be the person who gave too much than the person who gave up too easily." I looked into her eyes. "People who give up too easily don't have anyone at their funerals."

She crossed her arms. "Life is more than a contest to see who gets the biggest funeral."

"You're right." I grinned. "There's also the wedding. You want to have a lot of people there, because that's the one where you're still alive to enjoy it!"

She rolled her eyes. "You are so corny."

"If you think *that's* corny, wait 'til you hear my speech at your wedding."

She blushed. "Mom! I'm only sixteen."

The oven timer beeped, and she ran to the kitchen to pull out the pizza.

When she returned, she said, "I'm still concerned about Maisy Nix. Just because someone's a witch doesn't mean they're a good person. Auntie Z might have been keeping you away from her and the coven for good reason."

"I guess we'll find out when she gets back from her vacation." My magic wasn't fully recovered, so I used matches to light the candles.

After a moment, Zoey asked, "Does he know about me?"

I sucked in air between my teeth. This new development, of Zoey knowing about her father, was new, and questions about him kept catching me off guard.

Rather than fill the room with pink fog, tempting though it was, I answered honestly. "I can't say for sure either way. I've been going over everything he said to me, and I don't know." I sighed heavily, making the candle flames flicker. "I don't think Ribbons knew about your paternity until recently, until after I knew. I believe the little syrup guzzler pulled it from my mind. I had a hard time keeping him out when he first came to live with us."

There was a flapping sound, and the wyvern entered the dining room flying.

Zoey and I grinned at each other. In unison, we said, "Speak of the devil."

"There's nothing like a good day of flying to work up one's appetite," the wyvern said. He was not at all insulted by being compared to the devil.

Zoey disappeared to get the rest of the food.

When we got ourselves seated, my daughter and I sat across from each other while Ribbons took a spot at the head of the table. As usual for those nights the wyvern dined with us, we turned his chair backwards so he could perch on the back of it and still reach his food. We'd joked about getting him a children's high chair, or even a booster seat, but neither of those ideas had gone over well. And that's why we had one dining chair with deep talon scratches across the back of it. If anyone asked, I'd claim that our secondhand furniture must have belonged to a family with a parrot. A fat parrot.

We ate and talked about genies.

Ribbons was now able to speak telepathically to both of us at the same time. His connection with Zoey had been weak at first, which he'd blamed on her shifter blood. When I'd pointed out that technically I had a greater percentage of shifter blood than she did, since it was my father who was the fox, suddenly the wyvern's connection had strengthened. Whether it was the power of positive thinking, the placebo effect, or another of the wyvern's mind games, we Riddles would never know.

Even once he became able to, he didn't talk to Zoey much when I wasn't around. If anything, he was on edge around her. He'd flit into the air nervously if she moved quickly. Once, she'd shifted into fox form without warning and he'd made such a ruckus we thought he'd laid an egg!

Now that I knew he'd been aware of her genie lineage, his wariness made sense. According to Ribbons' stories, genies and wyverns had a long and complicated relationship in their home world. During the world's many wars, genies and wyverns had always been on opposite sides.

Thanks to Ribbons' access to the collective memory of his ancestors, he "remembered" being killed by genies. Or, even worse, being kept in a cage. Genies used the various body fluids and even the scales of wyverns to make powerful potions. There was one potion in particular, made with the venom of the female wyvern, that could kill gods and demons, melting them into goo. I knew about that one first-hand, and had seen it in action. Twice. Not a pretty sight.

When my daughter and I reviewed that detail, she became flustered. "If anyone kills my father before I get to meet him, they'll have to deal with me."

"Anyone?" I snickered. "Remember, your grandmother *did* take a chunk out of him," I said. "Via the neck." I gave her a double eyebrow raise. "You should take it up with Gigi next time you see her. That'll be fun."

"Right," she said flatly. "Fun."

"So much family drama," Ribbons commented.

In unison, Zoey and I said to him, "You love family drama."

He paused, his cutlery in midair—he'd taken to using a fork and knife to eat human meals for reasons unexplained.

"No," Ribbons said defensively. "Human family drama is boring, because all human affairs are boring."

Zoey and I exchanged a look. She rolled her eyes. For someone who complained how boring we were, Ribbons spent a lot of time hanging out with us.

"These cabbage entrails are not entirely unpleasant," Ribbons said, changing the subject. He preferred to make up his own terms for human food. *Cabbage entrails* sounded more fierce and wyvern-y than *coleslaw*.

We continued eating and talking about genies, then about sprites. I'd broken our no-books-at-the-dinner-table rule and had the DWM Monster Manual open next to me. I pictured my boss, Kathy, the head librarian, as I paraphrased the information to Zoey.

"Sprites aren't in this book at all," I reported. "Under sprites, it says 'see trolls.' The trolls page is pretty short. I guess our book editor, good old Jorg Ebola, didn't think much of them."

Zoey asked, "Are there pictures?"

"There's a bridge with a pair of eyes gleaming from the darkness underneath."

"Are you joking or is it really that offensive?"

"I'm not joking. I'm not even a troll or a sprite, and even I'm a little offended."

Zoey pouted. "I wish I could see it myself."

But she couldn't see it. I had to describe the glamoured contents of the book to her. Even though she had manifested some witch abilities, such as her telepathic connection with Ribbons, she wasn't yet able to see through the fake text. To her eyes, the Monster Manual was a textbook entitled Second Year Intermediate Economics, and I was reading it upside down.

"Ms. Carmichael doesn't seem like a troll to me," Zoey said.

I winced and held my finger to my lips. "Not so loud," I said, feeling guilty. "Maisy wasn't supposed to tell me, so you knowing about it is wrong on two counts."

Zoey waved her hand impatiently. "More information about trolls, please."

"Sprites."

"Whatever."

"Words matter. Would you want to be referred to as a werefox? A carnal beast who changes whether she wants to or not with the waxing and waning of the moon?"

"Gross."

"Exactly." I scanned the page before summarizing. "This creature's strongest talent is its digestive system. They can eat practically anything."

Zoey snickered. "We Riddles must be part troll. I mean sprite."

"Please. Don't even joke. Our family tree is already complicated enough."

"What else? Can they cast spells?"

"No. But their tongues are prehensile."

"Like monkey tails?" She stuck out her tongue and waggled it. "My tongue is not prehensile."

"They can also use their tongues like whips."

Ribbons chimed in. "They can regurgitate potions."

Zoey shot me a stunned look. "Is that true?"

"The book says their three stomachs produce different kinds of compounds." I rubbed my chin. "It doesn't say anything in here that would explain Kathy's weakness for stale birthday cake."

"That could just be a librarian thing," Zoey said.

"True. I've never met a librarian who could turn down..." I trailed off, distracted by the ghost who'd entered the dining room. Ishmael Greyson had come in, casual as could be, and taken a seat at the foot of the table. I cleared my throat. "Cake," I finished. "Speaking of which, what's for dessert?" I kept an eye on Ishmael. His throat was glowing, but he appeared to be calm enough, content to watch us eat.

"Dessert is apple pie," Zoey said, and she went to get it.

Ribbons sent me a private message. "Is the ghost back, Zed? Something is glowing."

"It's our friend," I whispered. "He's sitting at the foot of the table."

"That means the human detective hasn't finished his task, Zed."

"It hasn't even been forty-eight hours. Give Bentley a break. The guy's only human, after all."

"Puny human," Ribbons agreed.

Zoey returned with the pie. The scent of cinnamon filled the air.

I calmly informed my daughter that a certain *house guest*, wink wink, was sitting at the foot of the table, and that it would be polite to set a wedge of apple pie in front of him. She may have suspected I was playing a game to get an extra piece for myself, but she played along anyway. Whatever genie powers she had, they didn't give her the gift—or the curse—of seeing ghosts.

My daughter and I kept talking, acting as though nothing was wrong.

As we were finishing our second helpings of apple pie, Zoey said, "I think I'm lucky to have two powerful parents."

"Oh? Because of what you might inherit?"

"That, and also because if anything bad happened to me, both a witch and a genie would take vengeance!" Her voice took on a dramatic flair. "If someone messes with me, they'll have to deal with my family!" She hit the table with her open hand. The candles rattled. "Vengeance will be swift!"

She was sounding a lot like Ribbons. "My daughter the avenger." I shook my head.

"Speaking of *The Avengers*, that gives me an idea," she said. "Movies are a great way to do research. I'll hit the books, of course, but first, I'm going to watch every movie that has a genie in it, starting with *Aladdin*."

"Sounds fun," I said. "We could finish the weekend with a mini film festival."

"I'll come if there's popcorn," Ribbons said.

Movement at the foot of the table drew my eye. I turned to the ghost, though I didn't need to see him to know he was upset. I could feel his emotions affecting me. Thanks to his inner turmoil, I suddenly had muscle tension in my entire body. And the urge to grab the dining room table and flip it.

Ishmael's mouth was agape. His usually-buggy eyes were threatening to pop out of his head again. He got to his feet slowly, looking left and right with a panicked expression.

Ribbons sent me another private message. "What's happening, Zed?"

"He's freaking out," I replied. "I can feel it. He's angry and scared, all mixed together."

"Be strong," Ribbons said. "Look at me. Look into my eyes."

I turned to the wyvern. He had dropped his utensils and fanned out his wings. He curled his talons around the back of the chair, digging into the wood.

His black eyes bore into mine, and I felt a wave of serenity flowing from the wyvern and washing over me. I unshielded my mind and thanked him. I felt I could withstand the ghost's emotions now that I was prepared.

Now a question rose to my mind.

What had upset the ghost? We'd been enjoying a weird yet peaceful Sunday family dinner. Everything had been going well, but now something had changed.

I studied Ishmael. He got up from the chair and started pacing. He paced faster and faster, until he was practically running in circles, like a dog chasing its tail.

I tore my gaze away and looked at Zoey. She couldn't see Ishmael, but she could read my body language well enough to know something was up.

Zoey asked, "Is the ghost doing something?"

"Yes," I said.

"Did he take his head off?"

"Ew. No. He's pacing."

"That's not so bad." She went back to eating her apple pie. "Let me know if I should be concerned."

"Will do."

I closed my eyes and rubbed my temples. The rubbing of the temples wasn't magic, but it did help my memory.

Images from the weekend's investigation came to me in flashes. The twin streaks of blood on the wall. The head in the trophy cabinet. Family. Vengeance. Fire. Flying. Curved knives. Green busts made of gelatin. A Jersey cow chewing buttercups in an alpine meadow. The tattoo of a cougar. A car charging toward me. My hands, stuck to a hot table. Glowing eyes beneath a bridge. Family. My thoughts kept returning to family. And vengeance. That was what Zoey had been talking about a moment earlier.

My eyes flew open.

Zoey, who'd been looking at me, startled in her chair. "You scared me," she said, then, "Mom? You're not possessed again, are you?"

"I'm only possessed by a really good theory," I said.

"Oh?"

Ribbons chimed in, "Tell us, Zed!"

"Not until I'm sure," I said.

They both groaned.

"On the positive side, our dinner guest has just given me the information I needed." I pushed my chair back from the table. "If you'll excuse me, I have to do something." I got to my feet. "I have to find Bentley and tell him the killer's been under our nose this whole time."

CHAPTER 31

Five Days Later

Friday, July 22

5:25 pm

Five days after Ishmael Greyson's ghost gave me the key to solving his homicide, I was wandering around the DWM's underground headquarters by myself.

As I walked by an open office door, I muttered under my breath, "Where is that hallway? It's like a maze down here."

The person inside the office must have heard me, because he looked up from his desk.

"Steve," I said, my voice cheerful at my apparent relief in seeing a familiar face. "How do you find your way around this maze? Do you drop breadcrumbs to make a trail?"

His round face broke into a bright grin. "Oh, no. Management frowns on that. It attracts ants."

I stood hesitantly in the doorway and glanced around the lawyer's office. "You sure have a lot of candy on your desk. I notice it's all red candy."

"As you can see, some stereotypes are based on truth. We iguammits love our red candy." He waved for me to come into his office. "Would you like a piece, or would you rather not spoil your dinner?"

I came in, set down my heavy tote bag, and lifted the lid off a jar of red jawbreakers. "Don't make me laugh. Mr. Adebayo, you don't have enough candy here to spoil my appetite."

"Call me Steve," he said. "I insist."

"Thanks, Steve." I dug into the jawbreakers.

He opened the jar of red licorice, selected one, and gently tapped it against my jawbreaker in a toast gesture. "To pre-dinner candy," he said.

I made short work of the jawbreaker and immediately started the next one. He pushed up his tortoiseshell glasses and watched me. He was curious about what I was doing down there at the underground headquarters, but I didn't volunteer any information. *You first*, I thought.

"It's a shame they haven't made any progress on Ishmael's case," he said. "Are you... still working on that?"

"No need." I flicked one hand through the air. "It's all but wrapped up."

"They're closing the case, unsolved?"

I waggled my eyebrows. "The opposite." I leaned forward and whispered, "Can you keep a secret?"

He sniffed and grew taller in his chair. "I'm a lawyer."

"But you're not *my* lawyer."

He looked me steadily in the eyes. "Zara, I can keep a secret. What's going on?"

I reached for another jawbreaker but changed my mind and went for the jelly beans instead. "I can talk better around jelly beans than jawbreakers," I explained.

"Yes, yes," he said impatiently.

"So, here's the thing." I looked behind me. "Should we close the door?"

"I don't know. Should we?"

I shrugged. "You never know." I was closest, so I leaned back and pushed the door shut without getting up from my chair. I couldn't use magic, since Codex's dampening field was still in effect.

Once the door was closed, the interior of Steve's office felt eerily still and soundproof. The fake window behind him, showing a view of a wheat field, didn't do much to help me forget we were several stories beneath the surface.

"So, here's the thing," I said, using the juicy-gossip voice that always got my coworker Frank riled up. "It turns out there's a good reason those high-tech movie projectors weren't allowed off the department's premises."

"Oh?" Steve looked both surprised and interested.

"They're spy devices. They might have been broadcasting images, but they were actually sucking up way more than they ever sent out."

"What? Are you talking about," he lowered his voice in spite of the closed door, "surveillance?"

I nodded.

"Oh." He leaned back in his chair and tented his fingers. "Oh!" He leaned forward and grasped the edge of his desk as though steadying himself. "Oh," he said a third time, and leaned back, both hands curled into hooks against his chest. "Well, they can't do that," he said. "It's an invasion of privacy."

"It sure is. I'm surprised the news hasn't traveled down here to your department. I bet it's a real legal can of worms."

Steven hunched into his chair while his face went through a dozen variations on upset. "So many worms," he said.

"People are probably scrambling to cover their butts right now, but at least one good thing has come out of this. Ishmael Greyson had one of the units in his apartment. There's a very good chance it captured footage of his killer." I nodded down at my tote bag. "Assuming the killer wasn't another ghost, or someone invisible."

Steve said nothing. His glasses slid down his nose slowly.

"That's why I'm down here." I leaned over, picked up the tote bag, and placed it on my lap. "The box from Ishmael's was buried in red tape at the police station evidence locker. Bentley finally got it out today." I puffed up my chest with pride. "He deputized little ol' me to bring it here to the tech department for footage retrieval. According to the techies Bentley talked to on the phone, it's going to take a few days. We're not holding our breath or anything, but we might have our killer by Monday." I grabbed another handful of jelly beans and stuffed my mouth. "These beans are the perfect amount of stale, by the way. Nice and chewy."

"You're taking the box that was at Ishmael's apartment to the tech floor for data retrieval?"

I pointed a finger at the lawyer. "You got it." I turned my head toward the closed door. "That is, if I can find the techies in this maze."

"Oh," he said. "Oh! I could take you there. No. Even better. I could take the box. I'm heading there shortly. It's on my way."

"I don't know. Bentley told me not to dilly-dally."

"I'll take it straight there." He got up from his chair. "Right away."

I nodded, unzipped the tote bag, pulled out the plastic evidence bag containing the box, and set it on the desk between us. "Sure, why not? If you can't trust a lawyer, who can you trust?"

As Steve reached for the box, there was a series of urgent beeps coming from his computer.

"That sounds important," I said, nodding at the desktop machine.

He slowly turned and leaned down to read his computer monitor screen. "There's a memo here about undocumented surveillance and possible legal issues."

"Hah!" I pointed at my chest. "You heard it from me first."

He moaned. "It's just one mess after another."

"I guess that's why they pay you guys the big bucks." I got to my feet. "Not me, of course. I'm just a librarian." I opened the door. "Promise you'll take that box to the tech department right away? I don't mean to be dramatic, but being haunted by Ishmael's ghost is getting old. It's time for our buddy to move on."

"I couldn't agree more." Steve clicked off his computer monitor, picked up the evidence bag, and clasped the box to his chest. "I'm heading down there right now."

"Then what? Are you working late today or heading home?"

He frowned. "I'm not sure. Why?"

"Come stop by the cafeteria in," I checked the time, "exactly one hour."

He shifted from one foot to the other. "I'm somewhat busy."

I wagged a finger at him. "You can't say no to me. Not today. It's my birthday."

He sucked in air audibly. "It is? Happy birthday."

"It's not a big deal." I rolled my eyes. "Okay, it's kind of a big deal. The cafeteria made a special cherry cheesecake. A few of my other DWM friends will be there, too. They'll probably make me blow out an embarrassing number of candles. You have to join us." I stamped one foot. "You have to!"

"Okay, okay," he said. "One hour. Cheesecake in the cafeteria. I'll be there."

CHAPTER 32

One Hour Later

Light from the artificial windows filled the cafeteria with a golden glow that passed for summer sunshine.

The DWM's working-through-dinner crowd had cleared out, leaving only our group of five and our massive dessert. It was a football field of cherry cheesecake, dotted with candles. Too many candles, if you ask me, but I hadn't been in charge of that detail.

Seated around one rectangular table were a few of my friends who worked in or above the building: Charlize, Rob, Knox, and Bentley. Respectively, they were a gorgon, a bird shifter, another bird shifter, and a human.

Charlize was extremely powerful, able to turn living creatures into stone and back again. To the outside observer she was just a pretty blonde in a flashy silver catsuit. She looked about as menacing as an aerobics instructor. Our path to friendship had taken some twists and turns. When Charlize and I first met, she'd pranked me by pretending I'd been in a coma for years. It wasn't funny at the time, but we laughed about it now. I had originally been jealous of her easy friendship with my shifter neighbor, Chet Moore, but as my crush on him faded, my appreciation of Charlize had grown. We became friends. It didn't hurt that I'd saved her sister's life, and then Charlize had saved mine, bringing me back from the brink of death with her gorgon powers. Sure, she'd also betrayed my trust at least twice, but we were moving past it. Our friendship had its ups and downs, but what relationship doesn't? It certainly wasn't boring.

Sitting next to Charlize was Agent Rob. In his human form, Rob looked like a guy who worked in an office, at a desk. You'd never guess by his small frame and slim arms that he could transform into an enormous black bird. His shifted form was similar to a crow, but much larger, and with supernatural strength.

Next to Rob was his best friend, Knox. Out of the three DWM agents, Knox was the only one who looked tough in his human form. He was tall, broad, and roped with muscle. He had dark-brown skin, large facial features, and a smooth-shaved head. His shifted form of a giant eagle was intimidating, but his human form came pretty close—unless he was smiling. If Knox had a grin on his face, which he often did, thanks to his wisecracking sidekick Rob, it gave away his nature as a gentle giant.

Sitting to my right, on the birthday girl's side of the table, was Detective Theodore Bentley. I'd teased him about dressing up special for the occasion, though he wore his usual gray suit. Bentley didn't know the other three agents well, but he'd been talking to them over the week to arrange the evening's very special birthday party.

"I have eaten too much cheesecake," Knox said, puffing out his six-pack abs. He patted his belly, pretending the wall of muscle was actually body fat. "I should be at the gym right now."

His best friend, Rob, laughed and clapped him on the back. "You just came from the gym, big guy! Have another piece of cheesecake. Pretend you're doing digestion reps. Give that stomach a workout."

Knox gave Rob a wary look. "I will have one more small piece... if you promise to meet me at the gym in the morning."

"Let me think about it," Rob said.

"You can sit in the hot tub after you lift weights for forty-five minutes."

Rob wriggled in his seat. "How about I lift weights for twenty minutes, then we sit in the hot tub?"

Knox reluctantly agreed to the terms.

Charlize chimed in. "Can anyone join you for the weights plus hot tub, or is it boys only?"

"You should come," Knox said. "The gym is good for everyone, men and women. I would be happy to have some company. A sweaty workout with friends is the best way to start your day."

"Sounds fun," Charlize said. "I'll be there." The blonde gorgon caught my eye across the cheesecake. "Assuming we are all still in one piece when the sun comes up." She glanced upward, then quickly back at me.

I held up my hands to show her my fingers were crossed.

She cleared her throat and flashed her powerful blue-gray eyes as she glanced at the cafeteria's entryway.

Steve Adebayo walked in, buttoning the single button on his fashionable, body-hugging suit jacket.

"Abeda-yooo," Charlize called out in a friendly greeting, as though cheering on a favorite member of a sports team.

"Lookin' good, my man," Rob said to the newcomer. "You got here just in time to get some cheesecake before it disappears. Knox is going to show us how fast he can eat the rest of it."

Knox frowned. "I could not eat that much of any kind of food in human form."

Charlize and Rob slid their chairs apart, freeing space around an empty seat for the lawyer. Steve looked at the seat, but then chose a spot next to me, at the end of the table.

"I can't stay long," Steve said, pushing his tortoiseshell glasses up his low-profile nose. "Happy birthday, Zara. Any special plans to mark the occasion?"

I laughed lightly. "Besides seeing how much cheesecake we can get into Knox? Not really." I rubbed my chin thoughtfully. "But I should do something special for myself. What do you think of me getting a tattoo from your girlfriend?"

"From Carrot?" Steve looked down as he served himself a small wedge of cheesecake. "If you do have your heart set on getting a tattoo, it should be from her. She's the best artist around. And she could use the business. People have been avoiding her since her brother died. It's a shame when people don't know what to say to someone in grief so they choose instead to avoid them."

"How's she doing?" I asked.

"Fine, considering." Steve took a bite of cake. "What sort of tattoo are you thinking about getting?"

"A broomstick would be too obvious, right?" Nobody laughed. I shot the others a look. Act jovial, I thought. Act jovial or Steve's going to know something's up.

Charlize seemed to receive my nonverbal message. "Zara, I know what you should get," she said, grinning. "A beautiful snake!"

The others murmured in an almost jovial way.

"Or you could get a crow," Rob said.

"Or an eagle," Knox said.

We all turned to Bentley. "Get whatever you want," he said grumpily. "Don't look at me. I'm not really a tattoo guy."

"Big shocker," I said, which got a chuckle from Charlize.

Bentley frowned and touched his faux bullet pendant through his shirt.

I turned back to Steve, who was already pushing the final bite of cheesecake into his mouth.

"Look at you put that cake away," I said. "You *do* get hungry when you've been working all day."

He gave the group a bashful look. "It's worse when I'm in my chimera form. I'll eat anything." He licked his lips. "As you may have heard."

I had heard. There was a lot more to the shifter chimera than met the eye.

In a casual tone, I said to him, "Speaking of chimeras, I have a question to ask you."

He pushed his chair back. "Another time. I really should get back to my work."

I leaned over, dropped my hand on his wrist, and squeezed, stopping him from getting up. "Not so fast," I said. "It's Friday afternoon, Steve. I'm sure that whatever you're working on can wait."

Steve glanced around the table at the others then down at his lap. "Very well, then. I can stay for a few of these questions of yours, as long as they're not too personal."

"Great. There are props, too. Hang on." I reached into my big tote bag and pulled out the karambit I'd borrowed from Maisy Nix. The blade was wrapped in a burlap coffee sack, tied with twine. I pulled off the makeshift sheaf and placed the weapon on the table. The glinting blade curled around Steve's empty dessert plate.

Steve's chair scraped on the cafeteria floor as he recoiled, shifting back another inch. "What's that doing here?" He cast an angry glare around the table. "What's going on?"

"Dr. Lund says the blade wasn't affixed to the bone handle by any man," I said, trying to keep my tone even. "He says the blade and bone appear to have grown together." I picked it up by the handle. I held the handle between two knuckles as I curled my hand like a cat's paw. "Meow."

The table was utterly silent. At the edge of the cafeteria, a lone janitor was mopping near the buffet station. The slip slop of the mop over the floor was the only sound. Slip slop. Slip slop.

I pawed the air with my single sharp blade again. "Check this out," I said. "I've got one tenth of a Wolverine costume."

Steve pushed his glasses up his nose. His face was covered in a sheen of sweat. In a low, gritty voice, he said, "I'm not sure where you're going with this, Zara. Halloween isn't for a few months."

I flipped the blade so I had a secure grip on the bone handle, brought it down on the table, and scraped the surface, leaving a deep, clean groove.

Nobody else was cutting in, so I continued, as per our plan.

"Dr. Lund believes this knife is a hunting souvenir. It's made from the claw of a chimera," I said. "Specifically, a large iguammit."

Steve took in a deep breath, then let it out audibly. His glasses slipped down and he didn't push them up. "And I suppose you want me to change form so you can check that I still have all my claws?" He forced a laugh. "That's ridiculous. The iguammit this came from must have been two or three times my size. My own claws are tiny by comparison." He looked around the group. "That... That atrocity is not mine. It isn't."

Out of the corner of my eye, I saw Bentley nod. We almost had him.

I pressed on. "But you agree with Dr. Lund's assessment that it did come from an iguammit?"

Steve leaned forward, looked at the blade, then straightened up. "Sure. It could be. The curve is right."

Bentley spoke up. "It's a shame you didn't mention that observation to us the first time you saw the blade." He leaned back so he could look directly at Steve without me in the way. "Mr. Adebayo, you must remember the time I'm referring to. It was here, in the cafeteria, last week. We showed you the blade and you nearly vomited. I would imagine that to someone such as yourself, it would be like me seeing the severed hand of another man."

Steve whipped off his sliding glasses and stuffed them in his suit pocket. "I, uh... Perhaps I didn't make the connection on a conscious level."

Charlize spoke next. "Say, Adebayo, wasn't your father who recently passed away a lot larger than you? He'd been taking that serum Dr. Bob was producing. Gosh, with the amount he'd been taking, he must have been twice your size."

Everyone looked down at the karambit.

Steve leaned forward in his chair and started to stand. Agents Knox and Rob jumped up, swerved around the table, and got behind Steve so quickly they were a blur, even to my witch eyes. Each of the duo rested a hand on Steve's shoulders.

"Not so fast," Rob said. "Tell us why you killed Greyson. Was it to protect his sister?"

"I'm not answering any more questions," Steve said. "This whole line of inquiry is preposterous."

"It was revenge," Knox said, his deep voice booming.

"Revenge," Rob said. "That's right." To Steve, he said, "You don't have to answer with your mouth, smart guy. I can feel the truth in the vibration in your body. You must have found out Greyson was part of the hunting party that killed your father. That's how your father died, right?"

"My father died in an accident," Steve said through gritted teeth. "There was no need for revenge because there was no wrongdoing."

Charlize asked, "Then why did you give your girlfriend a sleeping pill last Friday night, then sneak over to Greyson's house and give him a close shave plus a, you know..."

Everyone looked at Charlize with puzzled frowns.

Charlize rapped on the table with her knuckles. "Shave and a *head cut*, two bits."

Knox said, "It's shave and a *haircut*, two bits." Then, a few seconds later, "Oh. Head cut."

Steve let out a high, long giggle. "Shave and a head cut," he said. "Good joke, everyone. Very theatrical. Thanks for the cake and the amateur theatre, but I can't play along. I didn't do anything to Ishmael Greyson."

"No?" It was my turn to spring the trap. "Then why did you sabotage the projection unit before you dropped it off with the tech department?"

The trapped chimera shifter blinked. "I did no such thing."

I pulled one more item from my purse. It was a battery-operated black light. I flicked it on, and aimed it at Steve's hands. His palms and fingers glowed bright blue under the special light. He gasped in shock and tried to rub the glow away but it wouldn't budge. That was sort of the point with invisible ink.

Bentley got to his feet, came over to look at Steve's hands, and nodded. "Bank Robbery 101," he said sagely. "There's always an invisible ink packet inside the things you're not supposed to touch. The interior of that little box Zara trusted to your care was rigged with simple invisible ink. Nothing high tech or even magical. It's the kind of mundane tool we use to catch the dumbest bank robbers."

Steve gave me a wide-eyed look. "You set me up. You weren't lost, Zara. You set me up!"

"Since we're letting the cat out of the bag, so to speak," I paused to chuckle at the irony. Steve was half lion, half cat. "The box doesn't do surveillance," I finished.

"But..." Steve's head jerked from side to side. "But what about the memo? The alert went out over the company-wide bulletin."

"Not really," Charlize said. "It only looked that way." She put her hands on her hips and huffed. "And what do you mean *amateur theatre*? We're professionals, Adebayo. Admit we got you. Heck, being a known killer around here isn't the grounds for dismissal you might think it is. When the department discovers special skills in agents, sometimes those agents get reassigned."

Bentley's jaw dropped. "What?"

Charlize blinked at the detective and smiled enigmatically.

Steve made a sputtering sound.

Knox tapped Steve's shoulder with one big hand. "We have to go somewhere else now. Rob and I will escort you. Please remain calm."

But Steve didn't stay calm. He tore free of Knox and Rob. He dove under the table, changing form as he did. With one massive lion's paw, he yanked Charlize's chair out from underneath her. Before she could hit him with her stone powers—before she could even cry out, he'd cracked her head against something hard. An instant later, Charlize lay still on the floor, her head tilted limply to the side, her blonde hair fanned out like a limp halo.

Through his enormous reptilian mouth, Steve growled, "Nobody move or I cut the gorgon's head off." Sure enough, he had one of those fierce claws fully extended. The curve would fit a human neck perfectly.

Bentley, who had his gun drawn and aimed already, fired off a shot. He managed to crack off two shots before the chimera with the body of a lion and the head of a reptile soared over the table and took down the detective. The shots sounded like they embedded in the beast's body, but didn't slow him. Bentley's third shot went wild. There was a crack, and a tinkle, and glass rained down from one of the false windows. An instant later, there was an electrical crackle, and all of the artificial windows went dark.

In the darkness, there was the awful sound of growling, snarling, flapping, and bones breaking.

When the backup lights flickered on, I almost wished they hadn't. There was blood everywhere.

Charlize was still unconscious, possibly dead. Two enormous birds lay on the ground near her outstretched hand. They barely resembled birds. They were a heap of dark feathers.

And Bentley. Poor Bentley. The human lay on his back, gasping for breath, his face twisted in agony. Both of his legs and one arm were—I could barely look at him long enough to make the assessment—broken in multiple places. Bones protruded from the fabric of his gray wool suit.

The only thing moving was Steve, walking toward me on four lion's paws. Now I saw every single one of the claws. Gleaming and metallic.

Closer he walked. Tick, tick went the claws on the floor.

I'd already tried blasting him with my blue plasma, as soon as he'd started changing. It hadn't worked then, and it still didn't work now. My magic was locked down. Why had we been so foolish to believe three agents and two humans with no powers could take down a mythical beast? We should have had more backup. So much more backup. Now we were all as good as dead.

But not yet. I still had my human strength. Aunt Zinnia had prepared me for this. A witch couldn't count on magic in every situation; she had to use her wits.

There was a weapon within my reach. I grabbed the curved karambit from the table and pointed the business end at the approaching beast.

I was fast, but he was faster. Before I could open my mouth to let off a verbal warning, he was on me. He pounced like a kitten, except he was no kitten. I fell backward helplessly. I managed to save my head somewhat, but it still struck the floor. My vision swam with stars. I couldn't move. I'd been pinned. Tough as I was, my arms were no match for the powerful forepaws of a lion.

"Stop this," I said. "You don't have to kill anyone else."

The reptilian face loomed over mine. Inhuman eyes stared down impassively.

"Their blood is on your hands," he growled. "Your hands, witch. You were the one who made the mistakes."

I spat in his scaly face. "At least I'm not a cold-blooded murderer."

He licked the side of my face with his long tongue. "Tasty," he said. "I do love eating delicious red candy."

I tried to kick him in whatever he had for a groin, but my legs wouldn't move. He had me completely pinned.

"Codex!" I yelled. "Hey, robot girl! A little help down here in the cafeteria?"

The eerie mechanical voice replied, "There is a security incident occurring in the cafeteria."

"I know! We need some help!"

She said, "The cafeteria is currently under lockdown."

And then I heard the banging on the other side of the door. Help should have been on the way, but it wasn't. It was just me versus one extremely angry iguammit. And I didn't even have the karambit in my hand. If only I had...

Bentley's gun!

I rolled my head, scanning the ground near Bentley. The gun was in sight. It was two feet from his bleeding hand, and about five feet away from mine. But it might as well have been a mile, because there was no way I could reach it. Not without any magic.

What a shame the dampener field doesn't shut down shifters, I thought bitterly. It wasn't so much a dampener field as an anti-witch field.

I closed my eyes and focused on a name. Ishmael Greyson. *Ishmael, if you're going to help avenge your death, if you can do anything at all in the physical plane, come and do it now!*

When I opened my eyes, there was only my injured friends and the reptilian face hovering above mine. No Ishmael.

Steve was talking. Blathering on about how he'd only gone to the apartment to talk to Ishmael, but something had taken control over him. It must have been the ghost of his father. Blah blah blah. I couldn't even hear him over the pounding of my pulse in my ears. The guy wanted me to believe he wasn't really a monster? I'd just seen him maim and possibly kill four of my friends. I was tempted to use my remaining strength to spit on him again, or headbutt him. But I needed to stay calm and keep thinking.

Where was that darn ghost?

Something moved over near Bentley's crumpled, broken body. Ishmael? No. It was Bentley, slowly moving one hand. He wasn't reaching for the gun, though. He was unbuttoning his collar. He was reaching in under his shirt. And then he was pulling out the talisman he wore on the chain around his neck.

The bullet.

Only it wasn't a bullet.

I blinked, the world swirled then settled around me, and the true form came into view.

His talisman was a vial of red liquid.

All at once, I realized what he was about to do.

"Bentley," I said. "Don't!"

The iguammit who had me pinned stopped whining. Dark eyes bore into me. With his face looming over mine, Steve breathed hot, cinnamon breath into my nose and mouth. "Nice try, witch. You want me to turn my head to see what the human detective is doing, and then what? You hit me with something?"

"You got me," I lied. "Bentley isn't doing anything you need to be concerned about. Nope. Nothing at all."

But Bentley was doing something. And if my suspicions were right, it would be of utmost concern to the killer who had me pinned.

CHAPTER 33

The bullet that was not a bullet went into Bentley's mouth, where he cracked it open with his teeth.

It wasn't a bullet because it was made of glass. It was a vial. A clear, glass vial. And that vial held something red.

What is red?

Cherry cheesecake sauce is red.

So are a variety of candies and juices.

And blood.

Don't forget blood.

And especially don't forget the kind of blood that comes from the dark veins of a creature of the grave.

That's the kind of blood that transforms a human being into something else.

Bentley was a lump of broken angles and pain, biting through a glass vial of dark blood.

Then the iguammit shifted, and its tawny lion's shoulder blocked my view of the detective.

I felt wind across my face. Wind inside a sealed cafeteria several stories underground. Magical wind.

When the beast above me shifted again to lick my face, I saw that the space where Bentley had been was now empty except for a pool of blood. And then, in a blink of the eye, the pool of blood was gone. The magic of his transformation must have done something. I'd seen so many strange things, yet it took me several seconds to process what was happening. The blood must have magically wicked back into the detective's body.

The world was turning black. I couldn't breathe—hadn't been able to for some time already, thanks to the weight of the beast on top of me, but it was only now taking effect.

Steve was still whining, still pleading innocent. "If I hadn't taken out Ishmael, he would have been a liability to the department. A guy like that can't be counted on. He was insecure, a braggart."

"Shut up," I managed to say. "If you're going to kill me, just do it already. I can't... listen... to..."

He stared down at me with incredulity in his large, black eyes. The blackness around his head was seeping toward the center of my vision. The weight grew even heavier on my chest, and the blackness closed in. I couldn't see anything.

But for a brief moment, I could still hear. I heard everything.

The janitor was whimpering behind something in the kitchen, talking to someone on a phone, or maybe praying to whatever gods he still believed in.

Charlize was groaning, breathing heavily as she pushed herself up.

And something went click. It went click, and then it went bang. My face was hit with something hot. Even as I lost consciousness, I knew it was blood. The iguammit's blood. And I knew Bentley had pulled the trigger.

As I pulled away from the pain and the confusion, down into the ocean of calm, I knew something else.

That night in the cafeteria, Bentley—the Bentley I knew and had even come to like—died.

He died to save me.

* * *

I regained consciousness shortly after Charlize and Bentley shoved the corpse of the beast off me.

He was dead, they reassured me. "You can't be too careful," I growled, and kicked him a few times to be sure.

Next, I turned my attention to the two great birds who lay tangled in each other's broken wings. My hands should have been tingling with healing powers but I felt nothing. It wasn't from the physical attack. My powers were still grounded.

I lifted my face to the ceiling, where I assumed the cameras were located. "Codex, lift the dampener field on the cafeteria," I said. "I need to—" My voice choked in my throat. Was there any use? Was there enough life still in Rob and Knox for me to try? They couldn't shift back to human form while injured.

The voice replied, as I knew it would. "The cafeteria is under lockdown."

I felt a cool hand on my shoulder. Charlize's hand. "I can turn them to stone," she said. "It's like putting them in suspended animation." She looked at them, grimaced, and quickly looked away. "It'll be hard on their systems, but... it's protocol whenever there's a grave injury in the field and I'm on the team. It's my job."

I took a step back. Hoarsely, I said, "Do your job."

* * *

The rest of the night was a blur. Backup eventually burst through the door, nearly shooting me in their confusion.

Charlize went with the granite birds to the medical bay, leaving me to explain why there was a dead chimera with the body of a lion and the head of an iguana lying on top of a smashed cherry cheesecake.

I turned to Bentley for corroboration of my story, but there was no Bentley. He was gone. Vanished into thin air. I looked up at the broken artificial windows. One was still shattered, but the other three were semi-functional, showing the most beautiful sunset.

* * *

When I got home that night, around midnight, Ishmael Greyson was standing on my porch. He had a packed suitcase at his side, and a rifle slung over his back.

"What are you up to?" I asked. "Don't tell me you're going on some hunting expedition in the afterlife."

He grinned.

"I guess you can't tell me anything, can you?"

He shrugged, picked up the suitcase, and vanished in a flash of light.

"Send me a postcard," I said to the empty porch. Then I thought of something my aunt and I had talked about before her vacation. About how people always ask for postcards but nobody really likes getting them. "Or not," I said to the stillness.

CHAPTER 34

I slept through most of Saturday.

By Sunday afternoon, life happily returned to what passed for normal in the Riddle household. Except it wasn't truly a regular Sunday.

It was the one day a year that, to me in particular, was not like the others.

Thirty-three years had passed since my birth.

Friday had been my fake birthday, but now the real one was upon us. July 24th. Smack-dab in the middle of summer. The perfect time for backyard parties. I had so many fond memories of water balloon wars staged between an army of preteen girls led by me versus a smaller band of teen boys led by my friend Nash. Such innocent days those had been, when none of the girls cared how many calories were in cupcake icing and the worst thing that happened was a lost contact lens.

In honor of the special day, my mother and Zinnia called me together with a video chat. They were overseas, so it was as close to in-person as they were going to get. I took the call in bed, since I hadn't gotten up yet. They worked out the time difference and gave me a hard time for sleeping in. Then my mother gave one of her almost-apologies.

"Such a shame we couldn't be there," Zirconia Riddle said, making a tsk-tsk sound.

"You've missed six of my birthdays in a row," I said.

The former redhead who now had ebony hair rolled her pretty eyes. "It's not polite to keep score."

Zinnia elbowed my mother and pushed in so her own face filled my screen. "What my sister is trying to say is we are sorry to miss your birthday." She winced and bit her lip in a girlish gesture I hadn't seen my aunt do much. "Promise you'll do something special to celebrate yourself, Zara. Birthdays are important. We ought not let them pass by without notice."

"This one won't pass by without notice." I smiled at the screen. "Zoey has arranged for a very special cake."

Zinnia blinked repeatedly. "But that's not terribly special. The two of you eat cake nearly every day."

My mother widened her eyes in horror, making the hollows below her cheekbones even darker. "Oh, Zara. Tell me it's not true. Cake every day?"

I pressed my lips together and said nothing. Protesting that we didn't have cake every day, since sometimes we ate pie, was not going to help my situation. I kept my mouth shut and received the lecture from my mother, calmly and gratefully. I'd missed her nagging during the years she was allegedly dead.

We talked for a while, about nothing in particular. Seeing their look-alike faces side by side, the long red hair mingling with the long black hair, filled me with love and longing. I lied and told them I didn't mind that they were gallivanting around Europe without me. It was good for them to have their sister time and space to catch up with each other.

My mother abruptly asked, "What about Teddy?" Teddy was what she called Bentley. Teddy, or even Teddy B.

If I'd had hackles, they would have gone up. "What about him?"

304

My undead mother narrowed her hazel eyes at me. "Something has happened with him."

"What makes you say that?" I felt a twinge of guilt over not calling her the moment I got home late Friday. I should have let her know that Bentley must have opened the "gift" she'd left him.

She used one pale, bony finger to stroke the indentation between her collarbones. "Call it a sixth sense. A mother's intuition."

Zinnia leaned half out of frame and gave her older sister a puzzled look. Zinnia didn't know about Bentley, or what had happened. But my mother did. She knew darn well.

I gave her what I thought was a mature look. "Mother, why would you ask a question when you already know the answer?" I caught sight of my face in the small window and winced. My *mature* look was the same one my teen daughter gave me during her rare bratty moments.

We stared off as best we could, considering the computer's camera was offset from our actual eyes by several inches. My mother was much better than I was at frowning fixedly at the tiny camera hole.

Zinnia broke in. "What's going on with Bentley? Have you started dating him, Zara? It's about time you moved on from the shifter. Their kind doesn't mix well with ours. The detective is a much more appropriate choice for you."

"Ew," I said. "I'm not interested in my mother's exes."

"He's not my ex," my mother said. "Although..." Her thin, dark eyebrows almost touched. "If Teddy has done what I sense he has, then he's sort of like a brother to you now."

Zinnia's eyes flew wide open. "What?"

My mother turned to her sister and explained, "Before I left town, I gave Teddy B a vial of my blood, concentrated in a lab by Dr. Ankh. I obscured most of his memory, but left him with explicit instructions to break the glass in case of an emergency." She touched one of her upper incisors casually. "I sense that the vial has been opened." She looked directly at me through the camera. "Trouble unsealed," she said ominously.

Zinnia's hands flew to her mouth. "Bentley's a vampire?"

"What?" I gave my mother an even brattier look. "Zinnia can say the V-word, but I can't? That's not fair. If you're going to glamour me, you should glamour everyone in the family."

Zinnia gave me a dumbfounded look. "Zara, what happened?"

I shrugged. "There was a shootout at the O.K. Corral, so to speak." I waved my hand. "Everyone survived."

My mother gave me a dark look. There was something besides anger in her eyes. Sadness. She quickly looked away.

She didn't have to say it. I knew what she was thinking. *Not everyone* had *survived.*

Zinnia peppered me with questions. I started at the beginning, seven days ago, and explained everything that had happened since Ishmael Greyson's first ghostly visit. I skipped over the key fact that I'd rezoned myself so that Ishmael couldn't interact by possessing me. We could discuss that when my mentor returned to town. I also left out my first broom flight with Maisy Nix, and how much I knew about the coven.

When I got to the end, Zinnia was leaning in so close to the camera, her face filled my screen. "What about Charlize? And the other agents?"

"They're okay," I reported. "I talked to Charlize already this morning. Everyone's going to make a full recovery."

Zinnia shook her head. "I hope this has taught you a lesson about being more careful."

My mother pushed her out of the way. "Zara, you should have a vial, too," she said. "I will FedEx one to you."

"Gross! Don't you dare FedEx me your... Ugh." I made a gagging face.

The two sisters turned to each other. They exchanged a look that said *What are we supposed to do about Zara?*

"I'm fine," I said. "Everybody's fine here. I even sent Bentley a text message inviting him to come join us for cake tonight. Does that make you happy?"

They turned to face me and sighed in unison.

"It's a Black Forest cake," I said. "From Gingerbread House. Zoey arranged it with Chloe, who made it for me personally." I scratched my chin self-consciously. "She made it with an orange liqueur filling instead of the usual stuff. For some reason, I've lost my appetite for cherry filling."

Diplomatically, my aunt said, "That was very considerate of Chloe. I feel better knowing you have some good friends there with you. Friends are important."

"Indeed," I said. "As important as birthdays."

"Indeed," she agreed.

My mother said nothing. Her gaze drifted upward. She stared into the distance dreamily while she traced a vertical line over her breastbone.

The three of us continued to talk for a while, but the conversation had already ended.

When it came time to end the call, Zinnia teared up, exactly as I knew she would. *The tougher they act, the harder they fall.*

When the connection clicked off and my laptop's screen went black, I struggled to keep my own eyes dry.

Why so emotional? Maybe because I was catching up to Zinnia in years. Was it aging that made people sentimental? Did all the small losses of life accumulate in such a way that one emotional tug could cause an avalanche?

I closed the laptop. In the silence, the weight of everything that had happened threatened to crash down on me. I could have easily slid back down under the covers and slept my birthday away. Instead, I cast a spell to whip my covers away, and I got up to face my birthday.

* * *

Zoey and I set the dining room table in preparation for my intimate party. Chloe would be arriving with the cake, accompanied by her sister Charlize. If Bentley showed up, there would be five of us. I hadn't invited my coworkers. I adored them, but I also saw plenty of them during the week. Chloe had baked two cakes so I could bring one to the library on Monday for a belated celebration.

As I set out five placemats, I found myself humming.

Zoey picked up the placemats I'd just set down, made a tsk-tsk sound, and unfurled a festive striped tablecloth over the table's scratched and dented surface.

While she smoothed out the wrinkles with her hands, she asked, "Where do you think he went?"

"Heaven, maybe." I used magic to take back the placemats and resettle them. "If there are Hell worlds, there must be Heaven worlds. Unicorns and rainbows must come from somewhere." I remembered the ghost's rifle. "He'd better not be shooting unicorns, wherever he went."

"I didn't mean Ishmael Greyson," she said.

"Oh. You meant Bentley?" I checked my phone. "Speaking of whom, he hasn't gotten back to me about coming for cake tonight. Oh, well! More cake for us."

She frowned. "But seriously. Where do you think he went after he shot that guy in the cafeteria?"

"Honestly, I don't know where he skulked off to after the... transformation. Don't they like graves? After we're finished eating birthday cake, you and I can go for a moonlight stroll by the cemetery. We can check for fresh dirt."

She gave me a pained look. "Mom, you're being very offensive to their kind."

"I make jokes, Zoey. Dark humor jokes. To help everyone deal with the horrors that are visited upon us every single day. I don't know if you've noticed, but it's sort of my thing."

"I may have noticed that about you," she said coolly. "But where do you think he went?"

"In my wildest fantasy, he snuck out of the cafeteria and went straight to the computer mainframe room where he gave Codex a lobotomy." I clenched my fists, remembering the frustration of being without my magic. "If I'd had my powers, nobody would have gotten hurt that night."

"Mom, you can't save everyone all the time."

"Why not?"

She gave me a blank look.

"I'm serious," I said. "If I'm not supposed to be saving everyone all the time, then why do I have these amazing powers?"

"Nobody is *supposed to be* doing anything. Don't you believe in free will?"

"Hmm." I reached up and swept away a stray cobweb from the chandelier.

The doorbell rang.

"Doorbell," I said, grinning.

"I believe in free will," Zoey said.

"Doorbell."

She struck one finger in the air. "I'll get the door, but only because I *choose* to get the door, of my own free will."

I nodded. "Doorbell."

It rang again.

She sighed and left to answer the door.

She returned a few minutes later with three people. Two blonde gorgons and one formerly alive detective.

"Look what the cat dragged in," I said.

Chloe and Charlize each set a cake on the table.

Detective Theodore "Teddy B" Bentley held out a fat bottle of champagne. "Happy birthday," he said. He looked different, though I hadn't quite worked out everything that had changed. A hint of a smile curled his lips. That was new.

"Thanks," I said, taking the champagne. "Getting older sucks, but it sure beats the alternative!"

Bentley raised one eyebrow. It lifted higher and faster than it had before. "Oh? And what is the alternative to getting older?" The steely gray eye beneath the raised eyebrow was now silver, the light tones on the iris shining like the facets on a cut diamond.

I was temporarily speechless. There were two alternatives to getting older: Being dead, or being something that didn't age. I hadn't seen Bentley in two days, and now we'd only exchanged a few words, and I'd struck a nerve already.

Or had I?

He didn't seem at all offended by my gaffe. If anything, the curve on his lips had deepened.

Someone—my daughter—clapped her hands. "Champagne flutes," she said. "I'll get some if you let me pop the cork."

Without taking my eyes off silver-eyed Bentley, I said, "They're above the refrigerator, behind the Frisbee we use to eat in the tub."

Now Bentley's second eyebrow raised. "You use a Frisbee to eat in the tub? I'd like to see that."

"You can't," I said quickly. "You can't see me naked. Only family is allowed to see me naked."

"We're practically family," Bentley said. "My maker is your mother."

His maker. My mother. Practically family. I managed to pull away from the tractor beam of his gaze and latch onto something safer. The gaze of a gorgon. Charlize.*Help me*, I pleaded with my eyes.

"You're okay," Charlize said softly, soothingly. "It's always a big adjustment when someone you know makes a transition. Bentley's still the same person, I swear."

"He's still Bentley, but he's..." *Not* Bentley. Not placid, predictable, striving, gray-wool-suit-wearing Bentley.

Charlize kept talking, reassuring me. I didn't hear a word she was saying. Chloe chattered happily about the cake and the recipe she'd adapted.

Suddenly, there was a loud BANG!

I was so startled, I managed to catch the champagne cork in mid-air and explode it into confetti.

Zoey squealed with glee and clapped her hands. "Nice one! I didn't know you could do that!"

I caught some of the falling confetti in my hand. It crackled against my palm. I hadn't known I could do that, either, but I didn't let on to the group. Instead, I smiled at my friends and complimented the baker on her handiwork.

Next, I endured countless jokes about the number of candles on my cake, and how next year they would have a fire crew standing by.

Zoey dimmed the chandelier, lit the candles, and they sang to me. I looked around at their faces, one at a time. Boa had joined us and was sitting politely on a chair. Ribbons had come for the cake and was not-so-politely hanging upside down from the chandelier like a bat. As I looked at each one of them, it hit me that one year ago I hadn't known any of them. Last year, it had been thirty-two candles on a store-bought cake, and my daughter and I had agreed to skip the singing that year, since it was, yet again, just the two of us. How things had changed.

"Blow out the candles before you burn this old house down," Charlize said.

"Let's see how many she can blow out in one breath," Bentley said. "Then we get to count all Zara's boyfriends."

Everyone made childish oooh-oooh sounds, except for Ribbons, who said, "You have boyfriends, Zed? More than one?"

I sucked in my breath and held it a moment.

"Make a wish," someone said.

Later, when I reflected back on that night, I wouldn't be able to tell you who told me to make a wish. I couldn't even say if it had been a man, a woman, or a wyvern. But I heard the command, and I looked across the glowing candles at my beautiful, kind, patient daughter, and I knew exactly what to wish for. I didn't even need to take a second breath to think about it.

I wished, I closed my eyes, and I blew.

Through my eyelids, I saw the bright light grow dim. The candles guttered, but not every one of them extinguished.

I opened my eyes to the sight of two candles burning defiantly.

There was another chorus of oooh-oooh, then, "Zara's got two boyfriends!"

"Oh, please." I huffed and rolled my eyes. "Who'd want to date a bossy old witch like me?" I took another breath and blew out the other two.

In the darkness, I said, "Cake time! Zoey, would you get the lights?"

"I'm trying," she said. There was a click-click sound of the switch being flicked. "We must have blown a fuse," she said.

"I'll blow a fuse if I can't see this cake to cut it," I said.

The chandelier came on. Nobody was standing anywhere near the switch. In fact, my daughter was at the doorway, presumably on her way to check the electrical panel.

Charlize gave me a knowing look. "Another ghost?"

I scanned the dining room. "I don't see one." I pointed to the hanging light fixture, and the scaled creature swinging from it. "We can probably pin this one on Cirque de Wyvern."

Everyone laughed.

Zoey was returning to her chair when the doorbell rang. She and I locked eyes. We weren't expecting anyone. Something about the sound of the doorbell at that particular moment sent an unwelcome shiver down my spine. I felt pressure on my lungs, like the chimera beast was standing on my chest again.

Without a word, Zoey ran to answer the door.

Everyone gathered at the table sat absolutely still, as though they sensed it, too.

Doom.

Impending doom.

My daughter's voice floated into the dining room. "Good evening, Mr. Moore! Is everything okay with Corvin? Do you need me to watch him for a few minutes?"

He answered her in a murmur too soft for us to hear.

Next to me, there was a hiss of multiple snakes waking from their magical slumber. The gorgon nearest me, Charlize, grabbed my hand with hers and squeezed. "That's not Chet," she said.

Chloe said, "If it's not Chet, then it must be..." She didn't say the name, but she didn't have to. There was a genie strolling around in a body he'd cut from Chet Moore's. He called himself Archer Caine.

Bentley stared at me across the table. "Zara," he said, his voice slicing through my confusion like a sharp blade. "What did you wish for?"

I looked down at the cake with the burnt candles and muttered my answer.

"Zara," he said again. "Tell us what you wished for."

I lifted my chin and met his eyes. "I wished that my daughter could have what I didn't. I wished she could get to know her father."

Nobody said anything.

313

Ribbons swung upward from his perch on the chandelier, flipped in mid-air, and landed on the table two feet from the cake. "And you say I stir the pot, Zed. You're the one who stirs the pot and shakes the hornet's nest and lights the firecrackers."

Two people appeared in the doorway. My daughter, her pale face even more pale than usual, and Archer Caine.

"Everyone," Zoey said hesitantly. "This is—"

She was cut off by Bentley, who hurled himself through the air in a supernatural move that defied all laws of physics. He struck the genie with the full force of his body, and the two went tumbling backward, snarling and growling and making an unholy racket.

Ignoring them for the moment, I picked up a knife and held it over the shaved chocolate curls and whipped cream in front of me. My hand was trembling. "Cake, anyone? Cake?"

For a full list of books in this
series and other titles by
Angela Pepper, visit

www.angelapepper.com

Made in the USA
Columbia, SC
21 October 2020

23211091R00174